Daniel Corrick is an editor and literary historian with a specialist interest in nineteenth-century literature, especially the evolution of Gothicism and the Decadent movement. He has worked on a number of volumes including the collected fiction of Montague Summers, and unpublished works of Edgar Saltus and Edward Heron-Allen. In addition, he has edited several anthologies, including *Sorcery and Sanctity: A Homage to Arthur Machen* (Hieroglyphic Press, 2013), and *Drowning in Beauty: The Neo-Decadent Anthology* (Snuggly Books, 2018).

NIGHT'S BLACK AGENTS

AN ANTHOLOGY OF VAMPIRE FICTION

EDITED BY DANIEL CORRICK

THIS IS A SNUGGLY BOOK

ISBN: 978-1-64525-131-6

CONTENTS

INTRODUCTION

THE vampire is the most glamorous of Gothic figures; an immortal prince of the night possessed of sinister beauty and a hypnotic power over the living. Film, music, visual art and even fashion give testament to our ongoing fascination with the thirsting dead. Yet readers will look in vain for mention of the vampire in any of the original works of the high Gothic; both the great English novelists and the multitudinous writers of Germanic "shudder literature" make next to no mention of this being. This absence cannot be due to unfamiliarity, for belief in vampires was so prevalent throughout European culture that a century after the rise of Newtonian physics nations were still having to pass laws restricting the exhumation and destruction of corpses under suspicion of *magia posthuma*, nor for literary indifference, for many writers of the Grand Tour recorded the belief with interest. It was in the decades following the French Revolution that the growing Romantic movement cast a new look at the phenomenon of vampirism, transforming the vampire from the walking witch corpse of evil legend to a kind of Satanic Overman, who obtains immortality and dominion over others through partaking in a blasphemous parody of the sacrament of Christ's Blood, in a poetic recapitulation of the anxieties of the prior century.

The stories selected for inclusion in this anthology showcase the development of the vampire both as a literary figure and a spiritual symbol over the course of the nineteenth century, the period during which vampire fiction was at its most vigorous, and into the twentieth, before its incorporation into modern horror fiction and cinema.

For various reasons to be discussed later on the new "Gothic" vampire was linked to the evolution of the figure of the libertine in the eighteenth and seventeenth centuries. Whilst many of us now would consider that term synonymous with "hedonist" and even consider it applicable to their own lifestyles, prior to the nineteenth century the libertine had a more sinister association, that of someone who not only views others as mere objects in pursuit of his pleasures, but who also takes an active satisfaction in defiling the virtuous; the thought being that over-indulgence of an appetite leads to one growing jaded and thus being driven to seek more and more twisted ways of satisfying it. Because of this perceived attack on virtue libertinage had a sacrilegious aspect, something which was gleefully highlighted, such as in the poetry of John Wilmot, second earl of Rochester, or in the practices of and legends surrounding the Hellfire Club. To the Puritan, the libertine's seduction is in essence also an attack on Christianity, for in seducing the innocent he wilfully and intentionally robs them of their salvation.

These elements of blasphemy and cruelty were made most explicit by the French anti-clerical pornographers of the late eighteenth century, the most notorious of which of course was the Marquis de Sade, whose works consist almost exclusively of obscene parodies of Catholic ceremonies and raptures on the suffering of the virtuous. Whilst it would be excessive to credit de Sade with a direct influence on the literature of vampirism, his oeuvre completed the final transformation of the libertine from amoral pleasure seeker to diabolical predator. Readers might note with interest however that *Justine* contains a character who not only obtains pleasure and a kind of sexual revitalisation from the spilling of blood, but who has taken a young wife whom he holds captive for this purpose, something which would become a trope in early vampire art.

The aesthetics of de Sade were those of eighteenth century materialism; however, those of the Romantics were decidedly not. A fascination with the extremes of psychology and morality, and an increased appreciation for various national folk mythologies lead to the diabolical libertine being combined with a monster of Eastern legend. Although some would credit this literary leap to a happy biographical accident in the life of one of the first writers, the seeds for this rebirth of the vampire were sown earlier in Romantic poetry. The Romantic vampire inherits the glamour of Milton's Satan without the high-minded aspects. He is defiant, his very existence is a defiance of the natural order and thus a triumph of his will over divine creation; his appetite, and in consequence his potency (in all senses from the sexual to the territorial), is insatiable and thus not subject to limitation, he is seductive in that his hypnotic allure inspires his victims to offer themselves to damnation willingly. In many respects he encapsulates the egotistical fantasies of freedom from restraint and power over others which some of the Romantics saw as dooming the Utopian dreams of the late Enlightenment. It should come as no surprise that one of the models for Nietzsche's Overman, the character of Arkady Ivanovich Svidrigailov from Dostoevsky's *Crime and Punishment*, with his mesmeric presence and unnatural youthfulness, was described as a vampire.

But whilst the Overman is a trans-moral character, the vampire is of its nature evil—a being which is not amoral but allies itself with the powers of darkness. He represents a new kind of villain with a new kind of eschatology. Although the various formulae of exorcism make reference to ghosts of the damned permitted to torment the living, classical Christian doctrine has little to say about the use the Archenemy might make of supremely wicked souls, those who actively sought to do his work in life. The figure of the vampire fills this spiritual lacuna, for he is a mortal man who has assumed a form of demonhood, more intimate and subsequently more disturbing than that of the fallen angels. The Romantic revaluation of the vampire emphasises his most Satanic characteristics to the point where his existence is a sort of prolonged Black Mass. His consumption of human blood to sustain unending life mirrors the worshipper's spiritual rebirth upon receiving Holy Communion, his corruption and eventual transformation of his virgin prey echoes the Sacrament of Marriage, and his very existence as the walking undead parodies the central miracle of Christianity—the Resurrection. This diabolical pedigree has echoes in the traditional association of vampirism with witchcraft and practitioners of dark magic. One suspects it is due to this overt embodying of evil that the vampire was never developed within the context of the Gothic novel proper. For all their gruesome and shocking content, the works of Spiess, Radcliffe, Lewis and Grose were written to instruct according to Enlightenment principles, in which knowledge equalled good conduct. Their protagonists and villains might be mired in vice, they may even be sworn to Lucifer himself, but it is as unwilling bondsmen rather than willing votaries; the idea that anyone would freely choose such wilful evil required more morally turbulent time to see consideration.

The first major work of fiction to introduce such a re-imagined vampire was John Polidori's 1819 novella *The Vampyre*, the circumstances surrounding the writing of which are almost too well-known to require recounting. Polidori, a former friend and companion to Lord Byron, developed his work from a short fragment of Byron's about the sinister oath a traveller is sworn to by his dying friend, drawing from the scandalous portrait of that nobleman in Lady Caroline Lamb's roman à clef *Glenarvon* to flesh out his own grave-defying hero-villain. Upon release it was taken to be Byron's own work, an attribution that came all too easily to the public mind as he had already referenced the vampire in his earlier poem "The Giaour" and presented a Faustian version of himself two years prior in *Manfred.* The vampire of the novel, Lord Ruthven, is every inch the libertine diabolist; he gives freely to encourage the sins of others, brings good luck to the vicious and ill fortune to the virtuous, and spurns worldly woman in favour of the corruption of the innocent. Polidori emphasises the vampire's part as a seducer by assigning him a Bluebeard like aspect wherein he will attempt to marry his intended victim.

The character and plot proved vastly popular, with Lord Ruthven becoming as iconic a villain as another aristocratic son of the night would a century later. Prequels and sequels flowed from the pen of admirer and opportunist alike. In France the great Romantic writer Charles Nodier spread the enthusiasm for vampires to that stage with his adaption *Le Vampire*; the result being a sudden craze for vampire tragedies, melodramas and even comedies. Nodier's play inspired a loose prequel from the London playwright James Robinson Planché entitled *The Bride of the Isle,* which brought the fiend to the English theatre, temporarily making the vampire a preferred stage villain. The secret to this success was partly due to a twofold appeal to both conservative and revolutionary tastes: to the traditional moralist the vampire was a religious horror representing the perils of libertine seduction; to the radical, a chance to portray the aristocrat as a corrupt libertine praying on the pious and good-hearted commoners.

As the various playwrights scrambled to compete with one another for the next season's success, the vampire found himself included in other popular settings such as the highwayman or nautical melodrama. One particularly flamboyant example of this is "The Wood Devil; or, the Vampire Pirate of the Deep Dell", originally a play by Edward Fitzball, the writer of a great number of melodramatic horrors, which was soon adapted for the Penny dreadful papers by the father of that format, Thomas Prest, himself destined to co-write another great vampire novel, *Varney the Vampire.* "The Wood Devil" is chaotic and colourful, stitched together from various traditions—the vampire of the title, Genano, is the Mephisthophelean devil of the Gothics in all but name, tempting the characters with promises of wealth and eternal youth. It is interesting to note that of the characteristics of the vampire derived from Polidori, those most central to the plot are those subsequently forgotten by later writers, namely the resurrection condition and Bluebeard aspects.

A far graver and more serious development of the stage vampire in prose form is the short novella, here titled in translation as "The Pale Lady's Story," from that titan of French literature, Alexander Dumas *père.* Although not published until the 1840s, the climatic scenes of this work were inspired by a performance of Nodier's play Dumas saw decades before and were to be reused in his own dramatic sequel to that adaption. Within the narrative Dumas develops the diabolical vampire beyond the Lord Ruthven model and associated setting, transplanting him within the brand of historical romance he was so famed for. The piece shows skilful burrowing from Friedrich Schiller's incredibly popular play *The Robbers,* with its bandit-lords and morally dualistic siblings, though the choice to relocate the events from a Levantine or high-society setting, then traditional hunting grounds of the thirsting dead, to the wilds of the Carpathian Mountains was soon to form an important prescient all of its own. The dramatic spectacle and bittersweetness of the ending scenes make one regret the formulaic laziness of stakes and coffins that besets vampire fiction to this day.

Following his popularity on the stage attempts were made by enterprising authors to write the vampire back into the Gothic. It was this trend, beginning with the imitations of the popular late German Gothic fiction published in *Blackwoods* and *The Ladies Magazine,* and continuing with stories in the Penny dreadfuls, which eventually culminated in vampire fiction as we know it. One of the earliest instances of this, maybe the earliest in the English language, is the 1840 story "Zuverlein; or, The Prediction", which gives away its pedigree with the sub-title "A Sketch After the German Fashion". The plot is undoubtedly inspired by one of Johann August Apel's ghost stories, "The Family Portraits", about a knight cursed to place a fatal kiss on the brow of his decedents; but whereas in Apel's story such an act is an omen of death, here it is a sanguine physical predation from an infernal nobleman with surprisingly familiar characteristics. Those who relished the depiction of the vampire in early horror films might be surprised to see just how early certain tropes, the thunder storm, the flames flickering lower at the banquet, the ill-omened guest who refuses both meat and wine et cetera, were already being formed in the popular conscience.

It will not have escaped the reader's notice that up until this point the vampire has been spoken of as male, a deliberate choice, for at these early stages there are important archetypal differences between the two sexes. If anything the female vampire had already achieved recognition as a literary subject before the male, first appearing in some of the major works of romantic poetry such as Goethe's "Bride of Corinth" and Southey's "Thalaba", in each case in the near Eastern setting originally associated with blood-drinking undead. As the diabolical nature of the vampire involves an element of sexual violation, and as women have traditionally been cast in the role of the beloved rather than the lover, the female vampire is presented initially in the mode of a temptress, a siren of the underworld. She does not destroy innocence with indecent passion as much as exploit existing passions, twisting them to foul purposes and leading the victim to destroy themselves. In this she is a sort of supernatural amalgamation of Lilith, Delilah, Jezebel, Hecate, all of the sinister women of Scriptural and Classical history. This is the female vampire as she first appeared in prose within the novellas of Théophile

Gautier and Ernst Raupach; a figure which, unlike the male, seldom appeared on stage, one suspects for fear of it proving too titillating.

Like the witch she is a votary of the powers of darkness but unlike the witch she enters into no commerce the Devil, instead taking the role of the Fallen One herself in offering a terrible quasi-sexual union as part of one's initiation into a forbidden state. An early Penny dreadful "The Bruxa" (soon pirated as "The Vampire Mother") makes explicit this connection between vampirism and witchcraft, as well as the female vampire being a threat to virtue, even indirectly, as a panderer and facilitator of (heterosexual) seduction; this story is also one of the first to describe the vampire as being able to take a bat-like form. Because of woman's unquestioned status as the beloved defiance of the divinely sanctioned laws of time and mortality are more often presented as the motive for vampirism than immediate dominion over others, such as in Edwin F. Roberts' Countess Báthory inspired, "The Vampyre Bride", wherein wounded vanity begins the fall to witchcraft and blood ritual. Although one might take the appeal of eternal youth as a crudely misogynistic comment on female vanity, in actuality it is another indication of the diabolic parody aspect of vampirism, in that the undead state is a kind of immanent immortality, enduring existence within the world and corporeal perfection, as opposed to the transcendent immortality beyond time offered by most religions.

As unrestrained appetite and passion are part of the vampire's allure it is inevitable that the vampire should become an object of overt romantic desire. Sometimes, as in Dumas' novella, this *eros* is just another form of the lust for dominion, but in other instances where it is tragically reciprocated the vampire actually becomes an object of pathos, a reminder of an ancient dictum of Western philosophy, that nothing can be completely evil in essence, especially if it attaches value to anything beyond its own ego. The vampire though is a demon lover; even if the undead comes to regret its nature its love is a blasphemous parody of real love, one of the teloses of which is the creation of new life, whilst that of the vampire only corrupts or destroys existing life. Even as the popularity of the vampire as a stage villain faded, this potent mix of Eros and Thanatos ensured it remained a powerful motif, the figure of the female vampire in particular finding additional resonance with the development of *femme fatale* archetype within the mid-nineteenth century revival of romantic painting and poetry that would eventually grow into Aestheticism. The increased literary interest in psychology had by then lead to more nuanced views of gender power dynamics, which threw into question the notion of female sexual desire as primarily passive, until by the end of the century the female vampire enjoyed a dominant allure if anything greater than the male. A quintessential example of this can be seen in the short novella "The Dead Are Insatiable" by the Austrian writer, Leopold von Sacher-Masoch, which blends Slavic vampire lore with other folk legends of an infernal Venus, who enslaves her lovers' souls even after death. Part Gothic homage and part self-satire Sacher-Masoch's work has a strong claim to being the first piece of vampire erotica, as well as making ironic reference to that author's infamous tale of Fetishism, *Venus in Furs*.

The accursed nature of vampirism made it a vessel to explore socially taboo themes such as racial relations and differing sexualities in a literary device we might refer to as the *pathos of evil*, by which a villain figure is presented in a comprehensible, if not unsympathetic light as a metaphor for those society has deemed pariah. In the short story, "Manor", originally published in 1886, the German writer Karl Heinrich Ulrichs, one of the first public champions of gay rights, gives a scandalously explicit portrait of homosexual love between a youth and a young sailor with a tragic aftermath that defies the grave; the male vampire taking on the demon lover role more commonly reserved for the female. Given how, for better or for worse, Sheridan le Fanu's "Camilla" went on to popularise the "lesbian vampire" trope in film and fiction one regrets that Ulrichs' piece has not received appropriate cinematic treatment, especially given the increased interest in historical queer art.

By the beginning of the twentieth century vampire fiction had experienced extreme exponential growth, with the vampire itself evolving into different forms such as the psychic vampire, "scientific vampire", vampire animals and even the extra-terrestrial vampire. One particularly patriotic or opportunistic Pulp writer was even to write a novel about soldiers of the Great War being resurrected as vampires in a dastardly Hunish plot to invade the British Isles. Despite this plethora of stories, one gets the impression that the vampire was losing its potency as a literary symbol. For one thing its uncertain whether many of these new species of vampire were really deserving of the name, as they often failed to respect the vampire's status as undead or the air of diabolism which surrounds it. Even many of the Edwardian writers who kept the traditional vampires form burrowed far too heavily from Stoker and le Fanu, to the point at which their stories were really just rehashes of several scenes from those writers' novels. One can make a strong case that *Dracula* was in fact the last great work of vampire fiction and maybe its logical conclusion, tacitly connecting as it did the vampire with the figure of the Anti-Christ.

But perhaps this is too pessimistic an assessment. Invariably experiments in novelty yield more failure than success and the former will obscure the latter; likewise attempts to reinvent a subject may fail but exploring it in connection with new styles and themes often yields interesting results. The pieces from this period, which one might call "the twilight of the vampires", have been selected in virtue of their varying styles, from clever antiquarian ghost story touching on the unsavoury aspects of college life to *moderne* attempts to link vampire with "vamp" in an age of gratuitous wealth. A story from the years immediately following the Great War by the German Weird Fiction writer Leonhard Stein captures the nascent Expressionist movement's fascination with venereal disease and clinical anxiety with its descriptive emphasis on the bodily horror of a vampire's predations. This piece also shows how the falling away of old institutions and cosmopolitan rootlessness had stripped away the last elements of passivity from the female vampire, in this case an anonymous quasi-sexual predator.

The vampire remains a popular cultural icon to this day. It would not be unfair to say that since the 1960s more vampire fiction has been written in any given single decade than throughout the entirety of the nineteenth century. Through a process of visual commodification, mass media has transformed the vampire into everything from a children's party costume to an emoji. Maybe this is why the aesthetic impact of the vampire was languished whilst its popularity has grown, for the vampire is in essence a metaphysical horror; an inversion of Catholic symbolism and ultimately an artefact of Satanism. One need not believe in any of the creeds in question, but at least being able to recognise the symbols involved goes a long way to allowing one to understand their resonance and power. There is always a chance the great modern vampire novel has already been written and is waiting to be discovered. Until then we must look to the past to understand the genesis of the most beautiful and sinister of night's black agents.

—Daniel Corrick

A NOTE ON THE TEXTS

UNLESS otherwise stated all stories included herein appear in the forms in which they were originally printed, with minor amendments being made to standardise punctuation and spelling. The text for Alexander Dumas' "The Pale Lady" is taken from the 1849 translation of *Les Mille et Un Fantômes* and corrected against the French original, with various lines omitted by the translator restored. The text of Thomas Prest's "The Wood Devil" was taken from John Thomas Haines' *The Ocean of Life; or, Every Inch a Sailor*, Royal Danish Library of Copenhagen.

The editor would like to thank the staff at that institute, as well as Cyrus Pacquin, Venus Raven, Quentin S. Crisp and Simon Hesselager Johansen for their help in making this volume possible.

NIGHT'S BLACK AGENTS

WE HAVE MADE A COVENANT WITH
DEATH AND WITH HELL WE HAVE
SIGNED A PACT.

Isaiah 28:15

THE VAMPYRE

by John William Polidori

IT happened that in the midst of the dissipations attendant upon a London winter, there appeared at the various parties of the leaders of the *ton* a nobleman, more remarkable for his singularities, than his rank. He gazed upon the mirth around him, as if he could not participate therein. Apparently, the light laughter of the fair only attracted his attention, that he might by a look quell it, and throw fear into those breasts where thoughtlessness reigned. Those who felt this sensation of awe, could not explain whence it arose: some attributed it to the dead grey eye, which, fixing upon the object's face, did not seem to penetrate, and at one glance to pierce through to the inward workings of the heart; but fell upon the cheek with a leaden ray that weighed upon the skin it could not pass. His peculiarities caused him to be invited to every house; all wished to see him, and those who had been accustomed to violent excitement, and now felt the weight of *ennui*, were pleased at having something in their presence capable of engaging their attention. In spite of the deadly hue of his face, which never gained a warmer tint, either from the blush of modesty, or from the strong emotion of passion, though its form and outline were beautiful, many of the female hunters after notoriety attempted to win his attentions, and gain, at least, some marks of what they might term affection: Lady

Mercer, who had been the mockery of every monster shewn in drawing-rooms since her marriage, threw herself in his way, and did all but put on the dress of a mountebank, to attract his notice:—though in vain:—when she stood before him, though his eyes were apparently fixed upon hers, still it seemed as if they were unperceived;—even her unappalled impudence was baffled, and she left the field. But though the common adultress could not influence even the guidance of his eyes, it was not that the female sex was indifferent to him: yet such was the apparent caution with which he spoke to the virtuous wife and innocent daughter, that few knew he ever addressed himself to females. He had, however, the reputation of a winning tongue; and whether it was that it even overcame the dread of his singular character, or that they were moved by his apparent hatred of vice, he was as often among those females who form the boast of their sex from their domestic virtues, as among those who sully it by their vices.

About the same time, there came to London a young gentleman of the name of Aubrey: he was an orphan left with an only sister in the possession of great wealth, by parents who died while he was yet in childhood. Left also to himself by guardians, who thought it their duty merely to take care of his fortune, while they relinquished the more important charge of his mind to the care of mercenary subalterns, he cultivated more his imagination than his judgment. He had, hence, that high romantic feeling of honour and candour, which daily ruins so many milliners' apprentices. He believed all to sympathise with virtue, and thought that vice was thrown in by Providence merely for the picturesque effect of the scene, as we see in romances: he thought that the misery of a cottage merely consisted in the vesting of clothes, which were as warm, but which were better adapted to the painter's eye by their irregular folds and various coloured patches. He thought, in fine, that the dreams of poets were the realities of life. He was handsome, frank, and rich: for these reasons, upon his entering into the gay circles, many mothers surrounded him, striving which should describe with least truth their languishing or romping favourites: the daughters at the same time, by their brightening countenances when he approached, and by their sparkling eyes, when he opened his lips, soon led him into false notions of his talents and his merit. Attached as he was to the romance of his solitary hours, he was startled at finding, that, except in the tallow and wax candles that flickered, not from the presence of a ghost, but from want of snuffing, there was no foundation in real life for any of that congeries of pleasing pictures and descriptions contained in those volumes, from which he had formed his study. Finding, however, some compensation in his gratified vanity, he was about to relinquish his dreams, when the extraordinary being we have above described, crossed him in his career.

He watched him; and the very impossibility of forming an idea of the character of a man entirely absorbed in himself, who gave few other signs of his observation of external objects, than the tacit assent to their existence, implied by the avoidance of their contact: allowing his imagination to picture every thing that flattered its propensity to extravagant ideas, he soon formed this object into the hero of a romance, and determined to observe the offspring of his fancy, rather than the person before him. He became acquainted with him, paid him attentions, and so far advanced upon his notice, that his presence was always recognised. He gradually learnt that Lord Ruthven's affairs were embarrassed, and soon found, from the notes of preparation in —— Street, that he was about to travel. Desirous of gaining some information respecting this singular character, who, till now, had only whetted his curiosity, he hinted to his guardians, that it was time for him to perform the tour, which for many generations has been thought necessary to enable the young to take some rapid steps in the career of vice towards putting themselves upon an equality with the aged, and not allowing them to appear as if fallen from the skies, whenever scandalous intrigues are mentioned as the subjects of pleasantry or of praise, according to the degree of skill shewn in carrying them on. They consented: and Aubrey immediately mentioning his intentions to Lord Ruthven, was surprised to receive from him a proposal to join him. Flattered by such a mark of esteem from him, who, apparently, had nothing in common with other men, he gladly accepted it, and in a few days they had passed the circling waters.

Hitherto, Aubrey had had no opportunity of studying Lord Ruthven's character, and now he found that, though many more of his actions were exposed to his view, the results offered different conclusions from the apparent motives to his conduct. His companion was profuse in his liberality;—the idle, the vagabond, and the beggar, received from his hand more than enough to relieve their immediate wants. But Aubrey could not avoid remarking, that it was not upon the virtuous, reduced to indigence by the misfortunes attendant even upon virtue, that he bestowed his alms;—these were sent from the door with hardly suppressed sneers; but when the profligate came to ask something, not to relieve his wants, but to allow him to wallow in his lust, or to sink him still deeper in his iniquity, he was sent away with rich charity. This was, however, attributed by him to the greater importunity of the vicious, which generally prevails over the retiring bashfulness of the virtuous indigent. There was one circumstance about the charity of his Lordship, which was still more impressed upon his mind: all those upon whom it was bestowed, inevitably found that there was a curse upon it, for they were all either led to the scaffold, or sunk to the lowest and the most abject misery. At Brussels and other towns through which they passed, Aubrey was surprized at the apparent eagerness with which his companion sought for the centres of all fashionable vice; there he entered into all the spirit of the faro table: he betted, and always gambled with success, except where the known sharper was his antagonist, and then he lost even more than he gained; but it was always with the same unchanging face, with which he generally watched the society around: it was not, however, so when he encountered the rash youthful novice, or the luckless father of a numerous family; then his very wish seemed fortune's law—this apparent abstractedness of mind was laid aside, and his eyes sparkled with more fire than that of the cat whilst dallying with the half-dead mouse. In every town, he left the formerly affluent youth, torn from the circle he adorned, cursing, in the solitude of a dungeon, the fate that had drawn him within the reach of this fiend; whilst many a father sat frantic, amidst the speaking looks of mute hungry children, without a single farthing of his late immense wealth, wherewith to buy even sufficient to satisfy their present craving. Yet he took no money from the gambling table; but immediately lost, to the ruiner of many, the last gilder he had just snatched from the convulsive grasp of the innocent: this might but be the result of a certain degree of knowledge, which was not, however, capable of combating the cunning of the more experienced. Aubrey often wished to represent this to his friend, and beg him to resign that charity and pleasure which proved the ruin of all, and did not tend to his own profit;—but he delayed it—for each day he hoped his friend would give him some opportunity of speaking frankly and openly to him; however, this never occurred. Lord Ruthven in his carriage, and amidst the various wild and rich scenes of nature, was always the same: his eye spoke less than his lip; and though Aubrey was near the object of his curiosity, he obtained no greater gratification from it than the constant excitement of vainly wishing to break that mystery, which to his exalted imagination began to assume the appearance of something supernatural.

They soon arrived at Rome, and Aubrey for a time lost sight of his companion; he left him in daily attendance upon the morning circle of an Italian countess, whilst he went in search of the memorials of another almost deserted city. Whilst he was thus engaged, letters arrived from England, which he opened with eager impatience; the first was from his sister, breathing nothing but affection; the others were from his guardians, the latter astonished him; if it had before entered into his imagination that there was an evil power resident in his companion, these seemed to give him sufficient reason for the belief. His guardians insisted upon his immediately leaving his friend, and urged, that his character was dreadfully vicious, for that the possession of irresistible powers of seduction, rendered his licentious habits more dangerous to society. It had been discovered, that his contempt for the adultress had not originated in hatred of her character; but that he had required, to enhance his gratification, that his victim, the partner of his guilt, should be hurled from the pinnacle of unsullied virtue, down to the lowest abyss of infamy and degradation: in fine, that all those females whom he had sought, apparently on account of their virtue, had, since his departure, thrown even the mask aside, and had not scrupled to expose the whole deformity of their vices to the public gaze.

Aubrey determined upon leaving one, whose character had not yet shown a single bright point on which to rest the eye. He resolved to invent some plausible pretext for abandoning him altogether, purposing, in the meanwhile, to watch him more closely, and to let no slight circumstances pass by unnoticed. He entered into the same circle, and soon perceived, that his Lordship was endeavouring to work upon the inexperience of the daughter of the lady whose house he chiefly frequented. In Italy, it is seldom that an unmarried female is met with in society; he was therefore obliged to carry on his plans in secret; but Aubrey's eye followed him in all his windings, and soon discovered that an assignation had been appointed, which would most likely end in the ruin of an innocent, though thoughtless girl. Losing no time, he entered the apartment of Lord Ruthven, and abruptly asked him his intentions with respect to the lady, informing him at the same time that he was aware of his being about to meet her that very night. Lord Ruthven answered, that his intentions were such as he supposed all would have upon such an occasion; and upon being pressed whether he intended to marry her, merely laughed. Aubrey retired; and, immediately writing a note, to say, that from that moment he must decline accompanying his Lordship in the remainder of their proposed tour, he ordered his servant to seek other apartments, and calling upon the mother of the lady, informed her of all he knew, not only with regard to her daughter, but also concerning the character of his Lordship. The assignation was prevented. Lord Ruthven next day merely sent his servant to notify his complete assent to a separation; but did not hint any suspicion of his plans having been foiled by Aubrey's interposition.

Having left Rome, Aubrey directed his steps towards Greece, and crossing the Peninsula, soon found himself at Athens. He then fixed his residence in the house of a Greek; and soon occupied himself in tracing the faded records of ancient glory upon monuments that apparently, ashamed of chronicling the deeds of freemen only before slaves, had hidden themselves beneath the sheltering soil or many coloured lichen. Under the same roof as himself, existed a being, so beautiful and delicate, that she might have formed the model for a painter wishing to portray on canvass the promised hope of the faithful in Mahomet's paradise, save that her eyes spoke too much mind for anyone to think she could belong to those who had no souls. As she danced upon the plain, or tripped along the mountain's side, one would have thought the gazelle a poor type of her beauties; for who would have exchanged her eye, apparently the eye of animated nature, for that sleepy luxurious look of the animal suited but to the taste of an epicure. The light step of Ianthe often accompanied Aubrey in his search after antiquities, and often would the unconscious girl, engaged in the pursuit of a Kashmere butterfly, show the whole beauty of her form, floating as it were upon the wind, to the eager gaze of him, who forgot the letters he had just decyphered upon an almost effaced tablet, in the contemplation of her sylph-like figure. Often would her tresses falling, as she flitted around, exhibit in the sun's ray such delicately brilliant and swiftly fading hues, it might well excuse the forgetfulness of the antiquary, who let escape from his mind the very object he had before thought of vital importance to the proper interpretation of a passage in Pausanias. But why attempt to describe charms which all feel, but none can appreciate?—It was innocence, youth, and beauty, unaffected by crowded drawing-rooms and stifling balls. Whilst he drew those remains of which he wished to preserve a memorial for his future hours, she would stand by, and watch the magic effects of his pencil, in tracing the scenes of her native place; she would then describe to him the circling dance upon the open plain, would paint, to him in all the glowing colours of youthful memory, the marriage pomp she remembered viewing in her infancy; and then, turning to subjects that had evidently made a greater impression upon her mind, would tell him all the supernatural tales of her nurse. Her earnestness and apparent belief of what she narrated, excited the interest even of Aubrey; and often as she told him the tale of the living vampyre, who had passed years amidst his friends, and dearest ties, forced every year, by feeding upon the life of a lovely female to prolong his existence for the ensuing months, his blood would run cold, whilst he attempted to laugh her out of such idle and horrible fantasies; but Ianthe cited to him the names of old men, who had at last detected one living among themselves, after several of their near relatives and children had been found marked with the stamp of the fiend's appetite; and when she found him so incredulous, she begged of him to believe her, for it had been, remarked, that those who had dared to question their existence, always had some proof given, which obliged them, with grief and heartbreaking, to confess it was true. She detailed to him the traditional appearance of these monsters, and his horror was increased, by hearing a pretty accurate description of Lord Ruthven; he, however, still persisted in persuading her, that there could be no truth in her fears, though at the same time he wondered at the many coincidences which had all tended to excite a belief in the supernatural power of Lord Ruthven.

Aubrey began to attach himself more and more to Ianthe; her innocence, so contrasted with all the affected virtues of the women among whom he had sought for his vision of romance, won his heart; and while he ridiculed the idea of a young man of English habits, marrying an uneducated Greek girl, still he found himself more and more attached to the almost fairy form before him. He would tear himself at times from her, and, forming a plan for some antiquarian research, he would depart, determined not to return until his object was attained; but he always found it impossible to fix his attention upon the ruins around him, whilst in his mind he retained an image that seemed alone the rightful possessor of his thoughts. Ianthe was unconscious of his love, and was ever the same frank infantile being he had first known. She always seemed to part from him with reluctance; but it was because she had no longer any one with whom she could visit her favourite haunts, whilst her guardian was occupied in sketching or uncovering some fragment which had yet escaped the destructive hand of time. She had appealed to her parents on the subject of Vampyres, and they both, with several present, affirmed their existence, pale with horror at the very name. Soon after, Aubrey determined to proceed upon one of his excursions, which was to detain him for a few hours; when they heard the name of the place, they all at once begged of him not to return at night, as he must necessarily pass through a wood, where no Greek would ever remain, after the day had closed, upon any consideration. They described it as the resort of the vampyres in their nocturnal orgies, and denounced the most heavy evils as impending upon him who dared to cross their path. Aubrey made light of their representations, and tried to laugh them out of the idea; but when he saw them shudder at his daring thus to mock a superior, infernal power, the very name of which apparently made their blood freeze, he was silent.

Next morning Aubrey set off upon his excursion unattended; he was surprised to observe the melancholy face of his host, and was concerned to find that his words, mocking the belief of those horrible fiends, had inspired them with such terror. When he was about to depart, Ianthe came to the side of his horse, and earnestly begged of him to return, ere night allowed the power of these beings to be put in action;—he promised. He was, however, so occupied in his research, that he did not perceive that day-light would soon end, and that in the horizon there was one of those specks which, in the warmer climates, so rapidly gather into a tremendous mass, and pour all their rage upon the devoted country.—He at last, however, mounted his horse, determined to make up by speed for his delay: but it was too late. Twilight, in these southern climates, is almost unknown; immediately the sun sets, night begins: and ere he had advanced far, the power of the storm was above—its echoing thunders had scarcely an interval of rest—its thick heavy rain forced its way through the canopying foliage, whilst the blue forked lightning seemed to fall and radiate at his very feet. Suddenly his horse took fright, and he was carried with dreadful rapidity through the entangled forest. The animal at last, through fatigue, stopped, and he found, by the glare of lightning, that he was in the neighbourhood of a hovel that hardly lifted itself up from the masses of dead leaves and brushwood which surrounded it. Dismounting, he approached, hoping to find some one to guide him to the town, or at least trusting to obtain shelter from the pelting of the storm. As he approached, the thunders, for a moment silent, allowed him to hear the dreadful shrieks of a woman mingling with the stifled, exultant mockery of a laugh, continued in one almost unbroken sound;—he was startled: but, roused by the thunder which again rolled over his head, he, with a sudden effort, forced open the door of the hut. He found himself in utter darkness: the sound, however, guided him. He was apparently unperceived; for, though he called, still the sounds continued, and no notice was taken of him. He found himself in contact with someone, whom he immediately seized; when a voice cried, "Again baffled!" to which a loud laugh succeeded; and he felt himself grappled by one whose strength seemed superhuman: determined to sell his life as dearly as he could, he struggled; but it was in vain: he was lifted from his feet and hurled with enormous force against the ground:—his enemy threw himself upon him, and kneeling upon his breast, had placed his hands upon his throat—when the glare of many torches penetrating through the hole that gave light in the day, disturbed him;—he instantly rose, and, leaving his prey, rushed through the door, and in a moment the crashing of the branches, as he broke through the wood, was no longer heard. The storm was now still; and Aubrey, incapable of moving, was soon heard by those without. They entered; the light of their torches fell upon the mud walls, and the thatch loaded on every individual straw with heavy flakes of soot. At the desire of Aubrey they searched for her who had attracted him by her cries; he was again left in darkness; but what was his horror, when the light of the torches once more burst upon him, to perceive the airy form of his fair conductress brought in a lifeless corpse. He shut his eyes, hoping that it was but a vision arising from his disturbed imagination; but he again saw the same form, when he unclosed them, stretched by his side. There was no colour upon her cheek, not even upon her lip; yet there was a stillness about her face that seemed almost as attaching as the life that once dwelt there:—upon her neck and breast was blood, and upon her throat were the marks of teeth having opened the vein:—to this the men pointed, crying, simultaneously struck with horror, "A Vampyre! a Vampyre!" A litter was quickly formed, and Aubrey was laid by the side of her who had lately been to him the object of so many bright and fairy visions, now fallen with the flower of life that had died within her. He knew not what his thoughts were—his mind was benumbed and seemed to shun reflection, and take refuge in vacancy—he held almost unconsciously in his hand a naked dagger of a particular construction, which had been found in the hut. They were soon met by different parties who had been engaged in the search of her whom a mother had missed. Their lamentable cries, as they approached the city, forewarned the parents of some dreadful catastrophe.—To describe their grief would be impossible; but when they ascertained the cause of their child's death, they looked at Aubrey, and pointed to the corpse. They were inconsolable; both died broken-hearted.

Aubrey, being put to bed, was seized with a most violent fever, and was often delirious; in these intervals he would call upon Lord Ruthven and upon Ianthe—by some unaccountable combination he seemed to beg of his former companion to spare the being he loved. At other times he would imprecate maledictions upon his head, and curse him as her destroyer. Lord Ruthven, chanced at this time to arrive at Athens, and, from whatever motive, upon hearing of the state of Aubrey, immediately placed himself in the same house, and became his constant attendant. When the latter recovered from his delirium, he was horrified and startled at the sight of him whose image he had now combined with that of a Vampyre; but Lord Ruthven, by his kind words, implying almost repentance for the fault that had caused their separation, and still more by the attention, anxiety, and care which he showed, soon reconciled him to his presence. His lordship seemed quite changed; he no longer appeared that apathetic being who had so astonished Aubrey; but as soon as his convalescence began to be rapid, he again gradually retired into the same state of mind, and Aubrey perceived no difference from the former man, except that at times he was surprised to meet his gaze fixed intently upon him, with a smile of malicious exultation playing upon his lips: he knew not why, but this smile haunted him. During the last stage of the invalid's recovery, Lord Ruthven was apparently engaged in watching the tideless waves raised by the cooling breeze, or in marking the progress of those orbs, circling, like our world, the moveless sun;—indeed, he appeared to wish to avoid the eyes of all.

Aubrey's mind, by this shock, was much weakened, and that elasticity of spirit which had once so distinguished him now seemed to have fled for ever. He was now as much a lover of solitude and silence as Lord Ruthven; but much as he wished for solitude, his mind could not find it in the neighbourhood of Athens; if he sought it amidst the ruins he had formerly frequented, Ianthe's form stood by his side—if he sought it in the woods, her light step would appear wandering amidst the underwood, in quest of the modest violet; then suddenly turning round, would show, to his wild imagination, her pale face and wounded throat, with a meek smile upon her lips. He determined to fly scenes, every feature of which created such bitter associations in his mind. He proposed to Lord Ruthven, to whom he held himself bound by the tender care he had taken of him during his illness, that they should visit those parts of Greece neither had yet seen. They travelled in every direction, and sought every spot to which a recollection could be attached: but though they thus hastened from place to place, yet they seemed not to heed what they gazed upon. They heard much of robbers, but they gradually began to slight these reports, which they imagined were only the invention of individuals, whose interest it was to excite the generosity of those whom they defended from pretended dangers. In consequence of thus neglecting the advice of the inhabitants, on one occasion they travelled with only a few guards, more to serve as guides than as a defence. Upon entering, however, a narrow defile, at the bottom of which was the bed of a torrent, with large masses of rock brought down from the neighbouring precipices, they had reason to repent their negligence; for scarcely were the whole of the party engaged in the narrow pass, when they were startled by the whistling of bullets close to their heads, and by the echoed report of several guns. In an instant their guards had left them, and, placing themselves behind rocks, had begun to fire in the direction whence the report came. Lord Ruthven and Aubrey, imitating their example, retired for a moment behind the sheltering turn of the defile: but ashamed of being thus detained by a foe, who with insulting shouts bade them advance, and being exposed to unresisting slaughter, if any of the robbers should climb above and take them in the rear, they determined at once to rush forward in search of the enemy. Hardly had they lost the shelter of the rock, when Lord Ruthven received a shot in the shoulder, which brought him to the ground. Aubrey hastened to his assistance; and, no longer heeding the contest or his own peril, was soon surprised by seeing the robbers' faces around him—his guards having, upon Lord Ruthven's being wounded, immediately thrown up their arms and surrendered.

By promises of great reward, Aubrey soon induced them to convey his wounded friend to a neighbouring cabin; and having agreed upon a ransom, he was no more disturbed by their presence—they being content merely to guard the entrance till their comrade should return with the promised sum, for which he had an order. Lord Ruthven's strength rapidly decreased; in two days mortification ensued, and death seemed advancing with hasty steps. His conduct and appearance had not changed; he seemed as unconscious of pain as he had been of the objects about him: but towards the close of the last evening, his mind became apparently uneasy, and his eye often fixed upon Aubrey, who was induced to offer his assistance with more than usual earnestness—"Assist me! you may save me—you may do more than that—I mean not my life, I heed the death of my existence as little as that of the passing day; but you may save my honour, your friend's honour."—"How? tell me how? I would do anything," replied Aubrey.—"I need but little—my life ebbs apace—I cannot explain the whole—but if you would conceal all you know of me, my honour were free from stain in the world's mouth—and if my death were unknown for some time in England—I—I—but life."—"It shall not be known."—"Swear!" cried the dying man, raising himself with exultant violence, "Swear by all your soul reveres, by all your nature fears, swear that, for a year and a day you will not impart your knowledge of my crimes or death to any living being in any way, whatever may happen, or whatever you may see."—His eyes seemed bursting from their sockets: "I swear!" said Aubrey; he sunk laughing upon his pillow, and breathed no more.

Aubrey retired to rest, but did not sleep; the many circumstances attending his acquaintance with this man rose upon his mind, and he knew not why; when he remembered his oath a cold shivering came over him, as if from the presentiment of something horrible awaiting him. Rising early in the morning, he was about to enter the hovel in which he had left the corpse, when a robber met him, and informed him that it was no longer there, having been conveyed by himself and comrades, upon his retiring, to the pinnacle of a neighbouring mount, according to a promise they had given his lordship, that it should be exposed to the first cold ray of the moon that rose after his death. Aubrey astonished, and taking several of the men, determined to go and bury it upon the spot where it lay. But, when he had mounted to the summit he found no trace of either the corpse or the clothes, though the robbers swore they pointed out the identical rock on which they had laid the body. For a time his mind was bewildered in conjectures, but he at last returned, convinced that they had buried the corpse for the sake of the clothes.

Weary of a country in which he had met with such terrible misfortunes, and in which all apparently conspired to heighten that superstitious melancholy that had seized upon his mind, he resolved to leave it, and soon arrived at Smyrna. While waiting for a vessel to convey him to Otranto, or to Naples, he occupied himself in arranging those effects he had with him belonging to Lord Ruthven. Amongst other things there was a case containing several weapons of offence, more or less adapted to ensure the death of the victim. There were several daggers and ataghans. Whilst turning them over, and examining their curious forms, what was his surprise at finding a sheath apparently ornamented in the same style as the dagger discovered in the fatal hut—he shuddered—hastening to gain further proof, he found the weapon, and his horror may be imagined when he discovered that it fitted, though peculiarly shaped, the sheath he held in his hand. His eyes seemed to need no further certainty—they seemed gazing to be bound to the dagger; yet still he wished to disbelieve; but the particular form, the same varying tints upon the haft and sheath were alike in splendour on both, and left no room for doubt; there were also drops of blood on each.

He left Smyrna, and on his way home, at Rome, his first inquiries were concerning the lady he had attempted to snatch from Lord Ruthven's seductive arts. Her parents were in distress, their fortune ruined, and she had not been heard of since the departure of his lordship. Aubrey's mind became almost broken under so many repeated horrors; he was afraid that this lady had fallen a victim to the destroyer of Ianthe. He became morose and silent; and his only occupation consisted in urging the speed of the postilions, as if he were going to save the life of someone he held dear. He arrived at Calais; a breeze, which seemed obedient to his will, soon wafted him to the English shores; and he hastened to the mansion of his fathers, and there, for a moment, appeared to lose, in the embraces and caresses of his sister, all memory of the past. If she before, by her infantine caresses, had gained his affection, now that the woman began to appear, she was still more attaching as a companion.

Miss Aubrey had not that winning grace which gains the gaze and applause of the drawing-room assemblies. There was none of that light brilliancy which only exists in the heated atmosphere of a crowded apartment. Her blue eye was never lit up by the levity of the mind beneath. There was a melancholy charm about it which did not seem to arise from misfortune, but from some feeling within, that appeared to indicate a soul conscious of a brighter realm. Her step was not that light footing, which strays where'er a butterfly or a colour may attract—it was sedate and pensive. When alone, her face was never brightened by the smile of joy; but when her brother breathed to her his affection, and would in her presence forget those griefs she knew destroyed his rest, who would have exchanged her smile for that of the voluptuary? It seemed as if those eyes,—that face were then playing in the light of their own native sphere. She was yet only eighteen, and had not been presented to the world, it having been thought by her guardians more fit that her presentation should be delayed until her brother's return from the continent, when he might be her protector. It was now, therefore, resolved that the next drawing-room, which was fast approaching, should be the epoch of her entry into the "busy scene." Aubrey would rather have remained in the mansion of his fathers, and fed upon the melancholy which overpowered him. He could not feel interest about the frivolities of fashionable strangers, when his mind had been so torn by the events he had witnessed; but he determined to sacrifice his own comfort to the protection of his sister. They soon arrived in town, and prepared for the next day, which had been announced as a drawing-room.

The crowd was excessive—a drawing-room had not been

held for a long time, and all who were anxious to bask in the smile of royalty, hastened thither. Aubrey was there with his sister. While he was standing in a corner by himself, heedless of all around him, engaged in the remembrance that the first time he had seen Lord Ruthven was in that very place—he felt himself suddenly seized by the arm, and a voice he recognized too well, sounded in his ear—"Remember your oath." He had hardly courage to turn, fearful of seeing a spectre that would blast him, when he perceived, at a little distance, the same figure which had attracted his notice on this spot upon his first entry into society. He gazed till his limbs, almost refusing to bear their weight, he was obliged to take the arm of a friend, and forcing a passage through the crowd, he threw himself into his carriage, and was driven home. He paced the room with hurried steps, and fixed his hands upon his head, as if he were afraid his thoughts were bursting from his brain. Lord Ruthven again before him—circumstances started up in dreadful array—the dagger—his oath.—He roused himself, he could not believe it possible—the dead rise again!—He thought his imagination had conjured up the image his mind was resting upon. It was impossible that it could be real—he determined, therefore, to go again into society; for though he attempted to ask concerning Lord Ruthven, the name hung upon his lips, and he could not succeed in gaining information. He went a few nights after with his sister to the assembly of a near relation. Leaving her under the protection of a matron, he retired into a recess, and there gave himself up to his own devouring thoughts. Perceiving, at last, that many were leaving, he roused himself, and entering another room, found his sister surrounded by several, apparently in earnest conversation; he attempted to pass and get near her, when one, whom he requested to move, turned round, and revealed to him those features he most abhorred. He sprang forward, seized his sister's arm, and, with hurried step, forced her towards the street: at the door he found himself impeded by the crowd of servants who were waiting for their lords; and while he was engaged in passing them, he again heard that voice whisper close to him—"Remember your oath!"—He did not dare to turn, but, hurrying his sister, soon reached home.

Aubrey became almost distracted. If before his mind had been absorbed by one subject, how much more completely was it engrossed, now that the certainty of the monster's living again pressed upon his thoughts. His sister's attentions were now unheeded, and it was in vain that she intreated him to explain to her what had caused his abrupt conduct. He only uttered a few words, and those terrified her. The more he thought, the more he was bewildered. His oath startled him;—was he then to allow this monster to roam, bearing ruin upon his breath, amidst all he held dear, and not avert its progress? His very sister might have been touched by him. But even if he were to break his oath, and disclose his suspicions, who would believe him? He thought of employing his own hand to free the world from such a wretch; but death, he remembered, had been already mocked. For days he remained in this state; shut up in his room, he saw no one, and ate only when his sister came, who, with eyes streaming with tears, besought him, for her sake, to support nature. At last, no longer capable of bearing stillness and solitude, he left his house, roamed from street to street, anxious to fly that image which haunted him. His dress became neglected, and he wandered, as often exposed to the noon-day sun as to the midnight damps. He was no longer to be recognized; at first he returned with the evening to the house; but at last he laid him down to rest wherever fatigue overtook him. His sister, anxious for his safety, employed people to follow him; but they were soon distanced by him who fled from a pursuer swifter than any—from thought. His conduct, however, suddenly changed. Struck with the idea that he left by his absence the whole of his friends, with a fiend amongst them, of whose presence they were unconscious, he determined to enter again into society, and watch him closely, anxious to forewarn, in spite of his oath, all whom Lord Ruthven approached with intimacy. But when he entered into a room, his haggard and suspicious looks were so striking, his inward shudderings so visible, that his sister was at last obliged to beg of him to abstain from seeking, for her sake, a society which affected him so strongly. When, however, remonstrance proved unavailing, the guardians thought proper to interpose, and, fearing that his mind was becoming alienated, they thought it high time to resume again that trust which had been before imposed upon them by Aubrey's parents.

Desirous of saving him from the injuries and sufferings he had daily encountered in his wanderings, and of preventing him from exposing to the general eye those marks of what they considered folly, they engaged a physician to reside in the house, and take constant care of him. He hardly appeared to notice it, so completely was his mind absorbed by one terrible subject. His incoherence became at last so great, that he was confined to his chamber. There he would often lie for days, incapable of being roused. He had become emaciated, his eyes had attained a glassy lustre;—the only sign of affection and recollection remaining displayed itself upon the entry of his sister; then he would sometimes start, and, seizing her hands, with looks that severely afflicted her, he would desire her not to touch him. "Oh, do not touch him—if your love for me is aught, do not go near him!" When, however, she inquired to whom he referred, his only answer was, "True! true!" and again he sank into a state, whence not even she could rouse him. This lasted many months: gradually, however, as the year was passing, his incoherences became less frequent, and his mind threw off a portion of its gloom, whilst his guardians observed, that several times in the day he would count upon his fingers a definite number, and then smile.

The time had nearly elapsed, when, upon the last day of the year, one of his guardians entering his room, began to converse with his physician upon the melancholy circumstance of Aubrey's being in so awful a situation, when his sister was going next day to be married. Instantly Aubrey's attention was attracted; he asked anxiously to whom. Glad of this mark of returning intellect, of which they feared he had been deprived, they mentioned the name of the Earl of Marsden. Thinking this was a young Earl whom he had met with in society, Aubrey seemed pleased, and astonished them still more by his expressing his intention to be present at the nuptials, and desiring to see his sister. They answered not, but in a few minutes his sister was with him. He was apparently again capable of being affected by the influence of her lovely smile; for he pressed her to his breast, and kissed her cheek, wet with tears, flowing at the thought of her brother's being once more alive to the feelings of affection. He began to speak with all his wonted warmth, and to congratulate her upon her marriage with a person so distinguished for rank and every accomplishment; when he suddenly perceived a locket upon her breast; opening it, what was his surprise at beholding the features of the monster who had so long influenced his life. He seized the portrait in a paroxysm of rage, and trampled it under foot. Upon her asking him why he thus destroyed the resemblance of her future husband, he looked as if he did not understand her—then seizing her hands, and gazing on her with a frantic expression of countenance, he bade her swear that she would never wed this monster, for he—— But he could not advance—it seemed as if that voice again bade him remember his oath—he turned suddenly round, thinking Lord Ruthven was near him but saw no one. In the meantime the guardians and physician, who had heard the whole, and thought this was but a return of his disorder, entered, and forcing him from Miss Aubrey, desired her to leave him. He fell upon his knees to them, he implored, he begged of them to delay but for one day. They, attributing this to the insanity they imagined had taken possession of his mind, endeavoured to pacify him, and retired.

Lord Ruthven had called the morning after the drawing-room, and had been refused with everyone else. When he heard of Aubrey's ill health, he readily understood himself to be the cause of it; but when he learned that he was deemed insane, his exultation and pleasure could hardly be concealed from those among whom he had gained this information. He hastened to the house of his former companion, and, by constant attendance, and the pretence of great affection for the brother and interest in his fate, he gradually won the ear of Miss Aubrey. Who could resist his power? His tongue had dangers and toils to recount—could speak of himself as of an individual having no sympathy with any being on the crowded earth, save with her to whom he addressed himself;—could tell how, since he knew her, his existence, had begun to seem worthy of preservation, if it were merely that he might listen to her soothing accents;—in fine, he knew so well how to use the serpent's art, or such was the will of fate, that he gained her affections. The title of the elder branch falling at length to him, he obtained an important embassy, which served as an excuse for hastening the marriage, (in spite of her brother's deranged state,) which was to take place the very day before his departure for the continent.

Aubrey, when he was left by the physician and his guardians, attempted to bribe the servants, but in vain. He asked for pen and paper; it was given him; he wrote a letter to his sister, conjuring her, as she valued her own happiness, her own honour, and the honour of those now in the grave, who once held her in their arms as their hope and the hope of their house, to delay but for a few hours that marriage, on which he denounced the most heavy curses. The servants promised they would deliver it; but giving it to the physician, he thought it better not to harass any more the mind of Miss Aubrey by, what he considered, the ravings of a maniac. Night passed on without rest to the busy inmates of the house; and Aubrey heard, with a horror that may more easily be conceived than described, the notes of busy preparation. Morning came, and the sound of carriages broke upon his ear. Aubrey grew almost frantic. The curiosity of the servants at last overcame their vigilance, they gradually stole away, leaving him in the custody of an helpless old woman. He seized the opportunity, with one bound was out of the room, and in a moment found himself in the apartment where all were nearly assembled. Lord Ruthven was the first to perceive him: he immediately approached, and, taking his arm by force, hurried him from the room, speechless with rage. When on the staircase, Lord Ruthven whispered in his ear—"Remember your oath, and know, if not my bride today, your sister is dishonoured. Women are frail!" So saying, he pushed him towards his attendants, who, roused by the old woman, had come in search of him. Aubrey could no longer support himself; his rage not finding vent, had broken a blood-vessel, and he was conveyed to bed. This was not mentioned to his sister, who was not present when he entered, as the physician was afraid of agitating her. The marriage was solemnized, and the bride and bridegroom left London.

Aubrey's weakness increased; the effusion of blood produced symptoms of the near approach of death. He desired his sister's guardians might be called, and when the midnight hour had struck, he related composedly what the reader has perused—he died immediately after.

The guardians hastened to protect Miss Aubrey; but when they arrived, it was too late. Lord Ruthven had disappeared, and Aubrey's sister had glutted the thirst of a VAMPYRE!

THE WOOD DEVIL;
OR, THE VAMPIRE PIRATE OF THE DEEP DELL

by Thomas Peckett Prest

MANY years ago, in the midst of a dreary and almost impervious forest in the Abruzzi Mountains, stood a cottage inhabited by old Urilda, her grandson Tom Walker, the wood-cutter, and Tom's betrothed, the pretty little Clara.

Urilda was supposed to be the most venerable woman in the world, being at that period 108 years old, and with her extraordinary age, came all the natural consequences—great infirmity, and a temper peevish, morose, and passionate, the effects of which, Tom had often felt and deplored.

Clara had been left in her infancy under the protection of Urilda, and she loved Tom sincerely. She was a fascinating, playful, and intelligent girl, and Tom looked forward to the time with much anxiety when he should call her his wife.

Urilda excited not that interest and veneration among those who knew her, that her great age might have been ex- pected to inspire, for there were strange stories whispered of her, and it was even said that she had prolonged her life by no good means; but the truth or fallacy of that report will appear in the sequel. Certain it is that when the old woman was not sleeping in her old armchair, as was her almost constant prac- tice, she was gazing continually upon a certain old fashioned portrait, which hung in the room upstairs, and which represented the likeness of Genano, a desperate pirate, who had suffered the penalty of his numerous dreadful crimes about half a century before, and whose spirit was still said to haunt the forest dell, and the mention of whose very name excited terror in the breasts of the hearers. This monster of the deep was said to have been Urilda's husband.

It was on a very tempestuous night, in the month of December, when the thunder rolled tremendously, and the lightning flashed its lurid fury around, that Tom Walker was hastening through the forest dell towards his humble home. He had reached a majestic tree, when he paused awhile to stand beneath its umbrageous foliage, which never faded from that tree; in order that he might shelter himself from the storm. But he started with terror on finding that it was the Wood Devil's tree, the one beneath which the pirate Genano had been taken, and which his phantom was said to haunt. Tom Walker could not boast of much heroism, and he therefore trembled with terror when he recognized the awful spot, and was immediately hurrying away, when he suddenly felt a singular and irresistible drowsiness come over him, and in spite of the terrors of the place he was compelled to lay down and commit himself to the arms of Morpheus. Terrific visions haunted the imagination of Tom, fiends seemed to dance before his eyes, his lantern appeared big enough to hold him, and at length he was aroused by loud and supernatural peals of laughter which seemed to shake the very forest, and quickly started Tom upon his feet. He gazed fearfully around, and his teeth chattered in his jaws with fear, but all was as he had found it when he went to sleep, and the storm continued unabated. Tom, therefore, once more shouldered his faggots, and with his lantern and axe in his hand was preparing to make the best of his way to the cottage, when his eye caught the name of Genano placed in the branches of the tree, and which was fixed there by some persons to point out the place where the pirate had been taken. As Tom gazed upon it, a sudden thought crossed his mind, which was that he would cut down the obnoxious name, and thus deprive himself and his neighbours of a portion of their terrors. He therefore raised high his axe for that purpose, and aimed one of the most powerful blows at it, but scarce had he made the attempt, when dreadful peals of thunder reverberated above; appalling and demoniacal shrieks rent the air; the forked lightning blazed with tenfold fury around, the trunk of the tree parted, and surrounded by a supernatural light, the form of the *Wood Devil; or, the Vampire Pirate* stood before the terrified woodman! Tom Walker's alarm was thoroughly depicted in his manners; with difficulty he stammered out a question as to who the frightful being was, who pointing above, Tom beheld in characters of fire the terrific name of GENANO!—

"Oh, oh, dear!—you—you—are th—the Devil then?" said Tom.

"Not exactly," said the Vampire with a sardonic grin, "but one of his family!"

"Oh, then I wish you a very good night!" ejaculated the woodman, and he was hastening away with all the speed his terror had prompted, when the awful voice of the demon arrested his steps.

"Hold!" cried he, "what compensation art thou going to make me for the injury thou hast done me?"

"Alas!" cried Tom, "I am so poor that I can scarcely get wherewithal to support myself; but I'm sure I beg your devil-ship's pardon, a thousand times—and——"

"This tree," continued the Vampire, "hath stood here one hundred and eight years."

"La! that's just the age of my grandmother, said Tom.

"True," returned Genano, "but thy grandmother is old and withered, and this tree remains blooming and fresh, as it was seen half a century ago. Thy grandmother has outlived four husbands, and spent four fortunes;—say, how like you poverty?"

48

"Not at all, your devilship—I beg your pardon, your honour," replied Tom.

"How should you like to be rich?" inquired the Vampire.

"Oh, I should like that very much," answered Tom, chuckling at the idea, "for then I could mount a high horse, and make my Clara a lady."

"Well, well," returned Genano, "attend to my instructions, and thou shalt be rich; meet me tonight when the moon tips the Bridge of Horrors, and I will present thee with a casket, containing all thou requirest!"

"No, will you, though," exclaimed the delighted Tom, forgetting for a moment his terrors in the golden idea; "but how much will the chest contain?"

"Ten thousand pieces of gold," replied Genano.

"Ten thousand pieces of gold!" cried Tom; "what a rich fellow I shall be to be sure; I mean to say you're a devilish good devil; but what return am I to make for this gift?"

"We'll talk of that hereafter," answered Genano, "thou wilt not fail to come?"

"Oh, no!" said Tom counting the ideal fortune on his fingers, "I'll be sure to come; but——"

Turning round he found Genano had vanished, and completely overcome by his fears, he now repented having promised to meet him. "Oh, Mr. Devil, Genano or whatever's your name," cried he, "I made a mistake; I—I shan't be able to come; I shall be ill in bed at that time." He was staggering off with these words, when a dreadful voice shouted in his ear "Remember!" and quite overpowered with alarm, the woodman sunk insensible on the earth, while the loud laughter of exultant fiends rent the air.

Upon regaining his senses what was his wonder to find himself on the floor of his own cottage parlour, and Clara standing over him, while his old grandmother seemed to be sleeping as soundly as usual in her old arm-chair by the side of the fire-place. Tom rubbed his eyes, and could scarcely believe he was awake. How he had got into the cottage he could not imagine, and Clara was equally at a loss to inform him, but of one thing she was positive, and that was that he had not entered at the door; so Tom naturally concluded that he must have fallen through the roof, although that seemed perfectly sound, and in the same state in which he had left it. He related to Clara all that had occurred to him in the forest dell, and of the appointment he had made with Genano, but Clara persuaded him not to go, advice he needed not, for he had already made up his mind to break his appointment with the Vampire. Clara now informed him that the old portrait his grandmother took such delight in gazing upon had blown off the nail to which it had been hung, and she therefore had taken the trouble to clean it; "See, here it is," said Clara, bringing forth the picture, "and I declare he looks quite fresh and youthful again, after his renovation."

Tom started when he looked upon it, and with alarm depicted in his countenance exclaimed, "Take it away, Clara, it is the likeness of Genano, as like him, aye, as two peas. Take it away, Clara, and replace it on the nail!" Clara yielded to the entreaties of her timid lover, and they left the parlour together to replace the portrait. As soon as they were gone, the old woman tottered from her arm-chair, in which she had appeared to sleep, but had in fact been listening attentively to all that passed, for the conversation awfully and deeply interested her.

"Genano has kept his word," said she; "the message delivered to my grandson was meant for me, and the falling of the old portrait is the signal he agreed upon to announce the time of his revisiting the earth."

At that moment a voice, loud as thunder, exclaimed: "Urilda!"

"Ah! 'tis his voice!" exclaimed the old woman,—"Genano, I come—I come!" and, with an uncommon firm step for one so aged, the guilty Urilda hastened from the hovel to meet Genano, the Vampire Pirate.

The astonishment and alarm of Clara and Tom was very great on their return to the parlour, to find the old woman gone, and Tom verily believed that she had been spirited away, for the last ten years she had done nothing but sit and sleep in the armchair, and he could not think it possible that she could now find the strength to take a walk, especially at that time of the night. Clara begged him to accompany her in search of Urilda, fearful that some accident might befall her, and they hastened towards the cottage door for that purpose, when it opened and there stood the decrepid form of Urilda, her furrowed face glowing with anger.—"Wretches," she cried, "dare but to follow me, or attempt to pry into my awful secrets, and dread my vengeance."

With these words, Urilda left the spot, leaving Clara and Tom still more astonished and alarmed. Notwithstanding the old woman's stern injunctions and threats, Clara was resolved to follow her footsteps, and accordingly left the cottage for that purpose.—After combating his fears, Tom followed her, but was unable to overtake her, till he met on the road one Gabbo, a simple vender of images, with whom he was acquainted, and who had been entrusted with a letter for Tom, to whom he was then bearing it. Tom hastily broke the seal, and him and Clara were delighted to find that it had come from the Baroness d'Ostia, a rich relative of his, whom he had never seen, but who had promised to befriend him. The letter informed him, that the baroness was then on her way to his grandmother's cottage, and that it was her intention to take him under her future protection, and to raise him from the poverty he at present lingered in, to a state of affluence. Clara and Tom were in perfect ecstasies at this intelligence, and thanking their Italian mercury, again set forth in pursuit of the aged Urilda.

The moon shone brightly on the Vampire's grave in the ruined monastery, as Urilda tottered into the solemn spot, on her mysterious and awful errand. In the back ground was seen the Bridge of Horrors, and in the distance Vesuvius reared its lofty head. With the greatest terror and emotion old Urilda gazed upon the well-known spot, and marked with a wild glance the tomb of her guilty husband. "Genano," she cried, "I attend your summons; if the power be granted thee, oh, appear to me!"—Quick as lightning the stone rolled from the pirate's tomb, and Genano stood before the trembling form of the aged Urilda, just the same as he had appeared fifty years before.

"Urilda!", he exclaimed, "I have kept my word with thee—Thou art now the oldest woman in the world!"

"Oh, Genano," uttered the feeble voice of the ancient sinner, "thou hast indeed kept thy word with me by heaping upon me years of life beyond those given to other mortals!—But alas, what years of wretchedness have they been to me!—I have outlived all I loved, or all that loved me in the world;—I see myself surrounded by those who hate me!—and conscience gnaws upon my heart, and is a never failing source of the most poignant anguish to me, recalling to me the deeds—the crimes—and the unpardonable errors of my youth!—Oh, that I could lay down and die, but yet I dare not—dare not—cease to exist!"

"Urilda," cried the Vampire, "thou knowest the power given to me; say shall I give thee death, or wouldst thou prolong thine existence for another century?"

"Oh, let me still live!—let me still live!" ejaculated the wretched Urilda, "much as I tremble to live, yet can I not muster the courage to die!—Let me live, Genano!"

"Take thy wish," cried the Vampire, placing his mantle before her; in a moment, Urilda found herself transformed into the person of a young, beautiful, and splendidly attired female, with all the action, vigour, and appearance of the most blooming youth.

"Heavens!" she cried, "can I believe my eyes?—This form—whose is it?"

"'Tis that of the young and beautiful Baroness d'Ostia!" answered Genano.

"What—my wealthy and haughty relation?" inquired the astonished Urilda.

"The same," said Genano, "she has but just fallen into the river, and is drowned, on her way to your hovel; her attendants have not yet missed her, you have, therefore, nothing to do but to join them, and her name and affluence are yours!—Quick, see, the attendants approach the bridge."

"But how to account to my grandson and Clara for my sudden disappearance?" inquired the now youthful Urilda.

"Leave that to me!" replied Genano, "away!"

Quickly Urilda disappeared to join the attendants—and the Vampire seeing Tom Walker and Clara approaching that way, assumed the late discarded red cloak of Urilda, and in all things looked like her himself. Tom and Clara upon their entrance, took the Vampire for Urilda, and accordingly went up to address her, but Genano imitating the voice of the late Urilda, as near as possible, said—"Get ye gone, ye impudent wretches!—Presume not to follow my footsteps, or I will make you dearly pay for it." The lovers were alarmed at these menaces, and Genano tottered away from their presence. He had not been gone many minutes, when the sound of horns was heard, followed by loud shouts of "the Baroness d'Ostia!"—and the rustic lovers, by the light of the moon beheld a long procession approaching that way, and prepared themselves to meet their wealthy patroness. Soon afterwards, the procession arrived at the spot, and Urilda entered, attended by a splendid train of followers, and bearing the exact appearance of the late baroness d'Ostia.

Tom and Clara bent in obedience to her, but the apparent

baroness approached them kindly, and greeted them in the most affable manner, intimating that it was her design to take them both back with her to her magnificent Castello, and to be their future guardian and friend.—She then inquired, with apparent concern, after Urilda, and Tom related to her the old woman's singular departure from the cottage; and the baroness expressed her astonishment, and was proceeding to order some of her domestics to go in quest of her, when to, the horror of all present, the old woman appeared tottering over the bridge, and from her feeble manner, threatening every moment to be precipitated into the rapid waters, which flowed beneath her.—Clara screamed—when a dreadful crash was heard, the bridge fell, burying the form of the old woman in the overwhelming current; Vesuvius sent forth one of its fiercest eruptions—the water seemed to turn to blood, and rising in the midst of it, to the terrified eyes of all, was revealed the terrific form of Genano, the Vampire Pirate, apparently exulting in the dreadful fate of the old woman!

We must now conduct the reader to the Castello d'Ostia, passing over several weeks since the occurrence of the awful events we have just narrated. There all was joy and revelry, and one of the most conspicuous of the guests was a certain Count Vintelli, a nobleman whose wit continually set the table in a roar, and whose gallant disposition attracted the attention of all the fair sex, who flocked to the Castello in great numbers, for the present baroness, the ex-Urilda, displayed one of the most gay dispositions, and her table was continually surrounded by all the fashionables of the neighbourhood. Gaming, and every species of debauchery and pleasure, was carried on at the Castello with an unbounded license, and chief of all the guests who shone in these wild and dangerous amusements, was the Count Vintelli. The reader will most probably already have in him recognized the so much dreaded Wood Devil, or Vampire Pirate, Genano, who had marked the lovely Clara for his next victim, and accordingly made the most forward advances towards the damsel, much to the annoyance of honest Tom, her sweetheart, who was now become a most fashionable personage, and began to think himself a man of no mean quality. Clara, however, was faithful to her first love, and endeavoured by every means in his power to crush the bold passion of Vintelli in its infancy. Urilda, too, with an anguish indescribable, marked the passion of the Vampire, but determined by every means in her power to avert the awful fate which threatened the poor girl. To Clara she was very much attached—she had taken her when an orphan, and sworn to her dying parent to protect her; and she was now resolved, let the consequences be ever so dreadful, if possible, that she would not break that vow!

It happened one day when the fatal time was fast approaching at which Genano was compelled to sacrifice a young and virtuous damsel, to prolong his mortal career, that he had been gambling to a considerable extent with one Rolano, a nobleman, and Montaldi, his friend, and as usual, had been successful, and won nearly every coin that they possessed. Stung with rage, and jealous of the favourable position Vintelli seemed to hold in the bosoms of the fair sex, they vowed revenge, and to gratify that, they followed the Vampire secretly to the ruins of an ancient temple, situated not far from the Castello, and seizing an opportunity, although Tom was present, they rushed behind Genano, and buried their poniards in his back! Genano staggered and turned ghastly pale, for he knew that his fate was sealed unless he could meet with someone on whom he might depend, and who would have the courage to follow his instructions. Tom was so alarmed at what he had witnessed, that he was about to retreat hastily, when the pirate's hollow voice called him back, and looking in his face he said:

"Thou hast a kind heart, wilt thou assist a wretched man? Thou hast the power to save my life; wilt thou do it? Quick, answer me, or it will be too late!"

"To be sure I will!" said the kind hearted Tom, "I would assist any person if I could, in distress."

"Enough, enough," said the Vampire, "I will trust thee! When I am dead, as I shall be in a few minutes, wilt thou promise to lay my body yonder, where the moonlight can stream full upon my face; then taking this phial, pour the contents in a circle around me; as a reward for which, I promise thee that thou shalt obtain whatever thou mayest wish for by dashing that phial to the earth!—Wilt thou obey?"

Tom took the magic phial, which contained a sort of green liquid, and hesitated, but seeing the fast declining condition of the supposed Vintelli, his humanity prevailed over every other feeling, and he promised that he would do as Vintelli requested. "Swear!" ejaculated the Vampire.

"I swear!" replied Tom.

"Enough! enough!" exclaimed the Vampire, and sunk into the arms of Tom a corpse.

Tom immediately obeyed the injunctions of the Vampire, and raising his body, he placed it upon a large stone, where the rays of the moon could play full upon him. He then with a trembling hand poured the liquid from the phial around the body in a circle, and what was his terror and astonishment to behold the corpse vanish instantaneously through the stone, and the next moment the form of the dreaded Vampire walked in from another part of the Pavilion, looking the same as before he had been slain. Tom was so terribly frightened that he did not wait to ask for an explanation, but rushed immediately from the spot.

At this moment Clara entered the Pavilion, and Genano

being now anxious to complete the conquest he flattered himself he had already made over her affections, repeated his vows of love, and urged the maiden to give her consent to their nuptials. Clara heard him out with the utmost coldness, and when he had concluded, she said, with an air of determination;

"Your lordship has already made too many advances towards a heart that cannot own you for its master; my heart is already engaged to another, and even were it not, recollect, my lord, I am but a poor friendless maiden every way unworthy of being united to one of your exalted station!"

"Oh, say not so, beauteous Clara," exclaimed Genano taking her hand, "thy charms, thy virtues, make thee a match fit for an emperor, then why think to bind thy brow in the peasant's flowery wreath, when it may be decked with a diamond coronet? Come, my love let us retire into yon Pavilion, where we can talk further," and the awful being was endeavouring to force the hapless damsel towards that fatal Pavilion, which when once within, she must assuredly become his victim but at that moment a voice cried "Forbear," the Vampire resigned his hold, Clara fled, and Urilda entered

"Urilda!" cried the Vampire, "why this interruption? Thou knowest I must obtain a victim to prolong my earthly existence, and why obstruct me?"

"Genano," replied Urilda, "that maiden must not, shall not be thy victim; I have sworn solemnly to protect her, and I will not break that vow; no, I will rather proclaim aloud thy dreadful secret and——"

The eyes of the Vampire flashed fierce with supernatural rage, as he cried; "Urilda, bride, thou talkest much of vows; remember, didst thou not swear to keep my secret?"

"Alas! too well I know it;" cried Urilda, "but oh, Genano, in mercy spare that poor girl! Slay me, rob me of the lengthened life of misery thou hast entailed upon me, but thou shalt not sacrifice my Clara! No, I will shout thy secret in the ears of every one, though lightnings should blast me!"

"Wretch! slave!" vociferated Genano, "darest thou to me talk thus? Beware, beware! Knowest thou not that it is in my power to accuse thee of crimes that will bring thee to the stake? But lest thy shallow memory should have failed thee, Urilda, I will thunder them in thine ear!" And the awful being dragged the wretched Urilda to him, and spoke a word in her ear that turned her whole mass of blood! Her countenance became ghastly pale, and trembling all over, she staggered from his presence, while he exclaimed:

"Now slave, wilt thou dare disobey? Thou art in my power, thou art the bride of Genano the Vampire!"

At that moment Clara entered and heard the last awful words of Genano: "A Vampire," she shrieked—"Oh heavens! save me!"

"Ah!" cried Genano, turning, "Thou hast overheard my secret, girl, and nothing can save thee!"

With these words Genano forced the terrified Clara towards the magic Pavilion; she shrieked, and attempted in vain to escape from his herculean grasp: "Monster," she screamed, "whither wouldst thou take me?"

"To yonder magic well!" replied the Vampire, "to the Halls of the Vampires, forty fathoms below the surface of the earth! Come girl! thou art mine; thou art mine; no mortal power can save thee!"

In vain poor Clara struggled in the awful Vampire's grasp; he had dragged her to the fatal Pavilion, just as Urilda, Rolano, Montaldi, and Tom entered.

"Oh, save her! save her!" shrieked Urilda, "she is in the power of the Vampire, Genano! save her! or she is lost for ever!"

The terrified and astonished spectators advanced towards the Vampire and his shrieking victim, but ere they could reach them, a loud peal of thunder rent the air, and they both vanished from sight.

With hasty steps Rolano, Montaldi, and a numerous host of domestics followed them down towards the magic well, and

Urilda was proceeding to do the same, when she was seized by the officers of the Inquisition, accused of innumerable crimes, and borne to a strong dungeon underneath the Castello.

✳

Here enduring the most dreadful tortures, both of body and mind, the miserable Urilda lingered, and was soon brought to her trial, and being found guilty, was condemned to the flames. It was now the horrors of conscience smote the wretched guilty woman more than ever; the dreadful crimes of her long life burst upon her reminiscence in awful array, and though she longed for death, yet did she fear to die to meet that Supreme Judge, whom she had so heinously offended. In the midst of these poignant sufferings, when the morning of her horrid fate had begun to dawn, she was suddenly aroused by hearing her name called in a loud voice, and on looking up, the terrific form of Genano stood before her.

"Urilda," said the Vampire, fixing his terrible eyes upon the countenance of the unhappy woman, "Urilda thou hast betrayed me, by revealing to the ears of mortals my awful secret; but nevertheless, am I disposed to save thee; if thou wilt therefore assist me in gaining the hand of Clara, I will open to thee the door of liberty, and thou shalt be free again."

"Genano," exclaimed Urilda firmly, "I again tell thee that I am resolved never to aid thee in thy designs against that unhappy damsel!—For myself I care not; I no longer wish to live;—I have prayed, Genano; I have prayed!"

"Remember Urilda," again said the Vampire—"the faggots are now piled in the court yard to burn thee to ashes, and in a short time no power on earth can save thee from thy appalling fate!"

"I have prayed, Genano!—I have prayed!" once more ejaculated Urilda with an air of calm resignation, and Genano scowled with rage.

"She is inexorable;" he soliloquized aside, "but yet is it in my power to take her life!—It shall be so!—Die Urilda! traitress!"—And he was rushing upon the defenceless woman with his drawn dagger, when a voice behind cried "Forbear!"—and Tom appeared at the iron grating of the dungeon with a couple of pistols in his hands, which he presented at Genano.

"Be off, you devil, vampire, pirate, or whatever you may be," he cried, "or by the Mass I have got a couple of as pretty bull dogs here as ever settled any scoundrel's business."

Genano laughed contemptuously. "Fool!" said he, "begone; thou knowest not I am invulnerable to mortal power."

"Well, I don't care for that," said Tom, "for I happen to have that little phial in my possession which you gave me, and if you say another word, I'll just wish you may be turned into a horse-shoe, to be trampled underfoot." With these words Tom exhibited the magic phial, which Genano beheld with evident consternation, and uttering a strange cry immediately vanished. By an extraordinary effort of strength, Tom then wrenched the iron bars away from the casement, and descending into the dungeon, he conducted Urilda to liberty, when they went in pursuit of Genano.

The hour was now fast approaching when the Vampire must sacrifice his victim or sink to dust; but yet he had not succeeded in bearing the terrified damsel to the Halls of the Vampires, in which the ceremony must be performed. He had reached an Italian mill, with a dried up well in the background, when he was overtaken by his pursuers, and finding himself surrounded by numbers he was compelled to make a desperate effort. In vain they attacked him with fire and sword, he was invulnerable, and at last succeeded in dragging Clara to the well, which he descended, bearing her in his arms. Urilda, Tom, Rolano, and the soldiers fearlessly followed, and after

descending an almost incredible depth, what was their astonishment to behold themselves in an immense hall, or palace,
surrounded on all sides with ghastly phantoms and roaring
torrents, while near a burning cauldron that stood before an
altar in the centre, stood the form of Genano endeavouring
to force the defenceless Clara to submit to his unholy rites.
They rushed upon him, and resigning the maid, he snatched
from the cauldron a large arrow and attempted to pierce the
breast of Urilda but it was dashed from his hand, and finding
all his attempts were futile, he cried, "Miscreants! I have still
the means of a deadly revenge left; this moment will I which
shall involve in one awful fate all but myself and my destined
bride!"

In a moment the fiend rushed to the back of the hall, and
snatching up a torch, he fired the fatal train; the flames as-
cended with awful rapidity, and a dreadful fate seemed inevitable, when Tom cried: "Now Vampire, it is my turn to triumph!—I will wish that thou mayest be destroyed, and that
we may escape!—"

He dashed the magic phial to the earth!—Genano uttered
a terrific shriek, and was in a moment plunged by innumerable fiends into the burning torrent; while Clara and the rest
were restored unhurt, to the spot from whence they had been
lured by the terrific Vampire Pirate.

Clara was soon after united to her faithful Tom, and Urilda
dying shortly after, with a full hope of forgiveness from above,
having received a pardon below, they fell into possession of
the Castello, and all the wealth of the late Baroness d'Ostia,
and passed together a life of uninterrupted bliss.

ZUVERLEIN;
OR, THE PREDICTION

by A. Bee

"BUT," said the Baroness, gravely, "doubtless there are instances of such things coming to pass."

"I hardly know," returned the Baron, "of one so well authenticated as not to admit of doubt. There are many tales related, I grant you, enough to freeze the blood in one's veins; but upon inquiry I could never trace one to its source. There is no certainty in them; they are told of a dozen different families; the time, too, of the fulfilment of these marvellous prophecies varies a century with each relater; in short, I place no faith in them, nor could I think that you were so credulous as your manner now leads me to infer."

These last words the Baron pronounced with a smile, which, however, met with no counterpart on the serious face of the Baroness. She was vexed with herself for having betrayed a tendency to superstition, which her good sense had hitherto taught her to repress. On the present occasion she had unwarily been led into discussion on a subject about which, although extremely interesting to her peculiar turn of mind, she seldom conversed, from a fear of exposing the credulity she was conscious of indulging to that ridicule which she felt she might merit, yet without having in her own mind power to endure. Brought up from infancy in a remote German province, in an ancestral castle, under the superintendence of an aunt whose knowledge of the world was limited to the forest around her, and whose ignorant and uncultivated mind gave full credit to every superstitious tale, it is not surprising that the Baroness imbibed some sentiments of credulity, though she possessed a well-informed mind, and accurate judgment. At an early age she had been united to the Baron de Rerenvelt, a noble of ancient descent, whose very limited fortune, the mere shadow, indeed, of former possessions, obliged him to abide almost entirely in his ancient castle, situated in a remote and secluded part of the country. As time passed on, his good sense and elegant acquirements greatly improved the Baroness; but as by carefully concealing the weak points of her character she received no correction from the judicious Baron, her superstitious fears flourished more than ever, whilst the passion for romance was fed by contemplation and secret study. Just as she had finished reading a certain wild legend of a prophecy which had been fulfilled in its minutest circumstances, when, moreover, her mind was deeply impressed with the recollection of the tale, she was suddenly summoned to the presence of her husband. Irresistibly impelled to speak of that which at the moment occupied her thoughts, with full frankness she narrated what she had read to the Baron and a conversation thereupon ensued, in which his sceptical notions led her to affirm a contrary belief, with an earnestness, too, which greatly astonished him; yet still regarding her sentiments rather as fit subject for mirth than serious admonition, he laughingly said—

"I suppose you will hardly forgive me for allowing you to be mistress of my castle so many years and still leaving you in ignorance of a mysterious, obscure, and, I doubt not, terrible prediction relating to our family, which has, I believe, been transmitted from father to son from the first founder, though by whom uttered is buried in oblivion. I have never heard that the report has in any way been made intelligible; but you, perchance, would carry such good faith to its unravelling that you may be the person destined to fathom its mysteries."

The Baroness could no longer attempt to conceal her emotions of the importance she attached to this ominous prediction, and starting up, exclaimed—

"Is it possible that you have so long kept me in ignorance of so extraordinary a circumstance, and yet treat it as so insignificant a matter? I entreat you to show me this prediction, if preserved in written characters, else relate it to me, if it exists only in oral tradition. You will not refuse."

"Certainly not," replied the Baron; "I have no such desire; but I am grieved to see you regard the wild ravings of some crazy hag, or half-mad dreamer, as likely to foretell the fate of so ancient a house as ours; for myself, at least, I have thought so little of the saying, that I solemnly assure you I know not where to seek for the MS.; yet am I ready to give you all the information I can on the subject; and, if you choose to rummage over the dusty recesses and chests of the library, far be it from me to forbid you. I remember hearing this prophecy from my grandfather; and from him I learnt that it had been carefully preserved for some centuries in the family archives. At my urgent request he produced it, and, as far as memory serves, it was contained in a very ancient looking cover, once splendidly ornamented, but then woefully tarnished. There was about it a fastening of three large and clumsy clasps, opening which, a single sheet presented itself resembling parchment, but what it was could scarcely be told, it was so greatly injured by time; on it was traced, in some extremely ancient character, a few lines apparently in metre, of which I could not make out a syllable. There were also several pages in a character of more modern date—attempts doubtless at explanation, or a translation of the prophecy, by men learned in ancient mysteries; as far, however, as I recollect, their interpretations did not agree, and my grandfather, who, to say the truth, seemed to attach no small importance to the subject, deeply lamented that the whole matter must still remain a profound mystery. The MS. was subsequently removed, and, although no doubt placed in some very secure receptacle, yet from that day I have scarcely thought of it."

The Baroness who had listened with breathless attention expressed great disappointment, yet could nothing prevent her endeavouring to discover it; and her lord was rather pleased than otherwise that in the solitude of Rerenvelt she had found a pursuit to interest her.

It is needless to say with what anxious curiosity the search was begun, though the Baroness almost shrank from the undertaking, when entering the spacious library her eyes wandered over heaps of dusty volumes, large chests filled with mouldering manuscripts, and drawers into which papers and parchments had been thrust in the greatest possible confusion. In vain she unfolded each separately; in vain she dived into each recess covered with dust and cobwebs; the wished-for volume eluded discovery. The Baron for some days good-humouredly assisted her, till weary of the toil and not being greatly interested, he relinquished the pursuit to resume his usual habits; and in chasing the wild-boar, and other animals with which the forest abounded, he passed those hours during which the Baroness was thus busied in the old and dark library of the castle. It happened one day that fatigued and disheartened, whilst seated in the recess of a window, resting momentarily from her labours, she was revolving useless conjectures in her mind respecting the ancient prophecy, her son the little Earnest von Rerenvelt entered, leading his twin sister, Paula—

"Why do you stay in this dull, dark room all day, mother," said Earnest, "instead of playing and walking, as you used, with Paula and me. The sun is as bright and as warm as if it were quite summer, and I am sure there are already some flowers in the forest; so come along with us; pray come, dear mother," he continued, pulling the Baroness's robe to attract her attention; but as he marked her eyes fixed upon him with a look as vacant as if she did not observe him, he again repeated, "Mother, mother, what are you seeking for always? Let me help you, and Paula will help you, and when we have found what you want, you *will* come with us, won't you?"

"I fear, Earnest," said the Baroness, roused by his importunity, "you will not be very successful; but if you wish it, you shall look over the contents of this old chest in the corner, provided the dust does not smother you and dear little Paula. You must turn over all the papers carefully; and should you meet with a very old-looking little book, with three clasps, you will be a very useful little boy, indeed, for that is the thing I am giving myself so much trouble about."

Little Earnest eagerly climbed up the tall sides of the huge chest, then helped his sister over, and they employed themselves for some time with great perseverance, turning over the heaps it contained, when Earnest suddenly exclaimed—"I have not found the book, but here is something very curious. See, mother, here is a little trunk in one corner with a lock; and here is an old key covered all over with dirt and dust which I think will open it, but I am not strong enough to turn it."

The delighted parent stepped forward, and having with some difficulty unlocked the box, what words can paint her joy and surprise at seeing, safely concealed at the bottom, an ancient volume, whose appearance exactly corresponded with the Baron's description. There seemed, too, something strange and marvellous, that its discovery should be denied to her minute and careful search, and yet be accomplished at the first glance of Earnest, the heir of Rerenvelt. With mingled feelings of awe and curiosity, she withdrew the tarnished volume from its place of concealment, and kissed her son, whose fate she dreaded might, perchance, be traced in its mysterious contents. The Baroness having quickly dismissed the children, hastened to her own chamber to examine the MS., and to dive if possible into its mysteries. One peep, however, sufficed to shew that it was sealed to her comprehension. The characters were unlike any she had ever seen, and the fluid with which they were traced, were so pale through age, that the letters could be seen only by a strong light. There were likewise several other, pieces of parchment, which, on inspection, proved to be the before-mentioned explanations and translations of monks and learned men. After careful examination, the Baroness at length selected two, bearing names of high authority, which, corresponding nearer than the rest, on these the Baroness fixed her attention, as most likely to give her some useful clue: they may be thus rendered into English—

> "When the grim Black Raven lies in its nest,
> Loving and close to the White Dove's breast,
> Then let the Rerenvelts beware:
> 'Blood! blood! blood!' thus saith the seer,
> And yet no mortal foe is near;
> But the birds will droop, and the towers will fall,
> When a shadow rests in their ancient hall."

The Baroness read and re-read those mysterious lines, but she could understand no more than that some dreadful fate hung over her house, which yet was so obscurely declared, that neither human wisdom nor foresight could prevent it. Sometimes it crossed her fearful mind, that from her son being so singularly the instrument of bringing it to light it might have some mysterious connection with his fate; but after hours of deep reflection, she could perceive nothing in its evidently figurative allusions particularly applicable to the young heir.

The Baroness hastened to obtain the Baron's opinion of those dark denunciations, but he owned his inability to fathom them.

Time passed on with but little change in the Rerenvelt family. The Baron pursued the chase with his usual ardour, and the Baroness remained as much at home as ever, brooding over the defaced characters of the ancient book, though the impression on her mind became daily fainter and fainter, as she saw how completely her utmost efforts were baffled to comprehend the meaning of them. As to Earnest and Paula, each year they grew more and more interesting and lovely, and with dispositions as kind and winning, as their persons were graceful and beautiful. It was nearly three years from the time of the first conversation, when the Baron and his lady, seated at table at a far later hour than usual, for the Baron had till twilight been pursuing a wild boar, that their attention was suddenly arrested by a loud ringing at the castle bell. It doubtless announced the arrival of a visitor of consequence, for as they lived in great seclusion, they were seldom intruded upon without due warning, especially at so unseasonable an hour; they were, therefore, greatly surprised, and the Baroness somewhat alarmed. The arrival of the old seneschal with a letter soon, however, unravelled the mystery. The bearer, he said, remained without the castle gate, till the Baron should have read the packet and had time to return an answer. Thereupon the Baron, breaking open the wax which fastened the silken string, read aloud as follows:—

So many years have rolled away since Leonce von Wolfstein has met with Earnest von Rerenvelt, that he would almost fear to address him, did he not place implicit confidence in his former friendship, and judging the heart of Earnest by his own feel certain that he will with gladness seize the opportunity of complying with a request of the companion of his youth. On my own affairs, and why I have so long neglected to communicate with one I have ever loved and esteemed, I have not now time to enter. You may hear all you wish to know from the dear and valued friend to whose hands I commit these lines, whom, too, I am eager to recommend, for my sake, to your hospitality and protection. He is one of the most superior of men; but persecuted and oppressed by the country which ought to revere and cherish him, he seeks a temporary asylum, where, free from malignant observation, he may determine upon his future course. Certain of your active benevolence, of your tried friendship, I have besought him to receive from you that succour which, I am persuaded, you will readily grant him. A short period will enable him to rise above all the malevolent efforts of his enemies, but he will for ever retain the impression of your kindness. Farewell, my earliest friend, and esteem Count Zuverlein, as you once did.

LEONCE VON WOLFSTEIN.

When the Baron had finished this letter, his noble countenance glowing with fond recollection of his early friend, he hastily desired the Count Zuverlein to be ushered into the hall. It was a large and lofty room, was dimly lighted by one lamp in the centre and others placed along the walls at wide intervals, and these cast but a melancholy glimmer upon the heavy dark oak of which the chamber was constructed, so that when the large door was thrown open, the Baroness's eager eyes could discover nothing but the outline of a remarkably tall person, enveloped in a dark mantle, clasped around his throat, and on his head a covering like a helmet, over which waved a high thick plume of the blackest feathers, which he slowly lifted from his head, and then replaced. As he stood in the gloom, with the faint rays of the lamps but partially falling on his figure, his appearance was so extraordinary, that to the eyes of the Baroness he looked more like a phantom than an earthly being, and an undefined feeling of fear led her to shrink from his presence, at the same time that she made a profound salutation. What added to the singularity of the scene was, that owing to the wind admitted by the unclosing of the castle gate, or to some other singular cause, a sudden rush of air whistled through the old hall, and the lamps flaring, and then changing to a bright blue, wavered and quivered for an instant and then suddenly expired, leaving the party in darkness, excepting for the dull gleams that shot forth from the huge pine logs in the chimney. This accident was, however, speedily remedied, and the Count, yielding to the hearty welcome of the hospitable Baron, advanced forward, and after a little ceremony, took his seat at the table. As he placed himself there, a rattling sound attracted the attention of the Baroness; and the Baron inquired if his guest would not disarm himself, now that he was in perfect security. He declined, however, in a voice so peculiar, that the Baron and Baroness both involuntarily looked up to see if the other had observed it. "You will surely, Count," said the Baron, "allow me to ease you of this enormous helmet; after a long journey it must press heavily upon your brow." The Count bowed, and slowly lifting it from his head, yielded it to one of the attendants, who, not aware of its weight, would have dropped it on the floor, had he not been at the instant relieved by a fellow-servant. The arrival of lights at this moment enabled the eager Baroness to raise her eyes, and gaze upon her guest's countenance. It was, indeed, the most extraordinary and singular that had ever met her gaze: with complexion pale even to wanness, lips totally colourless, large eyes, as if fixed and glassy, forehead and brow perfectly smooth, and cheeks fallen in towards the mouth, as visible with the dead. When addressed by the Baron, he answered in a low tone, as if conscious of its remarkably deep and hollow utterance; but there was something indescribably fascinating in his manner, and in the half smile which, for a moment, played faintly over his ghastly cheek. The Baron spoke of Leonce de Wolfstein, of their long separation, of his desire to be informed concerning his situation and pursuits, and the gratification he should feel if the Count would favour him with details when recovered from the fatigue of his journey: The stranger answered with his peculiar smile, that his journey had, indeed, been from a far country, but he entered not into further particulars. In vain was the table replenished for the refreshment of his guest; although the Count suffered the Baron to place viands upon his plate, yet he not only sent them away untouched, but he seemed to shudder as the odour of the meats and wines rose up in the hall. He even appeared to the curious gaze of the Baroness to grow paler and paler; but that might be the effect of the lamps, which, in spite of the trimming of the old butler, persisted in burning with spiral blue flames, flickering and quivering in the most unmanageable manner. The Baron himself, somewhat fatigued with his day's exercise and at a loss how to entertain his guest, who grew more and more taciturn and abstracted, early proposed that they should retire to rest, and the Count was accordingly shown to the chamber prepared for him.

After he had retired the Baroness made no remarks upon the singular demeanour of their new inmate; and the Baron himself also kept silence. Perhaps their feelings were too undefined even to themselves, and they were willing to await the effects of longer observation before they spoke. In the morning the Baroness arose with a sort of dread respecting her guest, and she shuddered as she entered the hall and found him already there. His tall figure was enveloped in his sable mantle, and he stood motionless in one of the recesses of the window, drawn up to the full extent of his remarkable height, with his arms folded, and apparently in deep contemplation. On the entrance of the Baroness he started, and advancing with slow steps, respectfully touched the hand which she courteously extended towards him. But what a hand and what a touch met hers! It froze her with its marble coldness; it was bony and thin to transparency, and yet the white skin seemed dragged over it with unnatural tightness. Again the very blood of the Baroness receded from her heart though she could not explain from what cause. After a moment's pause she invited the Count to the breakfast-table, and when she dared to lift her eyes to his countenance, it looked still more wild and peculiar in the bright light of the morning sun, than it had even the evening before. But he relaxed from his silence, and again the Baroness was astonished; she had never before heard such eloquence as that which adorned his speech. The simplest subjects became of interest; the richest imagery, the most poetical language flowed carelessly, as if he were unconscious of his superiority, and the voice which uttered them was at once the most fascinating and singular that ever struck on human ear. As if spell-bound, the Baroness listened, and as she listened, delight mingled with the awe with which this extraordinary person had so unaccountably impressed her, and she warmly expressed her hope, that he would find in her husband's castle the safe asylum he was seeking, and that he would look upon them both as most sincere in their wishes to serve him. The entrance of the Baron prevented an answer. The conversation, however, which had so enchanted his hostess was continued; and it was not long before she saw that the effect upon the Baron was the same as that produced upon herself. Accordingly, the Baron's good-humoured countenance lost its gravity and expanded into smiles of delight, as the Count, with admirable readiness, suiting his subject to his hearer, spoke of the chase and the wild inhabitants of the forest, with a minuteness of detail which shewed his tact and skill. In short the Count completely mastered the prejudices of both, although in the mind of the Baroness, more especially, there remained some inexplicable feeling of awe, which served only to increase the intense interest he had excited.

Another circumstance in which her maternal vanity was concerned likewise contributed to increase the Baroness's favourable disposition towards him. Earnest and Paula entered the room, and no sooner had the Count perceived them, than the most singular change took place in his countenance. His wan cheeks flushed, the colour rushed into his white lips, his large glassy eyes moved quickly with animation, and his whole frame quivered as if agitated by some deep emotion.

"You love children, Count," said the fond mother, smiling; "these are my little twins, Earnest and Paula;" and as she spoke she led them towards him: She was not a little fearful that they might shew some reluctance to approach so singular a being; they, however, on the contrary, quitted their mother's hand, and, advancing, seemed to be as pleased and fascinated as their parents were. The Count, too, extended his bony hands and pulled them towards him with extraordinary impetuosity, whilst his countenance assumed such a remarkable expression of eagerness, bordering upon ferocity, as for a moment alarmed the Baroness. The Count, now suddenly arose from his seat, and apologising for the inquietude which the aspect of these beautiful children had caused him, bringing, he said, to his mind certain painful recollections, left the room, having first made his peace with the Baroness. It occasioned no little wonder to the Baroness that the sight of Earnest and Paula continued to produce a decided effect upon this singular person; they never approached him but the same alteration took place in his countenance with the same apparently convulsive efforts to retain them; but he as constantly re-strained himself, and either left the room or retired to a distance.

The wonder of the Baroness (for the Baron was no acute observer) was also excited by the abstemiousness of their guest. He scarcely partook of the social meal, and when she ventured to remark it, he hinted at some religious vow which bound him to avoid eating in society, and said that he applied to the superintendent of the household for the small portion of bread which sufficed for his nourishment. This, upon inquiry, the Baroness found to be true, but she was also told that the scanty portion he demanded was often found untouched in his chamber, or scattered beneath the casement of his window. It chanced one day, that the conversation turned upon the Baroness's favourite subject, apparitions, and the power of foretelling future events, and this she had purposely introduced, because she had a strong desire to shew the old prophetic rhymes to one whom she fancied peculiarly calculated, from his almost universal knowledge, to explain their meaning. Their guest conversed about these mysterious subjects with reluctance, but it was evident to the Baroness that he inclined to give them full credence, and she was delighted that he attached great importance to them. When, therefore, she produced her treasured volume, and opening it asked him to peruse the characters and, if possible explain them, she watched his countenance with almost breathless anxiety. As she fully expected, it underwent one of its remarkable changes, of which, fully aware, he seemed anxious to screen his face from observation, for stooping forwards he concealed his brow with his hands. Awhile pondering over the parchment with profound attention and then looking up with a smile of sadness and deep emotion, he asked if no light had ever been thrown upon the mysterious denunciation.

"None whatever," replied the Baroness, herself in turn becoming exceedingly pale, for she felt as if the moment of explanation had arrived.

"I have divined a part," resumed the Count, in a solemn voice, "and a part is yet to me dark and inexplicable; but doubtless the time approaches, when everything mysterious will be cleared away."

The Baroness, trembling with agitation, now eagerly exclaimed—

"Reveal to me what you know."

"You know not what dread secret it is you wish to become acquainted with," answered Zuverlein; "but," and again the same horrid smile quivered over his deadly lips, "yet will you persist until I consent; I will therefore yield to your wishes. Mark well, then, the first lines of the prediction—

"When the grim Black Raven lies in its nest,
Loving and close to the White Dove's breast,
Then let the Rerenvelts beware.

"I marvel that words, thus clear in their import, should have eluded your powers of comprehension. Tell me, I pray, the distinctive symbol of your house."

"A Raven," replied the Baroness. "Do you not mark it sculptured over the portal, and wrought in stone along the walls of this very chamber?"

"Well," continued the Count Zuverlein, "your son, Earnest von Rerenvelt, I hold to be designated under the figure of the grim Black Raven, the family badge; the White Dove is sure- ly his sister Paula, described as plainly by the circumstance of her remarkable fairness and gentleness, as her brother by his dark complexion and manly spirit. His lying in the nest by this gentle bird surely describes the peculiarly close con- nection between them; for if I understood you aright, you declared them to be twins."

"It is too true," replied the Baroness, weeping bitterly; "the prophecy must too surely allude to my own children. How could it happen that I never discovered what now ap- pears to me to be so obvious. But I implore you, fathom also the meaning of the dreadful denunciation which completes it. Who knows but that watchfulness and precaution might avert their ill-starred fate."

"I have told you," replied the Count, gravely, "that it is not for me to unfold the mystery further. Nay, I may be complete- ly mistaken in my conjectures as to the meaning of the first lines; and it will therefore be unworthy of your spirit to attach undue importance to an opinion, for declaring which, I surely have not sufficient grounds."

These empty words gave not consolation to the unhappy Baroness, who was now firmly persuaded that her own children were too surely pointed at by the terrible prediction, and neither rest nor peace longer inhabited her bosom. Nevertheless she kept from the Baron her own fears, as a profound secret, pondering in silence and solitude over her dreaded misfortune, too late, indeed, perceiving that the fore-knowledge of misfortune is the bitterest curse, and that sufficient for the day is the evil thereof.

It was not now to be wondered at that the spirits of the Countess were often greatly depressed, her good state of health consequently broken, and that she frequently hoped to be released from this world's affliction before the sad issue of her children's fate. It appeared, moreover, as if they alone were not to be victims in this prediction; for about this time an extraordinary mortality occurred in the families of the Baron's vassals, under very singular and unaccountable circumstances. Fears were first awakened by the death of a young child, who had strolled into the neighbouring forest, in high health and spirits, to pick flowers. Alarmed at its protracted absence, the mother sought it and discovered it lying on a bank apparently in a deep sleep. But on attempting to rouse it, she was horror-struck at finding it lifeless. There was no disease, nor mark of violence. The limbs lay composed, a smile still dimpled the cheek, on which a lily hue had only displaced that of the rose which usually animated and adorned it. The next day the child of another peasant was found under nearly similar circumstances; and from this time scarcely a day elapsed without the Baroness being informed of the death of some little victim within the Baron's dominions. There were sometimes perceived faint traces of blood about the child's lips, but no wound of any sort to account for their fate. In vain did wretched parents confine their tender offspring within

76

their own miserable huts. If they left them a moment to pursue their necessary avocations, if they fetched water from the spring, or went to collect a handful of fuel, that lapse of time was sufficient for the cruel hand of death to do its invisible work; for so sure was the wretched mother, upon her return, to find her sight greeted by the aspect of a lifeless corpse, instead of being cheered by the smiles of the gay little cherub she had so lately left. Thus then a cloud of gloom seemed to settle over the lands and towers of Rerenvelt, until the Baron himself began at length to catch the general infection. The Baroness, too wretched to take further pleasure in that conversation which had so lately delighted her, now passed her days chiefly in her own apartment with her beloved children; and the Count spent much of his time in wandering through the forest, from the earliest dawn of day till twilight, in solitary self-communion. During his rambles he sometimes met peasants and serfs who lived in and about the forest, and his remarkable form produced fear and terror upon their superstitious minds. They thereupon began, in some inexplicable manner, to link him with the calamities which befell their offspring; and no sooner did they set eyes upon his tall, dark figure, with plumes waving amongst the forest trees, than they avoided him as some unholy thing. To so great a pitch did their feelings of alarm carry them, that several amongst them went in a body to entreat the Baron that he would no longer shelter a being who, they were convinced, had some forbidden communication with the powers of darkness. Singularly enough, it happened that the Baron had, on that very morning, prevailed upon the Baroness to reveal to him the cause of her altered spirits and daily increasing dejection; and, acquainted with the reason, he had expressed, in no very gentle terms, his displeasure, as he termed it, at the folly of his guest, who had so unwarrantably embittered the happiness of her life by his own fanciful explanation of the prediction. With this cloud of vexation on his mind, though he smiled at the superstitious fears of his vassals, he was not disinclined to join with them in their wishes that the Count Zuverlein would seek some other asylum, although his sentiments of what was due to hospitality, and his regard for his friend Leonce de Wolfstein, forbade his openly declaring his wishes. It chanced that same evening, as the Baron, his wife, and the Count were assembled in the old hall, listening in silence to a tremendous storm which shook the towers of Rerenvelt to their foundation, the Count suddenly turned towards them, and declared that the termination of his visit was nearly arrived.

"I perceive," he sarcastically said, "that my presence is unwelcome; never-the-less, I am not unmindful of the hospitality that has been extended to me. Before tomorrow's dawn I shall be far away, for ere then my mission will be accomplished, and I must return whence I came."

At the conclusion of these mysterious words, he folded his dark mantle around him; and when the lightning gleamed fiercely through the windows, he looked yet more ghastly and terrific than on the night when he first entered the castle. The Baron, rather embarrassed at this strange turn of affairs, muttered forth some indistinct words but expressed himself more intelligibly when he pressed upon his guest offers of assistance and accommodation on his journey. These were, however, declined, and the remainder of the evening was spent by all the three in awkward silence and abstraction. In truth the night was not calculated to excite even the light-hearted to mirth. The storm continued terrific as before, nay, it even increased in awfulness: the pealing thunder cracked over the castle as if it would burst the very fabric walls—lightning illumined the sky in sheets of liquid fire, succeeded by the blackest darkness—whilst the boisterous hurricane dashed impetuous through the forest, tearing up, in its progress, trees of the largest dimensions, filling the heavens themselves with turmoil and confusion.

"The night wears on," remarked the Baron, "and though I fear we may not sleep in this war of the elements, I recommend that we retire to the solitude of our chambers." The Count hastily arose, saying, he should be far distant before his hosts were stirring in the morning; and again thanking them for the courteous reception they had given him, bade them both an earnest farewell.

The Baron and Baroness each now pressed him to delay his departure, for it seemed unlikely that the storm would have entirely subsided by dawn. Nevertheless he peremptorily though courteously declined, remarking that storm and sunshine were equally immaterial to him, saying which, he bowed profoundly, and, taking his lamp, withdrew to his chamber.

"It is strange," said the Baron, as he walked along the passage leading to their own apartment, "it is strange, Paula, that all this noise and hubbub should not rouse me from the drowsiness which oppresses me, but I am overpowered with sleep."

"I would I were so also," replied the Baroness, sighing; "but my spirits are more than ever depressed. What a dreadful night. Each moment seems as if these old towers would fall."

"Never fear," said the Baron, "they will last our time; ay, and our little Earnest's also, in spite of Zuverlein's wise discovery."

The Baroness shook her head and answered not. The Baron, extended on his couch, was soon asleep; but the Baroness endeavoured, in vain, to compose her mind, as she seated herself near the huge stove, alarmed at the violence of the still continuing storm, and thinking about the singular guest she should, probably, see no more. In the midst of these ruminations, she, too, imperceptibly sunk into an unquiet doze, from which ere long she awoke in an excess of terror she could not control, although she could not retrace, with any degree of accuracy, the visions which had disturbed her slumbers. They were, however, connected somewhat with her children, some danger seemed to hang over them, though it was but obscurely depicted to her mind; when, at that moment, the old castle clock struck twelve, and its hollow tone piercing through the howling of the tempest, fell on her ears

like a death-knell. She started from her chair, resolved to proceed to her children's apartment and satisfy herself of their
safety. Cautiously she unclosed their own door that she might
not disturb the Baron, and shading her lamp with her hand
from the gusts of wind which swept along the passages, she
went on her way to the opposite turret, which was occupied
by Paula and Earnest.

The children, indeed, slept in a spacious chamber opening
from the stair-case, and a door at the end communicated with
another room, occupied by their attendants. The Baroness's
first surprise was to find the outer door open, but a dead silence reigned within, and she supposed it had been burst open
by the wind. As she entered that apartment she fearfully cast
her eyes around, but the surrounding darkness was so slightly dissipated by the nearly expiring rays of the lamp, which
flared fitfully on the marble table in the centre of the room,
that nothing was clearly perceptible. But when her eyes grew
accustomed to this state of obscurity, she perceived, indeed,
a tall, dark mass leaning over the side of Paula's couch, and
by the flowing sable mantle and waving plumes, she knew
it to be Zuverlein! With a shriek that seemed to burst her
heart, she flew to the spot, and with her eyeballs starting from
her head, gazed upon the dreadful sight. Slowly he turned his
livid face towards her; his glassy eyes shone with horrid animation, his lips alone were red and glowing, yet stained with
large drops of fresh crimson blood.

"Know me now," he triumphantly exclaimed, and his
voice sang through her ear like the funeral echoes in a vault,
wilder, too, than the raving of the storm; "know me now for
the fulfiller of thy house's destiny—

"'Blood! blood! blood!' thus said the seer,
And yet no mortal foe is near;
But the birds will droop and the towers will fall,
When a shadow rests in their ancient hall.

80

"Behold that shadow, that phantom of the tomb, that demon of the grave, who, curst with ten thousand curses, rests not in the lonely sepulchre; but, sent forth by the power of evil, wanders over the earth to destroy. Yet on the mortal part alone I revel. Behold the last heirs of Rerenvelt, they lie lifeless and bloodless; yet their spirits I cannot control. They are gone where I am for ever excluded. Yet I have sucked the stream warm from the heart. Their destiny on earth is fulfilled!"

"Demon accursed!" shrieked the agonized mother. "Thou art, indeed, that terrific monster whose existence I could never even credit. Thou art that vampire, who, even in the tomb, delights in blood, and gorges on human victims." But she spoke to the air. A laugh of horrid power and wildness alone answered her. The demon had vanished.

Too surely did the long foretold destruction fall thus upon this unhappy house. Scarcely were the fair and lovely twins consigned to the grave, ere a similar fate awaited their unhappy mother; and the Baron, who in a state of extreme despair and sadness, had quitted the hall of his ancestors for a foreign land, with a view to alleviate his sufferings, perished on his passage over the seas. Thus disposed of were the whole family, when the ancient and deserted towers of Rerenvelt, as if instinctively following in the footsteps of general decay, fell a heap of ruins.

For such calamitous events the busy tongue of idle tradition sought out a cause, and it was said, that in the days long gone by, the early founders of that barony had been guilty of great and grievous crimes, and that this was a terrible expiation of the family offences; and the tongue of tradition handing down the same to each succeeding generation, the peasant wandering through the forest still points, with fearful shudderings, to the spot thus blasted and accursed by the presence of the Vampire Demon.

THE BRUXA,
A LEGEND OF PORTUGAL

by William H. G. Kingston

THE year of our Lord 1185, was drawing to a close, when that pious sovereign, Alfonso I., King of Portugal, the mighty conqueror of the plains of Ourique, ended his mortal career of glory to enter in the odour of sanctity, the realms of eternal bliss. Ought not, indeed, he to be considered a hero, if not rather be placed among the saints beatified in heaven to whom a celestial vision was especially vouchsafed, to afford him the joyful assurance of victory on the eve of that most hazardous and memorable of his battles, when two hundred thousand of the unbelieving infidels fell before the unfaltering swords of his hardy followers; who with sixty true and valiant knights once defeated before the walls of Palmela, no less than five hundred horsemen and forty thousand of the Moorish foot; who, moreover, founded the magnificent monastery of Al-cobaca, which in time, enlarged and beautified by the well-noted and justly-extolled piety of Lusitanian sovereigns, came to contain one thousand monks, whose greatest joy was to offer up masses for the repose of the soul of this holy founder? May his example be ever imitated. Nor must we omit to mention the miraculous powers of the mantle he wore in his days of victorious warfare, and which, preserved with religious reverence after his demise, possessed the power of curing the diseases of the faithful, and which none but the wicked sceptic will doubt still retains its sanative virtues in as great a degree as formerly, or what true Portuguese would hesitate to believe, that this ever adorable king, still remembering his ardent affection for his beloved countrymen, descended, habited in white armour, from the abode of the blessed to the choir of the church of the Holy Cross at Coimbra, to assure the holy brotherhood that he and his son Dom Sancho, were then proceeding to assist the Portuguese at the siege of Ceuta, and that owing to their miraculous aid, victory crowned the arms of the faithful? No, thanks be to St. Bernard and to all the saints, such facts can never be forgotten by the faithful.

If the Mahommedans were not completely exterminated, and utterly confounded, it was owing to no want of the strenuous endeavours of the pious king to effect that laudable purpose; but, alas, the pages of history confess that a large portion of the dominions he called his own, was still held by the accursed infidels, who, before the measure of their iniquities was filled up, were yet for a time destined to triumph over the Cross. During the reign of Alfonso the celebrated laws of Lamego were framed, that code so revered by the lovers of the ancient institutions of this country and the haters of modern innovations. He was succeeded by his eldest surviving son, the first Sancho, the third King of Portugal, who was as pious a man, if not so great a warrior, as his more renowned father; but piety availed not against the fierce Moors, who recovered many fortresses Alfonso's arms had won, though his valour was conspicuous at the siege of Silves, which he captured from the Africans, and long maintained against their forces. Indeed, the changing fortunes of war ultimately restored many of the cities he had previously lost to the dominion of the Lusitanian crown.

He possessed a daughter, lovely and graceful as the antlered deer, when in unrestrained freedom it ranges its native wilds. Her hand was sought, not only from policy, which often is the cause of royal nuptials, but from devoted love, by her cousin, Alfonso IX., King of Leon, and the young princess returned the sentiment with the fondest affection. Sancho feeling the advantages which would accrue to his kingdom by so powerful an alliance, approved his daughter's choice, and the nuptials were solemnised with the utmost pomp and magnificence so august a ceremony demanded.

At this time Celestine III. sat on the chair of St. Peter, and no sooner did he hear of the marriage, than declaring the parties to be within the degree of affinity prohibited by the canon law, he despatched Cardinal Gregory into Spain to enforce its dissolution. A council of the prelates and dignitaries of the church was assembled at Salamanca; who, after mature deliberation, four, however, dissenting, declared the marriage void. Cruel, hard-hearted men, doomed themselves never to know the soft endearments, the tender affection of married love, they decreed that the beautiful, the devoted queen should be for ever separated from her spouse. The haughty king, as well he might, was highly indignant; the fair Theresa was overwhelmed with grief; her father, the King of Portugal, was equally enraged that so great an indignity should be cast on his daughter. For a time love triumphed over the stern decrees of the church, and, regardless of consequences, the young couple refused to obey. The legate was furious, and threatened to place the two kingdoms of Leon and Portugal under an interdict, unless the king and queen agreed to see each other no more. They still continued firm in their resolve, for they felt that "those whom God hath joined no man hath a right to part asunder." But the pope was not one to be resisted with impunity, and forthwith he launched the fierce thunders of the Vatican against the devoted heads of the young sovereigns, as well as against the King of Portugal and their respective subjects, both countries being placed under the ban of the holy mother church. Still Alfonso and Theresa pertinaciously refused to alter their resolve; but though they were

84

regardless of the anathemas of the church fulminated against them, their subjects trembled at their awful consequences. No longer could they put themselves under the protection of Heaven, no longer could they expect the intercession of the saints for their sins, the priests were prohibited from performing the rites and ceremonies of the church, the powers of darkness were let loose against them, and evil spirits, ever on the alert to commit mischief, had now greater power than ever to revel in the abominations in which they delight; so said the priests, and who would presume to doubt the words of such good and pious men, to whom the fees and perquisites of their offices, now seldom forthcoming, were of course as nothing compared to the souls of the sovereigns and their people, souls periled by the papal interdict.

It was during these awful times, that in that province of Portugal called the Beira Alta, there lived an old woman. The north-eastern portion of the province was in those days the least fertile part of Portugal, abounding in wild sterile rocks, deep ravines, rugged and precipitous hills, barren plains, the abode of savage wolves, foxes, and other beasts of prey—here and there, too, were to be found dark and stagnant pools, whose opaque waters scarce reflected on their silent bosom the bright sky of Heaven, surrounded by marshes and thick borders of reeds and sedges, which allowed them with difficulty to be approached by human footsteps. But to return to the old woman. It must not be supposed that she was the only old woman in the country, for since the days when Eve became a great-grandmother, old women have existed in every land, and it is to be hoped will continue to exist, for a very useful and respectable part of the community they undoubtedly are.

The old woman to whom we more particularly refer was, however, an exception to the general rule, being, it was affirmed, not only not useful but exceedingly unornamental, harmful, pernicious, and dangerous. She lived by herself in a small hut. It was built of dark, rough stones on the side of a hill, under a jutting rock, which served to form part of the back and roof of her miserable habitation. It was, as may be supposed, in a solitary and wild situation, looking down a valley over a marshy lake, with a wide extent of uncultivated country beyond. At some distance off was a village, tolerably populous for that district, called after that holy apostle the son of Zebedee, St. João da Pesquera, St. John of the Fishery, doubtless, on account of part of the river in the neighbourhood being well adapted for fishing. St. John having, as is well known, previous to his ministry, followed the vocation of a fisherman. Those were troublous times, the Moors making frequent forays to the very borders of the Douro, having at one period, indeed, occupied a chain of fortresses on the lofty and rocky cliffs which form the south bank of the river, but that fact has little to do with this history, except to show the disordered and unsafe state of the country. This old woman, Josefa by name, had a grand-niece called Maria das Castanias, from an early fondness she showed to those nutritious nuts—chestnuts—or else, perhaps, because she sold them baked or boiled to her countrymen as they passed her cottage-door on their way to their daily labours in the fields. Maria, at an early age, lost both her parents; her father was killed by the Moors, and her mother was carried off by them into captivity, when she became a renegade to her faith and the wife of a Mahommedan officer. At this disastrous event the deserted orphan went to live with her aged relative, where, it is to be feared, she learned but little good, if she did not rather imbibe the first seeds of evil, but before she had resided in the mountain many weeks she became the bride of a young farmer, who had some time previously been attracted by her loveliness. Of this quality she possessed a larger portion even than ordinarily falls to the lot of a race justly celebrated for their personal beauty, the un-mixed tribes of the Goths, who, it must be remembered, had long inhabited the northern portions of the Peninsula. Maria possessed light brown hair, blue eyes, and a skin which, though tanned by the warm sun of her bright clime, showed the rich blood which flowed beneath. Her husband, Pedro Ozorio, was the master of a cottage and a few acres of land, which made him perfectly independent, owing allegiance to no lord except his sovereign King Sancho. In the process of time his wife became the mother of three children, sweet smiling cherubs, upon whom her warmest affections were bestowed, though her love for her husband appeared rather to diminish than increase. This at last became palpable even to the poor man himself, who laid the circumstance, and not without reason, to the door of old Josefa, whose constant visits to his wife he felt boded no good. He had always disliked the old woman, and nothing but his love for her niece conquered the repugnance he felt to her society; this she could not fail to perceive, so that she returned the feeling with the most spiteful and deadly hatred, vowing to wreak her vengeance on his head for the slights with which he had treated her. Those who heard her threats and knew her character, were assured that she would not fail to keep her promise. Others, besides her husband, began to perceive the change which had taken place in Maria's character; she was no longer the lively, laughing, cheerful girl she once appeared, her beauty was undiminished, but there was a frown on her brow, a bright spot on her cheek, and a wandering, wild expression in her eyes which told of troubled thoughts within. She was one day sitting in her cottage on a low stool, her distaff was in her hand, and her foot was rocking the cradle of her last born infant, when in hobbled old Josefa. The hag's blear eyes looked more wicked and sharp than ever, and a cunning leer was on her wrinkled and parchment-like features, as she sat herself down on a low bench, her long, bony hands grasping the staff which supported her steps, and her head, on which were a few grey hairs, bent down almost to her knees.

"So, *minha menina*, my child," she began, "still spinning away with your distaff, not tired of such dull work, you whose beauty might have made you the bride of one of the proudest lords of the realm. It was a sad day when you married Pedro Ozorio."

"It cannot be helped now, *minha tia*," answered Maria, rocking the cradle, and biting off a knot in her thread.

"Cannot be helped!" exclaimed the wicked hag, "I tell you it can be helped, and if you followed my advice you would become the wife of a rich and gallant cavalier, the mistress of a proud castle and broad domains, with hundreds of armed retainers to obey your orders."

Maria laughed outright. "No, no," she said, "such cannot happen, except my husband should die (and I do not want him to do that). I cannot marry anybody else, and as for marrying a hidalgo, that is absurd."

"And I tell you that it is no such thing," returned the hag. "You can marry a rich and gallant cavalier, and yet your husband may live, and be happy without you if he likes. Tell me, my child, are there not among the Moors cavaliers as gallant and handsome as any of the Christian knights, who would be ready to worship at your feet, and proclaim your charms throughout this empire."

Maria, blushed with pride, for she was not proof against the specious flattery even of an old woman, and the poison had already entered into her soul.

The hag continued this style of conversation for some time. "Now hear me," she said, "not far from hence a gallant band of Moorish cavaliers lie hid—their chief, a youthful and handsome noble, has, no matter how or when, seen you, and fallen desperately in love with you, for he knows not that you are married and have children. He found me out, and came to me not long ago, saying he should die if he could not see you again, though, of course, he could not venture here by daylight, except he came with his whole force to carry you off. I commiserated his agony and despair, and at length consented to assist him. I promised that tonight you would go out to meet him in a glen near here to hear him plead his cause, and to persuade him not to die."

More need not be said. Maria listened and hesitated—when a woman hesitates she is lost—her patron saint was not invoked to protect her, and in an unhappy moment she consented to accompany her old aunt to meet the Moorish cavalier of whom she spoke.

Now it must be made known, that all the accursed hag had been pouring into the ear of the too credulous Maria, was a tissue of falsehood, to work out her own terrific purposes. There was no Moorish cavalier in love with the unhappy girl, but there was one, ever greedy to devour the souls of mankind, who had marked her as his prey. At the appointed hour of midnight the doomed Maria slipped from the side of her unsuspecting husband, and hastily putting on her garments, hurried forth to a spot near the village, where her aunt, with fiend-like anxiety was awaiting her arrival. The wicked hag seized her hand, and hurried her rapidly along.

"Where are we going, *menha tia*? Where are we going?" she asked in an alarmed tone.

"To see your Moorish lover, to be sure," responded the hag, "he anxiously awaits your coming."

"But I no longer wish to see him," said Maria, trembling, but again she forgot to call on her patron saint, or the Holy Virgin for aid, and it was fear more than repentance which made her unwilling to proceed.

The hag laughed at her scruples, and regardless of her entreaties dragged her forcibly on. The scenery, as they advanced, became each step more savage and gloomy. On every side were lofty and rugged rocks, trees truncated and scorched by lightning, and dark pools, in whose icy waters no fish, or thing with life, would exist. At last they reached a spot on the borders of a lake, more wild and terrific than any they had before passed, surrounded on every side by frowning rocks thrown around in the strangest confusion. The wind whistled shrill and loud, forked flashes of lightning darted ever and anon from the troubled sky, and, as the crescent moon and stars were seen at intervals between the quick-passing clouds, they seemed to burn dim and blue, affording not their usual light to the world below. But what was still more extraordinary, at a little distance off burned on the ground a fierce fire, the bright flashes it threw up casting a lurid glare on the waters of the lake, while round the fire dark figures were seen moving in a circle with strange and wild antics.

Maria at the sight again hung back, for her worst suspicions were aroused.

"Come on! come on!" said her aunt. "The figures you see are a few Moors keeping themselves warm while they wait for their chief."

As they approached nearer, however, Maria saw to her horror that, instead of Moors, the dancing group were a collection of women, mostly old and hideous like her aunt, but others young and handsome as herself. A cold perspiration broke out on her brow, her knees knocked together; but a fate she could not control urged her on. She had heard of such things, but scarcely believed them true. They must be, they were the accursed, the dreaded Bruxas. With loud shrieks and croakings, the vile sisterhood welcomed the new comers as they saw them advancing; and seizing the hapless Maria by the hand, they drew her into their circle.

"She has come to meet her Moorish lover!" cried old Josefa, with fiendish glee.

"He will be here anon! he will be here anon!" they answered, with renewed shrieks of laughter, and continuing to dance furiously round, till Maria, giddy and exhausted, scarcely knew where she was, or what was occurring. At last a loud clap of thunder was heard, and the witches, for such they doubtlessly were, forming in a line, pointed with their arms to a huge dark rock in the distance.

"He comes! he comes!" they cried; and presently, after a continued roar of thunder and flashes of dazzling lightning, a vast blue flame was seen to issue from the base of the rock and ascend towards the sky; thick smoke then followed, and the solid rock opened with a loud crash.

Maria trembled more violently than ever, even the other women seemed agitated; and she expected to see the Prince of Darkness appear in his proper person, but what was her surprise when, instead, a tall and handsome cavalier stepped forth from the cavern, habited in the most superb Oriental costume. A golden crescent with a sparkling diamond decked his milk-white turban, a jewelled scimetar was by his side, and his vest and cloak were of the richest silks of India. With a smiling countenance he advanced towards Maria, whose fears speedily abated, as, bending on his knee, he took her hand and pressed it between his own.

"Lovely, adorable creature!" he exclaimed; "long have I wished for this happy moment, when I might utter all my heart has felt; for often, visiting your village in various disguises, have I gazed on you with delight, but never till now have I been able to present myself to you in my proper character. Sweet, sweet Maria!" and he looked unutterable things as he again pressed her hand to his lips. Those and other words of honeyed flattery had their due and fatal effect on the too susceptible heart of the fair Maria. Bewildered and confused, the poison crept into her soul; she felt not the burning touch of the deceiver's lips, she forgot to look down at his feet hid by the long grass which grew around, she saw not the high protuberance beneath his turban, and she thought not of calling on the Holy Virgin to shield her from evil.

In the meantime the women, as well as old Josefa, had disappeared; the fire, which appeared to be raised on a sort of rough altar, had burned low, and thus Maria and the young Moor stood alone by the silent lake in the darkness of midnight. With impassioned words the infidel urged his suit. Maria's heart melted within her; she confessed her love, but pleaded that she had already a Christian husband. Her lover laughed her scruples to scorn.

"What matters that?" he exclaimed, "another and a stronger tie shall bind you to me. Banish your senseless fears and doubts, lovely one, and be my bride—see, yon altar burns ready for our nuptials—say, charmer, but the word, and I will instantly summon the priest, who awaits my commands to perform the ceremony."

The thunder rolled, the lightning flashed, the night-birds shrieked, as Maria consented to become the Moorish stranger's bride. With triumph he led her back to the altar, before which stood two tall and swarthy men in white garments, but how they came there she did not perceive. The fire blazed up brightly, and by its light Maria perceived her aunt approaching, now, wonderful to relate, habited in rich and costly garments of an eastern fashion, and accompanied by a number of young and beautiful females and handsome Moorish cavaliers. Old Josefa took her niece's hand, and placed it in that of the Moor.

"Thus, noble prince," she exclaimed, "I fulfil my vow. Here is my blooming niece; I give her to you as your bride."

"Will you be my bride, sweet one?" asked the Moor, in a tender tone.

"I will," answered Maria, in a faltering voice.

Again the thunder rolled, the lightning flashed, and the night-bird shrieked.

"'Tis well," said the Moor; "but my race have a custom, that who-ever weds with us, there must be drawn from her arm a drop of blood, to sign with it, while yet warm, the compact. It is but a ceremony, loved one, and no pain will follow, be assured," and the Moor smiled sweetly as he pressed her hand.

On this, one of the dark priests advanced, and, with his dagger, punctured the arm which Maria unfalteringly held towards him; for the presence of her aunt, and the goodly company, had restored her spirits. Three drops of blood fell down, which the other priest caught in a golden cup. The Moor took a pen which was offered to him, and with it wrote some characters in a book held by the second priest, but what was their signification Maria could not tell, though, as she gazed wonderingly on them, they appeared to be of fire. At the same time one of the priests uttered these words—

> "For now and for ever
> No power shall sever
> The knot which has tied
> The bridegroom and bride."

A dreadful doubt, which had hitherto not occurred, now flashed across her mind. She looked down at her bridegroom's feet—horror of horrors! they were cloven!—that undisguisable sign of the Prince of darkness. The hapless Maria had become the bride of a demon. At the same moment, the lovely ladies and the gay cavaliers, with unearthly shrieks and cries, flew off in the shape of foul and hideous birds of prey, so vast of size that they obscured the moon in their flight. The priests and altar vanished in flame and smoke, with a terrific noise, and old Josefa, turning into a gigantic owl, followed the rest, while the Moor, still retaining his shape hurried the now repentant Maria towards the rock from whence he had first appeared. She now was fully aware of the fatal compact into which she had entered, and she knew that if once she accompanied the Moor her doom was sealed, if even there yet remained any hope for her. In vain she entreated to be released—in vain were her shrieks and cries for mercy—the fatal verses rung in her ear—

> "For now and for ever
> No power shall sever
> The knot which has tied
> The bridegroom and bride."

The rock opened with a loud crash, and, seizing her in his arms, the Moor bore her into the unfathomed recesses of the earth.

Before the morning dawned, Maria das Castanias found herself haggard, weary, and wretched, by the side of her mortal husband, in her own cottage at St. João da Pesquera. She rose early, and went about her household concerns as usual. As she gazed at her smiling infants, who, with rich bloom on their fair, rounded cheeks, lay tranquilly locked in each other's arms, all a mother's love gushed forth from her bosom. She kissed them again and again, and tried to banish, but in vain, all thoughts of the dreadful occurrences of the night. She dared not confess to priest or layman what had happened; the consolations of religion were excluded from her for ever. On no side could she look for comfort; and death, the last refuge of the miserable, to her she felt could bring nothing but despair. Yet even then she knew not what was to be the full measure both of her crime and her punishment. Her unsuspecting husband went about his daily labour in the fields, and scarcely was she left alone when in hobbled old Josefa.

"Well, *minha Sobrinha*, what thought you of your gallant Moorish bridegroom, eh?" And she gave way to a fit of croaking laughter like the concert of a hundred thousand frogs. It was not, then, a horrid dream which had occurred, as Maria had begun to hope, but a dread reality.

"You cruelly, vilely deceived me," answered Maria.

"Eh? did I?" said the hag, chuckling. "Not the first woman who has been thus deceived. I vowed to be revenged on your husband, and I have been. Ha! ha! ha! You will join our revels again tonight, pretty one, when a new member will be added to our sisterhood, and your gallant bridegroom of yesterday will have another bride. Ha! ha! ha!"

"Never, never, will I go to such a scene again," cried Maria.

"You will though, this very night," said the hag. "What, have you not discovered what you are?" And putting her mouth close to her ear, she whispered, in a hissing tone, "*You are a Bruxa.*"

And, having said this, she hobbled forth again into the open air, while Maria remained all day trembling with terror, yet with a strange anxiety to revisit the scene of the demon's revels. No sooner did night come on, and her husband was fast asleep, then, leaving her couch, she hurried forth to the wild glen, where she had met the demon Moor. With loud shouts of fiendish laughter she was welcomed by the vile sisterhood of Bruxas, who, as before, were madly dancing round a blazing fire, and, taking their hands, she also joined in their extravagant gyrations.

The number of revellers was soon increased by an equal number of demons of various hideous forms; and one, even more frightful than the rest, singled her out as his partner; nor did she resist or think of resisting his advances. The same dreadful scene as on the previous night was again enacted, except that a fresh victim was brought forward—a young girl whom Maria recognised as belonging to a neighbouring village, betrayed by a woman whom she also knew, and now for the first time discovered to be a Bruxa. Again the demon Moor appeared, or rather the Prince of Darkness, in that shape, and carried off his shrieking and helpless prey.

No sooner had the dreadful event occurred, then the Bruxas were borne away also by the demons, and at the conclusion of their disgusting orgies, Maria, like the rest of the hapless sisterhood, felt herself changing into the form of a vast bird of dusky hue, claws were on her feet, her arms became wings, and her face was sharp and pointed like a bat. Away she involuntarily flew over the dark lake, and now for the first time, as she skimmed along close to the waters, she beheld her hideous form reflected on its placid surface. Too well she knew herself, and though possessing all her human feelings in full force, yet these sanguinary propensities of the vile form she had been compelled to assume overpowered them completely. A thirst, and insatiable craving for blood, burnt up her soul; and, dreadful thought, not for the blood of animals, but for that of human beings, of young and tender beings who, while sleeping, might be destroyed.

After many gyrations over the lake, she found herself impelled, she knew not by what influence, to fly towards the village of St. João da Pesquera. Her own door stood open as she left it when she quitted her cottage. With difficulty she forced herself in, and found herself hovering over the eldest of her sleeping infants. The cool air as she fanned her wings lulled it to a sounder sleep, her sharp mouth was at its fair neck, and from a small puncture she sucked up huge draughts of the life's blood of her best beloved. Soon the rosy hue forsook its cheek; its rounded, plump form grew thinner and thinner; on she sucked with desperate haste; she knew all the time that she was destroying her child, yet she could not stay her insatiable propensity; more attenuated and shrivelled each instant became the once plump infant; life for ever fled, till nothing remained but an emaciated form of skin and bones, when with an agonised shriek of despair at the dreadful act she had perpetrated, the hapless mother flew back to the stagnant lake.

The next morning the miserable Maria rose from her troubled sleep, having been transported invisibly back to her home, well knowing the scene of horror she was about to witness. There on its couch lay her dead child, pallid and shrivelled, a small red spot, with a blue ring round it, full well attesting how it had died. Her husband was awoken by her cries and hurried to her side. No sooner did he see the fatal marks, then he exclaimed,

"A Bruxa—an accursed Bruxa has done this. Our pretty Pedro has been murdered by one of those vile beings."

Maria hung with desperate calmness over the little corpse, for, though conscious that she was guilty of her infant's death, she had not the power, even if she wished, to confess her crimes. As soon as the child's death was known, women came and decked it with robes of silk and silver; they put flowers in its hair; they painted its cheeks, to give it the appearance of life, and they placed it in a little blue coffin, without a lid, in which it was carried to the place of burial, though, as it must be remembered, the kingdom being under an interdict, no priest dared perform the service of the church over it. The neighbours, however, came not to mourn, but to congratulate the parents that this child was translated an angel to Heaven; and more acute was the anguish their words caused to the mother's heart, for she knew that she could never hope to meet her child in the realms of bliss. Repentance availed her not. The following night she again hurried to the rendezvous of her vile sisters in iniquity; and once more changed into her hideous form, she flew forth seeking for prey. Her cannibal propensities attracted her to her own cottage, which stood on the skirts of the village, and when she smelt the fresh breath of her two remaining infants. Alas, alas! was no watchful angel ready to guard their innocent lives? The second child fell a victim to the mother's thirst for blood.

The next morning poor Pedro was awakened as before. His grief and rage knew no bounds, as he beheld his little Maria thus cruelly murdered but a few feet from where he had been sleeping.

"This shall not happen again," he at length exclaimed, rousing himself from his grief. "I will watch every night till I have discovered the accursed Bruxa who has destroyed our children, and punish her for her vile wickedness."

It is impossible to describe the wretchedness and the agony of Maria; she grew thin and pale, till scarce a wreck remained of her former beauty. The neighbours remarked it; some pitied her, but others shook their heads, and whispered that, perhaps, she herself was of the sisterhood of the Bruxas.

Pedro kept his word: if he slept, it was in the day-time. Night after night he watched, with a lamp burning in his room, and his two-handed sword clenched firmly in his grasp, as he sat watching the door, to cut down the dreaded Bruxa should she enter. In consequence, for a long time Maria could not join the demon's orgies, but at last, after a day of unusual exertion, Pedro slept on his post, and his wife took the opportunity noiselessly to slip out, and to hurry eagerly to meet her sisters in iniquity. Now she was the companion of the chief of the devils himself, and while revelling in his unlawful orgies she for the moment forgot all her wretchedness. Quickly the time came for her to re-assume her bat-like form, and from afar she scented the fresh breath of her youngest infant. Pedro was asleep as she flew into the chamber—the soft fanning of her wings lulled him as well as the child into a deeper slumber. Soon, the life-blood drawn from its veins, the innocent babe was a lifeless corpse. The dreadful deed committed, she was about to quit the cottage, when one of her long wings struck against the door and closed it with a loud noise. The sound awoke Pedro, who, beholding the noxious bird in the room, the dreadful Bruxa, the destroyer of his children, made a stroke at it with his two-handed sword, and clove its skull in two. Instead of seeing the bird, as he expected, fall lifeless at his feet, he beheld his wife stretched dead upon the floor, a torrent of blood flowing from her head. At the same moment the whole house was shaken to its foundations by a terrific crash of thunder, and in a volume of smoke and flame a troop of demons carried off the body of the accursed Bruxa.

Scarcely had morning dawned when the hag, Josefa, hobbling up to the door, put her head into the room. "I told you I would have vengeance for the insults you offered me, ha! ha! ha! beware how you again offend a Bruxa," she croaked out as she pointed with her long skinny hand to the dead body of his last child, and away she went, and was never more seen in the neighbourhood. Poor Pedro was found by his neighbours in the morning sitting on his bed, with his bloody sword in his hand, while he gazed on the pool of blood at his feet, and raving mad. After some difficulty he was secured, for he threatened the life of every one who approached, his friends guessing, pretty correctly, the dreadful events which had occurred. He never recovered his senses, but died in the same un-happy state a few years afterwards, a warning to all men never to offend a Bruxa.

THE PALE LADY

by *Alexander Dumas*

I am a Polish woman, born at Sandonur, a country in which
legends are accredited like articles of faith, and in which we
rely as much on family traditions as on the Gospel. There is
not one of our castles but it has its ghost—not one of our cottages but it has its familiar spirit. The rich and the poor equally admit the friendly principle and the adverse. Sometimes
these two principles enter into a contest, and oppose each
other. Thence we derive those unaccountable noises in the
galleries, those terrific roarings in the old turrets, those quak-
ings of the walls, by which the tenants are driven from room
to room out of the castle; and all alike, noblemen and peasants, hurry to the church to seek the protection of the cross or
of the holy relics, as the only defense against the evil spirits,
by whom they are pursued.

But there, likewise, two other principles, more terrific,
more pitiless, more inflexible, meet together—tyranny and
liberty.

In the year 1825 one of those struggles broke out between
Russia and Poland, in which one might believe that the whole
blood of a people was shed like that of an entire family.

My father and my two brothers had risen against the new
Czar, and had stationed themselves beneath the standard of in-
dependence, so often thrown down, and so often raised again.

One day I was told that my youngest brother had been killed; another day they informed me that my eldest brother had been mortally wounded. At length, after a whole day's fighting, during which I had heard the roar of the cannon continually approaching, I saw my father return at the head of a hundred horsemen, the relics of three thousand whom he had commanded. He was come to shut himself within our castle, and determined to bury himself beneath its ruins.

My father, who had no fear for himself, trembled for my fate; and truly, he had nothing to dread but death, for he was sure not to be taken alive; but I had to fear slavery, dishonor, and shame.

My father selected ten of his little band, summoned the steward of the castle, gave him all the money and jewels we possessed, and ordered him to escort me to the monastery of Sahastru, situated amid the Carpathian mountains, where my mother had found a hospitable refuge at the second partition of Poland.

In spite of my father's great affection for me our farewell was a short one; for, according to all probability, the Russians would the next day come in sight of the castle. There was no time to be lost. I hastened to put on a riding habit, which I usually wore when I hunted with my brothers. The best horse in the stable was saddled for me; my father put his own pistols into the holsters, embraced me, and gave orders for our departure.

During that night and the following day, we went twenty leagues along one of those rivers which fall into the Vistula. After this advance, we had got beyond the reach of the Russians.

At sunset, we had seen the sunny peaks of the Carpathian mountains.

Toward the evening of the next day we reached their feet; and at last, on the morning of the third day, we began to penetrate into one of their gloomy passes.

Our Carpathian alps bear no resemblance to the mountains of the west. The wildest and grandest of nature's features here meet the eye, in its most majestic form. Their heads are lost in the clouds, covered with everlasting snow; their vast forests of fir trees lean over the smooth surface of lakes that appear like seas; and those lakes have never been furrowed by a boat, or disturbed by a fishing-net; the voice of man is scarcely heard at intervals, chanting a Moldavian song, to which the wild beasts respond with their cries. For many miles you travel under the gloomy roofs of woods, intersected by those unexpected marvels which solitude abounds in, and which carry the mind from astonishment to admiration. There danger is everywhere present, and consists of a thousand perils; but you have no time to fear, so sublime are those perils. Here, a cascade, formed by the melting ice, suddenly stops up the road you are traveling along; there, a huge tree, undermined by age, loses its hold upon the soil, and falls with a fearful crash; by and by a tornado encompasses you about with clouds, out of which the forked lightning is seen to leap like a fiery snake.

Meanwhile we drew closer to our journey's end. We had travelled forward without any accident for ten days. We began to perceive the top of Mount Pion, whose peak rises above all those gigantic hills, and on whose declivity is situated the convent of Sahastru, whither I was bound. In three days more we expected to arrive.

It was about the middle of July. The day had been intensely hot; and it was with exquisite delight that, about four o'clock, we had began to inhale the cool breeze of evening. We had just left behind us the mined towers of Niantzo. We were going down toward a plain that we had recently descried through the mountains. Already we beheld the Bistrizal with its flowery banks. We were riding by the side of a precipice, at the bottom of which the river flowed, but as yet only as a torrent. So narrow was the defile that our horses had scarcely room to go two abreast. The guide led the way, lying on his horse, and singing a low melody, the words of which I was listening to with a singular interest. The singer was the poet likewise. I cannot give you any idea of the wild sadness of the air, or of its sullen simplicity. But these were the words:

"In the marshes of Stavila,
Where flowed the blood of many soldiers,
Do you see that body yonder?
It is not a son of Illyria,
But a robber full of rage,
Who, deceiving the gentle Mary,
Exterminated, deceived, and burnt.

A ball sudden as the blast
Has struck the robber's heart—
A yatagan is in his throat;
But, strange to tell, for three days
His lukewarm blood moistens the earth,
And blackens the pale Ovigan.

Closed are his blue eyes for ever.
Let us fly; unhappy the man
Who passes him by in the marsh!
He's a vampire! The fallow wolf
Dares not come near the body;
And the vulture, too, dismayed,
Flies to the bald-headed hill."

Suddenly, the report of a firearm was heard, and a ball hissed through the air. The song ceased, and the guide, mortally wounded, fell over the precipice; while his horse stopped, shuddered, and, stretching his intelligent head over the brink, looked down for his rider.

At the same moment we heard a loud outcry, and discovered some thirty banditti start up on the side of the mountain; we were completely hemmed in. Every one snatched up his weapon; and although taken by surprise, as my defenders were all old soldiers accustomed to war, they were not dismayed; and I myself, setting the example, snatched up a pistol, and cried "Forward!" then spurring my horse, rushed toward the plain. But we had to deal with mountaineers, who sprang from rock to rock, like so many demons, firing at us while they leaped to and fro, and still maintaining the position they had taken upon our flank.

Besides, our manoeuvre had been foreseen. At one point in the road, where it opened into a plateau, a young man was waiting for us at the head of ten cavaliers. As soon as they caught sight of us they galloped up to our front, while those who pursued us ran down the side of the hill, and, cutting off our retreat, surrounded us on all sides. All these men, clad in sheepskins, wore large round hats crowned with natural flowers, like Hungarians. They had each of them a long Turkish gun in their hands, which they brandished about after they had fired it off, yelling and howling like savages. A sword and a pair of pistols were stuck in their belts.

As for their chief, he was a young man, hardly turned two-and-twenty; pale, with large black eyes, and hair which fell down in curls over his shoulders. His costume consisted of the Moldavian robe, trimmed with furs, and bound to the waist by a scarf of silk and gold. A sabre glittered in his hand, and four pistols were stuck in his waist. During the skirmish, he uttered hoarse, inarticulate cries, which seemed not to belong to a human being, but which, however, expressed his will, for his followers obeyed those yells, falling flat on their faces to avoid our soldiers' shots, and then rising again to return the fire, bringing down those who were still standing, finishing the wounded, and, in a word, turning the conflict into slaughter.

104

I had seen fall, one after the other, two-thirds of my defenders. Four still survived, and kept close about me, not seeking for that mercy which they were sure not to obtain, and only thinking of selling their lives as dearly as possible.

Just then their young leader sent forth a louder and more significant cry than the rest, pointing at us with his sword. Undoubtedly his order implied that we were to be surrounded and killed at once; for the long Moldavian muskets were all pointed at us spontaneously. I felt that our last hour was at hand. I raised my eyes and hands to heaven, with a final appeal, and waited for death. At that moment I saw a young man, not merely coming down, but rushing, bounding from rock to rock. He stopped upon a ledge of stone which commanded the whole scene; like a statue on a pedestal, he stretched his hand out over the field of battle, and exclaimed:

"Enough!"

At that voice they all looked up, and each appeared to obey this new master. One bandit alone returned his gun to his shoulder, and pulled the trigger. One of my escort uttered a cry of pain; the ball had broken his left arm. He turned round the next moment to rush upon the man by whom he had been wounded; but before his horse had reached the foe there was a flash above our heads; and the rebellious brigand fell down, his head shattered by a ball.

So many strains of feeling, so many causes of excitement, had exhausted my strength, and I fainted. When I recovered, I was lying on the grass, with my head supported on a young man's knees; all I could see of him was his white hand covered with rings, which he had put round my waist; while before me, with his arms crossed over his breast, and his sabre under one of his arms, stood the young Moldavian, who had led the attack.

"Kostaki," said the young man who was holding up my head, "draw off your men directly, and leave the care of this young woman to me."

He spoke this in a tone of authority, and in French.

"Brother," replied the leader of the band, "take care you do not fatigue my patience. I leave the castle to you; leave me the forest. At the castle you are certainly master; but here the power is mine. I have but to say the word, and you must obey me."

"Kostaki, I am the elder, and therefore master in the forest as well as at the castle. I spring from the blood of Brankovan as well as you—royal blood, accustomed to command, and I will be obeyed!"

"Gregoriska, command your servants, and let me give orders to my soldiers."

"Your soldiers are robbers, Kostaki. I will have them all strung up at the castle if they do not obey me this very moment."

"Well, try, then, if they will take orders from you."

Thereupon I felt the elder brother draw his knee gently away, and lay my head upon a stone. I looked after him anxiously and had time to contemplate the youth who seemed to have fallen from heaven to rescue us. He was a young man of four-and-twenty, tall, with large blue eyes, which revealed the greatest firmness and resolution. His long fair hair, an indication of the Slavonic race, fell over his shoulders, like those of Alexander; his cheeks were finely coloured with the tint of youth; his lips were curled with a smile of disdain, and disclosed a double row of pearls; his gaze was that of an eagle undaunted the sun's blaze. He had on a kind of black velvet tunic, a small cap with an eagle's feather upon his head, tight pantaloons, and embroidered boots. He wore a girdle round his waist, with a hanger in it; a small doubled carbine was slung over his shoulder.

He stretched out his hand, and said a few words in Moldavian. This address appeared to make a deep impression on the banditti.

After him the young leader spoke, in his turn; and I could see that his words were intermingled with threats and imprecations. But to this long ebullition of wrath the elder replied by one word only. The banditti bent their heads. He waved his hand; they fell into rank behind us.

"Well, be it so, Gregoriska," said Kostaki in French. "This woman shall not go to the cavern; but shall be mine, for all that. I think her beautiful; I have won her with my sword, and resign her I will not."

So saying, he sprang upon me, and snatched me up in his arms.

"This woman shall go to the castle, and be given up to my mother; nor will I leave her till then."

"My horse!" cried Kostaki.

The robbers hastened to obey, and brought their leader his horse. Gregoriska looked round, seized the bridle of a horse without a rider, and leapt upon it without touching the stirrups.

Kostaki got into his saddle almost as lightly, although he held me in his arms, and galloped off. Gregoriska followed; and the noble animal, sharing his rider's impulse, kept his neck and flank side by side with Kostaki's horse.

It was curious to see these two horsemen flying along in sullen silence, never losing sight of each other, though they did not seem to look, giving free rein to their steeds, whose wonderful velocity carried them over rocks, precipices, and woods. My head, which had fallen backward, enabled me to see Gregoriska's fine eyes fixed upon mine. Kostaki perceived this, raised me up, and then I saw no more than his wild and gloomy looks, which seemed to devour me. I closed my eyelids, but all in vain; for still I beheld his keen penetrating eyes piercing my heart like a lance. A strange hallucination too possession of my fancy: I thought myself the Leonora of the ballad, carried away by the phantom knight and horse; and when I felt that we had halted, I opened my eyes in alarm, so well assured I was that I should see nothing about me but broken crucifixes and open graves.

What I really saw was not much more lively. It was the inside of a Moldavian castle, erected in the fourteenth century.

Kostaki let me down from his arms, and almost immediately dismounted himself; but quick as he was in his motion, Gregoriska had anticipated him. It proved to be as Gregoriska had asserted, he was really master at the castle.

On seeing the two young men and the strange lady they had brought with them, the servants came running out; but though their attentions were truly divided between the brothers, it was obvious that the greatest respect was shown to the elder.

Two women came forward; Gregoriska gave them some order in Moldavian, and made me a sign to follow them. There was so much respect in his look, that I did not hesitate. Five minutes after, I was left alone in an apartment which, though it might have seemed bare and desolate enough to the least fastidious man, was evidently the best in the house. It was a large square chamber, with a sort of coarse green divan, used as a sofa by day, and as a bed by night; five or six elbow-chairs made of oak, a spacious chest, and a canopy in one comer of the room resembling a splendid cathedral stall. No curtains either on the bed or at the windows. One went up to this chamber by a stair-case, in which each in his own niche, stood three statues of the Brankovans, larger than the natural size.

A moment after, they brought in my luggage, and my trunks among other things. The women volunteered to help me; but, though I repaired the disorder which this event had produced in my toilet, I retained my riding-habit, as a costume more in keeping with that of my hosts than any other I could have chosen. These little alterations were scarcely completed before I heard a gentle tap at my door.

"Come in," said he in French; for the French language, you know, is almost a native tongue among Poles. Gregoriska entered.

"Ah, madame, I'm happy to find you speak French."

"And I, too, sir," answered I, "am happy to speak that language, since I have been able, thanks to that chance, to appreciate your generous conduct to me. It was in that language you defended me against your brother's designs, and it is in that language that I now offer you the expression of my very sincere gratitude."

"Thank you, madame; it was quite natural that I should interest myself in a woman in your critical situation. I was hunting in the mountains, when I heard several irregular and continuous reports of firearms. I guessed it must be some armed attack, and marched toward the scene of strife. I arrived in time, Heaven be praised; but will you give me leave to ask, madame, how it happened that a lady of your rank had ventured among our mountains?"

"I am a Polish woman, sir," answered I; "my two brothers have just been killed in the war against Russia. My father, whom I left ready to defend his castle against the enemy, has by this time probably joined them; and I, obedient to my father's order, was going to seek a refuge in the monastery of Sahastru, where my mother, in her youth and in equal straits, had met with a safe asylum."

"You are an enemy to the Russians; so much the better," said the young man; "that title will serve you as a powerful safeguard at the castle; and we require all our means and powers to sustain the struggle which is preparing for us. But first let me tell you, madame, who we are. The name of Brankovan is not a stranger to you?"

I bent my head:

"My mother is the last princess of that name, the last descendant of that illustrious chief who was murdered by the Cantimirs, those miserable courtiers of Peter I. My mother's first husband was my father, Serban Waivady, of noble birth, but of a less illustrious house.

"My father had been educated at Vienna, where he had been enabled to appreciate the benefits of civilization. He resolved to make a European of me. We set out, therefore, on a tour through France, Italy, Spain, and Germany.

"My mother—excuse a son for speaking on such a subject—my mother, who, during my father's earlier travels, when I was a mere child, had formed a criminal intimacy with a leader of a tribe, Count Gioriaki was his name, half a Greek, half a Moldavian—my mother, I say, wrote to my father, confessing all, and proposing a divorce; alleging that she, a Brankovan, would not continue to be the wife of one who was every day becoming more a stranger to his own country. Alas! my father had no occasion to grant his consent to this application, for he had just died of an aneurism, after a long illness, and it was I who received the letter.

"I had nothing to do but to wish my mother happiness, and to inform her that she had become a widow. By the same letter I solicited her permission to continue my travels, a permission which was granted me.

"My settled intention was to fix myself in France or Germany, in order to avoid the presence of a man who hated me, and whom I could never love—that is to say, my mother's husband—when suddenly I learned that Count Giosdaki had been assassinated, it was said, by the old Cossacks who had served under my father.

"I hastened to return, for I loved my mother; I knew how lonely she must feel, and how much she must require at such a juncture to have the fondest objects about her. Although she never evinced much tenderness for me, I was still her son. I returned unexpectedly one morning to my father's castle. There I found a young man whom at first I took to be a stranger, and whom I afterwards discovered to be my brother. It was Kostaki, the son of adultery, but whom a second marriage had rendered legitimate; Kostaki, that indomitable creature whom you have seen, whose passions are his only law, who holds nothing in this world sacred but his mother, who obeys me as the tiger submits to the arm that has conquered it, but with a sullen growl, and the secret hope of one day devouring me. Within the castle, in the halls of the Brankovan and the Waivady, I am still master, but once beyond its walls, and in the upcountry, he becomes the savage child of the woods and mountains, who wants everything to bend beneath his iron will. How he came to yield today, how his men came to submit, is to me a riddle; it was from an old habit of respect, doubtless. But I would not venture on another trial. Stay here; do not leave this chamber, this courtyard, or the inside of these walls, then I will answer for everything; but if you stir even a step out of the castle, I can no longer do aught but die in your defense."

"Shall I not be able to obey my father's wishes and continue my way to the convent of Sahastru?"

"Try, give your commands, and I will accompany you; but I should be sure to remain on the road, and you—you, alas! would not reach your destination."

"What, then, must I do?"

"Stay here, wait a while; let events point out the proper course; take advantage of the circumstances that may occur. Suppose yourself to have fallen into the hands of banditti, and with nothing but courage to extricate, and presence of mind to preserve you. My mother, in spite of her preference for Kostaki, the child of her wanton love, is good and generous. Besides, she is a Brankovan, and a true princess. You will see her; she will defend you from the brutal passions of Kostaki. Place yourself under her protection; you are beautiful, and she will love you. Moreover, who could behold without loving you? Come, then, to the supper room, where she is expecting us. Show neither distrust nor confusion; speak Polish; nobody here understands that language but myself. I will interpret what you say to my mother, and will say nothing that can give umbrage. Above all, not a word on these revelations; let none suspect the understanding between us. You do not yet know the cunning and dissimulation of the sincerest among us. Come, lady."

I followed him down the stair-case, lighted up with torches of rosin fixed in iron holders branching out of the walls. It was evidently on my account that they had contrived this unusual illumination. We entered the supper-room.

As soon as Gregoriska had opened the door, and, in Moldavian, had pronounced the single word, "Stranger", a woman of majestic mien came forward to meet us.

It was the princess Brankovan. She had on a small sable cap, surmounted with a tuft of feathers, the ensign of her princely extraction. She wore a sort of gold tunic, bestrewed with precious stones about the bosom, and, underneath, a long robe of Turkish stuff, fringed with dark fur like the cap. In her hand she held a chaplet made of amber beads, which she kept telling very rapidly. By her side was Kostaki, invested with the glittering and imposing Magyar costume, in which he appeared to me still wilder than at first. It consisted of a robe of green velvet, with very wide sleeves, reaching to the knee, morocco sippers, edged with gold lace; his head was uncovered, and his long black hair fell down over his neck, slightly concealed by a white silk shirt.

He saluted me awkwardly, and said something in Moldavian, which I did not understand.

"Speak French, brother," said Gregoriska; "the lady is a Pole, and understands that language."

Then Kostaki uttered, in French, a few words almost as unintelligible to me as his first speech, but the mother interrupted him by a gesture; and I could evidently see she was declaring to her son that it was her part to receive me.

Thereupon she delivered an address of hospitable welcome in Moldavian, which was easily interpreted by her looks. She pointed to the table, offered me a seat near herself, and signified by a gesture that her whole castle was at my disposal; she then took her seat with an air of dignified affability, crossed herself, and began to say a prayer.

Then each took his seat, according to etiquette; Gregoriska next to me, and Kostaki next to his mother, Smerande. That was the name of the princess.

Gregoriska was dressed nearly like his brother, but he wore, besides, a magnificent decoration round his neck: it was the nisham of Sultan Mahmond.

The rest of the inmates at the castle supped at the same table, each according to his rank as a friend or attendant.

The supper was very dull; Kostaki did not say a word to me; and his mother, though very attentive to supply me out of every dish, retained that solemn air which was always present to her. Gregoriska had truly spoken—she was a real princess.

After supper, Gregoriska went up to his mother, and explained to her that I stood in great need of rest after the excitement and fatigue of such a day. Smerande acquiesced with a nod, gave me her hand, kissed me on the brow as if I had been her daughter, and wished me a good night's repose.

I curtseyed reverently, and withdrew to the same apartment I had left an hour before. The sofa had been converted into a bed. That was the only alteration that had been made.

I dismissed the female attendants who had shown me into the room, letting them know by signs that I would undress myself. They retired with such testimonies of respect as plainly evinced they had received orders to obey me in everything.

Besides the door through which I had entered, and which opened on the stairs, there were two other doors in the chamber; they were, however, secured by means of heavy bolts, fastening within the room.

I opened the window; it looked out upon a precipice. Gregoriska, I plainly saw, had selected an apartment that bespoke his careful regard for me.

Finally, as I returned to the sofa, I found a table near the head of it, and a small folded note. It said in Polish:

Sleep tranquilly. You have nothing to fear as long as you remain *within* the castle.

GREGORISKA.

I followed the advice he gave me, and fatigue prevailing over all my thoughts and anxieties, I lay down on that Moldavian bed and slept.

✳

From that time forward I was settled at the castle, and the dramatic events I am about to relate begin from that day.

The two brothers became equally enamoured of me, each according to his character.

Kostaki, as early as the next day, told me that he loved me; declared that I should belong to him, and no one else; and that he would kill me rather than suffer another man to possess my heart.

Gregoriska said nothing; but he surrounded me with kind attentions. All the resources of a brilliant education, all the recollections of a youth spent in the noblest courts of Europe were invoked and exerted to please me. Alas! it was not difficult; at the first sound of his voice I had felt that that voice steal upon my spirit like music; at the first glance of his eye, I had felt his look penetrate into my heart.

Before the end of three months, Kostaki had told me a hundred times that he loved me, and yet I hated him; before the end of three months, Gregoriska had never said a word to me of love, and yet I felt I should be his the moment he required me.

Kostaki had suspended his predatory excursions; he now never left the castle. He had for the present abdicated in favour of a sort of lieutenant, who, from time to time, came to receive his orders, and immediately went off.

114

Smerande likewise loved me with a passionate fondness, the expression of which made me afraid. It was obvious that she favoured Kostaki, and she seemed more jealous of me than he was himself. Only, as she understood neither Polish nor French, and as I did not understand Moldavian, she could not press her son's suit very urgently; but she had learned to say three French words, which she repeated to me every time her lips touched my forehead:

"Kostaki loves Hedwige."

One day I heard a terrible piece of news, which made up the sum of my misfortunes; the four survivors among my escort had been set at liberty; they had returned to Poland, having pledged their honour that one of them should come back within three mouths to bring me tidings of my father. One of them did indeed return. Our castle had been taken, burned, and razed to the ground, my father having been killed while defending it. I was henceforth alone in the world.

Kostaki became more ardent; Smerande more indulgent and kind; but I appealed now to my mourning for my father. Kostaki insisted, saying, that the more desolate I was, the more need I had of a protector; his mother urged me still more pertinaciously.

Gregoriska had spoken to me of the command the Moldavians have over themselves, when they do not wish their thoughts to be read. He was a living example of it. None could be more certain of a man's love than I was of his; and yet had any person asked me what proofs I could adduce, I should have had none to expose; nobody in the castle had ever seen his hand touch my own, or his eyes directed toward me. Jealousy alone could reveal this rivalry to Kostaki, as my love alone could enlighten me as to his love.

Still, I acknowledge, this command and self- possession in Gregoriska made me uneasy. I certainly thought and believed but it was not enough, I wanted to be convinced—when, one night, as I had just entered my room, I heard a gentle tap at one of the two doors that bolted inside; I guessed by the mode of the appeal it was a friendly visitor. I called out:

"Who is there?"

"Gregoriska," answered a voice, whose tone could not be mistaken.

"What do you want?" I inquired, trembling.

"If you have any confidence in me," said Gregoriska; "if you believe me to be a man of honour, grant me my request."

"What is it?"

"Put out the light as if you were in bed; and, in half an hour, let me in."

"Return in half an hour," I replied. I extinguished the light and waited. My heart beat violently, for I was conscious that some event of great import was impending.

The half hour elapsed; I heard someone tap again, still lower than at first; I had withdrawn the bolts in the meantime; so I had nothing to do but to open the door. Gregoriska came in, and without his telling me, I pushed the door back and drew the bolts. He stood still and listened for a minute, and made me a sign to be silent. Then, when he had assured himself that no urgent danger threatened us, he drew me into the middle of that spacious apartment, and feeling by my quivering frame that I could not continue standing, he went and brought me a chair. I sat down, or rather fell upon the chair.

"Oh, heavens!" cried I, "what then is the matter, and what mean these precautions?"

"Because my life, which would signify nothing, and likewise your life, it may be, depend on the conversation we are going to hold."

I took his hand in terror. He raised my hand to his lips, looked at me the while, as if to beg my pardon for his boldness. I cast down my eyes—it was an assent.

"I love you," said he, in a voice as soft and musical as a song; "do you love me?"

"Yes," I replied.

"Will you consent to be my wife?"

"Yes."

He passed his hand over his brow with a deep sigh of acutest bliss.

"Then you will not refuse to go with me from the castle?"

"Wherever you go I will go."

"Are you conscious, my beloved, that we cannot be happy until we have fled from this?"

"Oh! yes!" I exclaimed; "let us fly."

"Silence!" he said, starting: "silence, dearest."

"You say well." And I approached still closer to him, shaking all over.

"This is what I have done," said he; "this is why I have delayed so long to tell you that I love you. I wanted, when once I should be sure of thy love, that our union should be quite unimpeded. I am rich, Hedwige—immensely rich—but, after the manner of Moldavian nobles, rich in lands, flocks, herds, and slaves. Well, I have sold to the monastery of Hango the value of a million livres, in cattle and villages. They have given me a part in jewels, a part in gold, and the rest in bills of exchange on Vienna. Will one million be enough for you?"

I pressed his hand.

"Your love had been enough for me, Gregoriska; judge, then."

"Well, hear me again; tomorrow I shall go to the monastery of Hango, to take my last measures with the superior. He is to have horses in readiness for me; these horses will wait for us from nine o'clock, concealed near the castle. After supper, return here as usual; put out the light; and I enter your room as I did just now. But tomorrow, instead of leaving it alone, you shall accompany me; we will make for the gate opening into the fields, where the horses will be waiting for us; we mount them instantly, and the day which breaks after tomorrow shall see us ninety miles away."

"Why is not this the day after tomorrow?"

"Dearest Hedwige!"

Gregoriska folded me to his bosom—our lips met together. He was a man of honour, to whom I had opened my chamber but he understood it well: if I could not belong to him in body yet I already did so in soul. He left me directly.

The night passed away, yet I did not sleep a moment.

I saw myself fleeing with Gregoriska, I felt myself carried by him as I had been by Kostaki, only this time the dreadful, terrifying deathly charge transformed itself into a sweet and ecstatic embrace in which the speed added to the voluptuousness, since the speed had a voluptuousness all of its own.

The day returned—I went down. I thought I detected something more sullen than usual in Kostaki's salutation. His smile used to look like irony; it looked now like a threat. During breakfast Gregoriska ordered his horses. Kostaki did not seem to notice the order.

About eleven o'clock he saluted us, saying he should not return till evening, and begging his mother not to expect him to dinner; then turning to me, he requested me also to accept his apology.

He departed. His brother's eye followed him to the door; and, at that moment, there shot from that eye such a vivid flash of hatred as made me tremble.

The day lingered on, amid fits of doubt, anxiety, and impatience. I had made no confident of our projects, scarcely even mentioning them in my prayers; for if I had dared to speak of them to the Creator, I should have thought that everybody knew them—that every eye that rested on me might penetrate into my heart, and read its most secret thoughts.

Dinner was a torture; gloomy and taciturn by nature, Kostaki seldom spoke at all; on this occasion, he only spoke two or three times to his mother, in Moldavian, and each time the tone of his voice made me shudder.

When I stood up to go to my chamber, Smerande kissed me as usual; and, as she did so, she repeated the words which I had not heard her use for a week:

"Kostaki loves Hedwige!"

This sentence rang in my ears like a knell; when I got to my room I thought I heard a fatal voice repeating: "Kostaki loves Hedwige!"

Yet, Kostaki's love, as Gregoriska had told me, was death!

About seven o'clock, as the day began to decline, I saw Kostaki cross the court-yard; he turned round to look toward me, but I fell back, in order that I might not be seen.

I was uneasy, for I had watched him as long as I could see him, and I had seen him take the direction of the stables. I ventured to withdraw the bolts, and to slide into the adjoining room whence I could survey all his motions. And truly, he went into the stables. He drew out his favourite horse, saddled it with his own hands, and with the greatest possible care. He wore the same dress in which I had first seen him. He had but one weapon with him—it was his sword. After he had saddled his horse, he cast his eyes once more up to my window. Then, not perceiving me, he leapt into the saddle, had the same door opened as that by which his brother had left, and rode off, at full gallop, in the direction of the monastery.

Then my heart sank deeply within me, for a terrible foreboding told me at once that Kostaki had gone forth to meet his brother.

I stood at that window for as long as I could distinguish the road, which, a mile beyond the castle, turned off, and was lost to sight within a wood. But the night grew darker every moment, and completely obliterated the view. But still I continued there. At length my uneasiness by its excess, restored my strength to me; and as it was evidently in the parlor I was to look for the first intelligence respecting either of the brothers, I went down.

My first look was for Smerande. I saw, by the composure of her countenance, that she had no apprehensions; for she was giving her usual orders for supper, and the covers of the two brothers were placed for them.

I dare not question any one. Besides, whom was I to interrogate? Not one of the inmates of the castle, except Kostaki and Gregoriska, spoke either of the two languages with which I was acquainted. The least noise I heard made me start.

It was habitually at nine o'clock we sat down to supper. I had come down at half-past eight. I kept my eyes fixed on the minute hand, and watched it as it moved along the large dial of the clock. The nimble hand sped along over the space between it and the quarter. The quarter struck. The vibration sounded sadly and gloomily; and then the hand resumed its silent march, and I saw it again measuring the distance with the regularity and slowness of a point in the compass.

A few minutes before nine, I thought I heard the galloping of a horse in the courtyard. The princess likewise heard it, for she turned her head toward the window; but the night was too obscure for her to see. Oh! if she had listened to me at that moment, how easily might she have guessed what was passing in my bosom! We had heard but the sound of a single horse, and that was natural. I knew very well that only one rider would return. But which?

Steps were heard in the ante-chamber. They were slow and faltering; each of them fell heavily upon my heart. The door opened. I saw a shadow beyond the sill; it paused a moment in the doorway. My heart upheaved. The shadow advanced; and gradually, as it came within the radius of light, I began to breathe.

I saw it was Gregoriska. Another moment of suspense and my heart must have broken. I saw Gregoriska, but he was as pale as death. The sight of him alone was enough to proclaim that something terrible had happened.

"Is that you, Kostaki?" inquired Smerande.

"No, mother," answered Gregoriska, in a hoarse voice.

"Ah! there you are," said she; "and pray, why must your mother be thus kept waiting for you?"

"Mother," said Gregoriska, looking at the time-piece, "it is only just nine."

"True," said Smerande. "Where is your brother?"

In spite of myself, I felt that it was the same question that God put to Cain.

Gregoriska returned no answer.

"Has any one seen Kostaki?" inquired the princess.

The vatar, or majordomo, made inquiries.

"About seven o'clock," said he, "the count went to the stables, saddled his horse himself, and rode out on the road to Hango."

At that moment my eyes met those of Gregoriska. I know not whether it was fancy or reality, but I thought he had a spot of blood in the very middle of his forehead. Gregoriska understood me when I raised my finger to my own forehead, thereby indicating the spot where I fancied I saw the blood. He took his handkerchief and wiped it.

"Yes, yes," muttered Smerande, "he must have met with a wolf or a bear, and diverted himself in the pursuit. That's the reason a child keeps his mother waiting. Where did you leave him, Gregoriska, speak?"

"Mother," replied Gregoriska, in a sad, yet firm voice, "my brother and I did not go out together."

"Very well,' said Smerande. "Let the supper be brought in; sit down all of you, and let the gates be shut; those who are out shall sleep out."

Smerande sat down at her usual place, Gregoriska took his seat on her right, and I on her left.

Then the domestics went out to execute her command by shutting the castle gates. But just then a great noise was heard resounding in the courtyard, and a valet, full of terror and affright, ran into the parlor, saying:

"Princess, Count Kostaki's horse has just entered the courtyard alone, covered with blood!"

"Oh!" muttered Smerande, starting to her feet, pale and menacing, "thus it was that his father's horse one night returned alone!"

I glanced toward Gregoriska—he was not pale now, but lividly white. For true, Count Koproly's horse had returned one night to the castle, all covered with blood; and an hour after, the servants had found his body and brought it home, full of wounds.

Smerande snatched a torch out of the hand of an attendant, passed out of the room, and descended into the yard. The horse, wild with terror, was held by three or four domestics, who were all endeavouring to quiet him. Smerande went up to the animal, looked at the blood upon his saddle, and discovered a wound at the top of his head.

"Kostaki's death was dealt from the front," she said, "in a duel, and by a single foe. Look now for his body, my children—by-and-bye we will look for his enemy."

As the horse had returned by the gate looking toward Hango, all the servants rushed out through that door; and there torches might be seen trailing over the fields and plunging into the forest, as, on a fine summer evening, you see the shining light-flies over the plains of Nice and Pisa.

Smerande, as if she had been convinced that the search would not be a long one, stood waiting at the threshold. No tear was in the eye of that desolate mother, and yet you felt that her despairing heart was silently groaning.

Gregoriska stood behind her, and I near Gregoriska. When we left the parlor, he intended, I saw, to offer me his arm, but he had not dared.

We had waited about a quarter of an hour, when we saw at the turn of the road first one torch reappear, then two, then all of them. But this time, instead of scattering themselves over the fields, they had clustered together around a common centre. That common centre, we soon perceived, consisted of a litter, with a man stretched upon it.

The funeral procession came slowly along but still it did come; and in ten minutes it had reached the door. On perceiving the desolate mother, who stood there waiting for her son, the bearers uncovered their heads instinctively, and then in solemn silence entered the courtyard.

Smerande placed herself behind the train, and we followed her. In this manner we reached the spacious hall, where they deposited the body. Then, majestically waving her hand, Smerande made the mourners fall back, when she herself approached the body, bent one knee to the ground before him, put aside his hair, which hung over his face like a veil, stood over and contemplated it for a long time, and still without a tear.

The wound was in the right side of the chest. It must have been made by a straight two-edged blade.

I recollected that I had seen that day that Gregoriska wore the long hanger, which he used as a bayonet for his carbine. I looked to see whether he wore it still—it was gone.

Smerande called for water, steeped her handkerchief into it, and cleansed the wound. A fresh current of blood came up and reddened the lips of the wound.

The spectacle before me presented at once something sublime and appalling. That spacious chamber, filled with smoke from the resin torches—those wild savage faces, those ferocious eyes, those strange costumes—that mother reckoning, by that still warm blood, how long death had deprived her of her son—that awful silence, broken in upon, from time to time, by the heavy sobs of the banditti, whose leader Kostaki had been—all this, I repeat, was at once both terrible and grand to behold.

At length Smerande put her lips to her son's forehead, and then rising again, and flinging back her long white hair, which was streaming over her face:

"Gregoriska," said she.

My lover started, shook his head, and emerging from his thoughts:

"Mother," he replied.

"Come here, my son, and listen to me."

Gregoriska shuddered, but for all that he obeyed. Gradually, as he approached the body, the blood, still more abundant and ruddy, kept flowing out of the wound. Fortunately, Smerande was not then looking that way; for, at the sight of that accusing gore, she would no longer have needed to look for the murderer.

"Gregoriska," said she, "I know that Kostaki and thou did not love each other. I know that thou art a Waivady by thy father, and he a Koproly by his; but, by your mother, you were both Brankovans. I know that thou art a man of the western cities, and he a child of the eastern hills; but still, by the womb which bore you both, you were brothers. Well, Gregoriska, I want to know whether we are to lay my son by his father's side before the oath has been taken; and whether I can weep for him in peace, as a woman confiding in you, who are a man, to pursue his murderer?"

"Name my brother's murderer to me, madame, and give your commands; I swear to you that in less than an hour, if you require it, he shall have ceased to live!"

"Swear, Gregoriska, sweat on pain of my malediction—hear that, my son—swear that his murderer shall die—that not one stone shall stand upon another in his house—that his mother, his children, his brothers, his wife, or his bride, shall perish by your hand. Swear, and as you swear, call down the anger of Heaven on you if you fail in your oath. If you fail in your sacred vow, expect misery, your mother's curse, and the execration of your friends."

Gregoriska stretched out his hand over the body.

"I swear that the murderer shall die!" said he.

At this extraordinary oath, of which I and the deceased alone, perhaps, understood the true meaning of, I saw, or thought I saw, the accomplishment of a terrifying miracle. The eyes of the corpse re-opened and fixed themselves on me more vividly than I had ever seen them; and I felt that double ray as if it had been palpable penetrate through to my heart like a burning rod of iron. This was too much for me to bear, and I fell back into a swoon.

✳

When I awoke I was in my room, lying on my bed; one of the two women was watching by my side. I asked where the Princess Smerande was; they answered me she was weeping over her son's body. I asked for Gregoriska; they told me he was gone to the monastery of Hango.

There was no more to be said of flight; Kostaki was dead. There was no more to be said of marriage; could I wed a fratricide?

Three days and three nights passed away in this manner, amid the strangest dreams; sleeping or waking, I continued to see those two living eyes in that dead countenance. It was a horrible vision!

It was on the third day that the funeral of Kostaki was to take place. On the morning of that day they brought me, on the biding of Smerande, a complete widow's habit. I dressed myself in it, and went down.

The house appeared to be empty; everyone was gone to the chapel. I could not continue to play the part of a disinterested spectator in that castle.

So I bent my steps toward the meeting-place. At the moment I was passing into it, Smerande, whom I had not seen for three days, crossed the sill, and came forward to receive me.

She seemed like the statue of Grief. As slowly and silently as a statue she set her cold lips to my forehead, and, in a voice which seemed already to belong to the grave, she uttered the usual words:

"Kostaki loves Hedwige!"

You cannot conceive the effect which these words produced upon me. This protestation of love, expressed in the present instead of the past tense—that love beyond the grave, which came to seek me in the living world—produced a terrible impression upon me.

At the same time a strange feeling seized upon me, as if I had been in effect the wife of him who was dead, and not the fiancé of him who was living. This gaping coffin drew me forward, in spite of myself, as painfully as they say the serpent attracts the bird which it fascinates. I looked about for Gregoriska, and saw him standing against a pillar. He was looking up to the sky. I know not whether he saw me. The monks of the convent of Hango surrounded the body, singing psalms of the Greek ritual sometimes full of melody, at other times dull and monotonous. I wanted to pray likewise, but the words expired on my lips; my mind was so disturbed, that I felt more like one present at a congregation of demons, than at a consistory of priests. When they bore away the body I attempted to follow it, but my strength would not permit me; I felt my legs give away beneath me, and I leaned against the door. Then Smerande came toward me, and made a sign to Gregoriska. Gregoriska obeyed, and drew near. Then Smerande addressed me in the Moldavian language.

"My mother commands me to repeat to you word for word, what she is going to say," said Gregoriska. "These are her words:

"You lament for my son, Hedwige; you loved him, did you not? I thank you for your tears and your love. Henceforward you are as much my daughter as if Kostaki had been your husband. You have a country once more, a mother, a family. Let us shed the tears that are due to the dead, and then become worthy of him we have lost. Adieu! return to your apartment. As for me, I will follow my son to his last home; when I return, I shall shut myself up with my grief, and you will not

126

see me until I have subdued it; and be assured I will conquer it, for it shall not kill me."

I could not answer the speech of Smerande, interpreted by Gregoriska, otherwise than by a groan. I returned to my bed-chamber—the mournful procession moved forward; I saw it disappear at the corner of the way-side. The convent of Hango was not above a mile and a half from the castle, in a direct line; but the natural obstacles of the ground compelled them to turn the road aside, and, by following that route, the distance was greatly increased. We were in the month of November. The days were become cold and short; at five o'clock it was perfectly dark. About seven o'clock I saw torches appear again. It was the funeral cortege returning. The body was at rest in the tomb of its fathers. All was over.

I have already told you the strange fancy which had haunted me since the fatal event which had put us all in mourning, and especially since I had seen those eyes, which death had closed, open again and settle upon me. On that evening, overwhelmed by the shocks and excitement of the day, I was still more dejected. I listened to the different clocks as they struck in the castle; and by degrees, as the hour returned when Kostaki must have died, my despondency increased. I heard the clock strike a quarter to nine, then a strange sensation came over me. It was a creeping terror that ran through my whole body, and froze it still; after which a something like an invincible desire to sleep weighed upon my senses; my chest heaved with oppression, my eyes were covered with a mist. I spread my arms open, and staggered back upon my couch.

Meanwhile, my senses had not so totally left me yet I could hear a kind of tread approaching the door; then I thought the door opened, after which I neither saw nor heard anything. Only I felt a sharp uneasy sensation in my neck, and then I fell into a complete lethargy.

At midnight I awoke. My lamp was still burning. I wanted to get up; but I was so weak that I had to repeat the attempt.

Still I conquered the weakness; and as I felt the same acute pain as in my sleep, I dragged myself along the wall to the looking-glass, and examined myself. Something like the puncture of a pin was visible on the artery of my neck. I thought that some insect had bitten me during my sleep, and, as I was borne down with fatigue, I lay down again and went to sleep.

The next morning, I awoke as usual. I wanted to get up as soon as I had opened my eyes; but I felt a weakness that I had never felt but once before in my life—the day after I had been bled. I went to the mirror, and was startled at my pallor. The day was sad and heavy. I felt a singular sensation; wherever I was, there I wanted to stay; every removal was felt as an effort.

Night came on. They brought me my lamp; my women, as I understood, at least, by their gestures, offered to stay with me; but I dismissed them with acknowledgments. At the same hour as on the previous evening I felt the self-same symptoms. I attempted to get up and call for help; but I could not reach the door. I heard, but not distinctly, the clock strike the quarter to nine; the tread was again outside the room—the door opened. I saw no more, I heard nothing, and, as the previous night, I fell back in a leaden drowsiness upon the couch. As the night before, I experienced a most acute sensation in the neck. Again I awoke at midnight; but I awoke weaker, paler still.

The next day I was haunted again by the horrid obsession. I had determined to go down to Smerande, weak as I was, when one of my women entered my apartment and announced Gregoriska. My lover was close behind her. I wanted to get up to receive him; but I fell back on my arm-chair. He uttered a cry when he perceived me, and wanted to spring toward me; but I had only sufficient strength to stretch my hand out toward him.

"What brings you here?" inquired I.

"Alas!" said he, "I was come to bid you farewell. I came to tell you that I leave this world, which would be unendurable to me without your love and society; I came to tell you that I was about to retire into the monastery of Hango."

"My society is withdrawn from you, Gregoriska," answered I, "but not my love. Alas! I still love you; and my greatest affliction for the future is to know that my love will be imputed to me as a crime."

"Then I may hope that you will pray for me, Hedwige?"

"Yes; only I shall not be able to pray long," added I, with a languid smile.

"What is the matter, then? Why, indeed, are you so pale?"

"God is taking compassion on me, and doubtless is calling me away to him."

Gregoriska came close up to me, took hold of my hand, which I did not seek to withdraw, and looking at me fixedly, said:

"This pallor is scarcely natural, Hedwige; what is the cause of it? Speak."

"Were I to tell you, Gregoriska, you would believe that I am insane."

"No, no; speak, Hedwige, I implore you. We are here in a country which is like unto no other—in a family different from every family. Say—say all—I implore you, beloved of my soul!"

So I related every particular; the strange hallucination by which I was visited at the hour when Kostaki must have died; the terror, the rigid drowsiness, the icy chillness, the overpowering prostration which made me fall back upon my bed, the tread I heard in the passage, the door which I could see opening, and finally that acute pain, followed by a pallor and debility which continually increased. I had expected that my narrative would appear a proof of incipient distraction to Gregoriska; and I felt a degree of embarrassment as I drew toward the close. But, on the contrary, I saw he paid the deepest and most earnest attention to the recital. After I had ceased speaking, he reflected a moment.

"So," said he interrogatively, "you fall asleep every evening at a quarter before nine o'clock?'

"I do indeed, whatever effort I make to banish sleep."

"And you fancy you see your door open?"

"Yes, although I fasten the bolts."

"And you experience a quick sanguine pain in the neck?"

"Yes, although my neck shows scarcely any sear I find."

"Will you allow me to look?" said he.

I laid my head sideways upon my shoulder.

He examined the cicatrice.

"Beautiful Hedwige," said he, after a pause, "have you confidence in me?"

"What a question!" I replied.

"Do you believe in my word?"

"I do, Gregoriska, as in the Holy Gospel."

"Well, Hedwige, on my honour, I swear to you that you have not another week to live, unless you consent to do, this very day, what I am going to tell you."

"And supposing I consent?"

"If you consent to be advised by me, you may perhaps be saved."

"Perhaps?"

He was silent.

"Whatever may come to pass, Gregoriska," answered I, "depend upon it I will do what you ordain."

"Well, listen to me," said he; "and, above all, take heart. In our country, as in Hungary, which is only separated from it by the wild Carpathians, there exists a certain tradition."

I shuddered; for this tradition had already occurred to myself.

"Ah! said he, "you foresee my meaning!"

"Yes," answered I, "I have seen in Poland some who were the victims of that appalling fatality."

"You allude to vampires, do you not?"

"Yes; when a child I saw them dig up out of the burial-ground, in a village belonging to my father, forty bodies of people who had all died in a fortnight, without any one being able to account for their deaths. Seventeen of the number exhibited all the signs of the vampire appetite; that is to say, they looked fresh and ruddy, and like living bodies; the others were their victims."

"And what was done to rid the country of them?"

"They drove a stake into their hearts, and burned them."

"Yes, that is the ordinary course; but for us it is not sufficient. In order to deliver you from the phantom, I must first discover him; and, by Heaven! I will. Yes, and if necessary, I will struggle with him for life or death, whoever he may be."

"Oh, Gregoriska!" cried I, terrified.

"I have said it, and repeat it, be he who he may. But, in order to bring this terrible adventure to a favourable conclusion, you must consent to whatever I require."

"Speak."

"Be ready at seven o'clock; go down to the chapel—go down alone. You must overcome this weakness, Hedwige—it is indispensable. In that sacred temple we will receive the nuptial blessing; do not refuse it, my beloved. In order to defend you, I must have received the right to watch over you, in presence of God and man. We will then return hither and wait."

"Oh, Gregoriska!" I exclaimed, "if it is he, he will kill you."

"Fear nothing, my beloved Hedwige: do but consent to be mine.'

"You know, Gregoriska, that I cannot deny you anything."

"This evening, then, dearest?"

"Yes, do on your side whatever you think requisite, and I will second you as well as I can, rely upon it."

My lover went out, and a quarter of an hour afterward I saw a horseman bounding along the road to the monastery; it was he.

Scarcely had he disappeared before I fell upon my knees and prayed, as people have ceased to pray in your impious countries, and waited for seven o'clock, offering up to God and the saints the holocaust of my thoughts; nor did I rise from that position until it struck seven.

I was as weak and pale as one dying. I threw over my head a black veil, went down, holding by the walls, and bent my steps toward the chapel, without having met anybody.

Gregoriska was waiting for me with Father Bazile, the superior at the monastery of Hango. He wore at his side a sacred blade, the relic of an old crusader who had been at the capture of Constantinople with the illustrious Hardouin Ville and Baldwin of Flanders.

"Hedwige," said he, striking the sword with his hand, "this weapon, with the help of God I shall break the charm that threatens your life. Approach then, without alarm; this holy man, having already heard my confession, is ready to receive our vows."

The ceremony began: never before, perhaps, had any one so simple and solemn at once been performed. None assist-ed the monk; with his own hands he placed upon our heads the nuptial wreaths. Both of us clad in mourning, we went round the altar with a taper in our hands; after which the pious monk, having spoken the sacred words, added:

"Go then, my children; and may God give you strength and courage to struggle with the enemy of mankind. You are armed with your innocence and with His justice; you will surely overcome the demon. Go, and may you be blest."

We kissed the sacred books, and left the chapel. Then, for the first time, I leaned on Gregoriska's arm, and it appeared to me that as I touched that valorous arm, and felt the contact of his noble heart, my life returned into my veins. I thought myself sure of triumphing, since Gregoriska was with me. We returned together to my chamber. It was half past eight.

"Hedwige," said Gregoriska to me, "we have no time to spare. Will you sleep as you usually do, and let the whole pass off while you are at rest? Or will you stay awake and see what shall happen?"

"Near you I fear nothing; I will stay awake and see what shall befall me."

Gregoriska took out of his breast a consecrated twig of box-tree, still humid with holy water, and gave it to me.

"Take this twig," said he, "lie down on thy bed, pray to the Virgin, and wait without fear. God is with us. Above all don't let the twig fall! for so long as you hold it, you shall be able to conjure Hell itself. Don't call upon me, don't cry out, hope and bide for events."

I lay down accordingly on my bed. I crossed my hands over my chest with the consecrated twig between my fingers. As for Gregoriska he hid himself behind the canopy of which I have spoken, and which stood in the corner of my bed-chamber. I counted the minutes as they flew by, and undoubtedly Gregoriska counted them likewise on his side. The quarter to nine struck. The vibration of the time-piece was still ringing, when I felt again the customary torpor, the same terror, the same chilling cold; but now I put the consecrated twig to my lips, and the first sensation died away. Then I heard very distinctly the slow and measured tread upon the stairs, and then approaching my door. After that, my door was opened slowly and noiselessly, as if acted upon by some supernatural power, and then——

"And then, I received Kostaki, as pale as when I beheld him stretched on the litter; his long black hair, scattered over his shoulders, dripped with blood; he wore his usual costume, but it was open at the chest, and exposed his bleeding wound. All about him was dead, like a corpse—flesh, clothes, gait; his eyes alone, those fearful eyes, were living. At that sight, strange to tell, instead of feeling my dismay increase, I felt my courage rise. God, no doubt, had given it to me, that I might consider my situation and resist Hell. At the first step the phantom took toward my bed, I looked at and confronted him boldly, with my gaze meeting those eyes of lead, and presented the consecrated twig. The spectre tried to advance; but a power stronger than his bound him to the spot. He stood still.

"Oh!" muttered he, "she does not sleep, she knows all."

He spoke in Moldavian; and yet I understood him as perfectly as if he had spoken in French or Polish. Thus we continued watching each other—the phantom and I; nor could I take my eyes away from him; when I saw, without requiring to turn my head round that way, Gregoriska coming from behind the screen, like the exterminating angel, holding his sword in his hand. He made the sign of the cross with his left hand and advanced slowly, presenting his sword to the phantom; the latter, at the sight of his brother, had likewise drawn his own with a terrific laugh; but scarcely had his sabre touched the consecrated steel, before the arm of the phantom fell down inert by the side of his body. Kostaki uttered a cry full of desperation and abhorrence.

"What wouldst thou?" said he to his brother.

"In the name of the living God," said Gregoriska, "I conjure you to answer."

"Speak," said the phantom, grinding his teeth.

"Was it I who waited for you?"

"No."

"Was it I who set upon you"

"No."

"Was it I who struck you?"

"No."

"You cast yourself upon my sword, and that was all. Therefore, in the eyes of God and man, I am guiltless of the crime of fratricide. You have not received a divine, but an infernal commission; and have come out of your grave, not as a sanctified shade, but as an accursed spectre; and now you shall return to your tomb."

"Yes, along with her," he cried, making a violent effort to seize upon me.

"You shall return alone," said Gregoriska, "this woman belongs to me."

And as he delivered the words, he touched, with the point of the consecrated steel, the unliving wound. Kostaki yelled aloud as if a blade of fire had touched it; and putting his hand to his left breast, he took one step behind. At the same time, as if following his movement, Gregoriska took a step forward; and then, with his eyes were steadfastly fixed on his brother's, and his sword to his chest, he began a slow, awful, and solemn march—the spectre recoiling from the holy blade, under the irresistible will of the champion of God; the latter following step by step, without uttering a word, both of them panting and ghastly pale, the living urging on the dead before him, and forcing him to abandon the castle which had been his abode during the past, for the grave, which was to be his dwelling for the future. Oh! that was a terrible sight to witness, I swear to you! And yet, moved myself by a superior power, a power at once unseen and irresistible, I arose and followed them without well knowing why.

We descended the staircase, lighted only by the burning eyeballs of Kostaki. In this way we crossed the gallery and the court-yard. Thus we crossed, too, the threshold of the house, with the same measured step; the phantom with a backward tread, Gregoriska with his sword arm outstretched, and I following. That singular advance lasted an hour, for it was necessary to drive the dead man back to his grave; but, instead of taking the usual path Kostaki and Gregoriska had pursued a direct course through the country, unheeding the obstacles which no longer existed; the earth became flat beneath their feet, torrents were dried up, trees fell back, rocks moved aside;

the same miracle was effected for me as for them; the sky appeared to me entirely overhung with a black veil, the moon and the stars had disappeared, and nothing in that night could I see but the flaming eyes of the vampire.

In this manner we reached Hango, and through the hedge of strawberry trees leading into the burial ground from the cloister. As we entered it, I distinguished Kostaki's tomb beside his father's grave; I did not know it was there, but yet I recognized it. On that night nothing was hidden from me.

Gregoriska stopped on the brink of the grave.

"Kostaki," said he, "all is not yet over with you; a voice from heaven tells me that you shall be pardoned if you repent; will you promise to return into your tomb, and not to leave it anymore; will you promise, in a word, to give to the true God that worship you have dedicated to the powers of Hell?"

"No!" replied Kostaki.

"Do you repent?' inquired Gregoriska.

"No!"

"For the last time, Kostaki?"

"No!"

"Well, call upon Satan to assist you, as I call upon God, and we shall see, once for all; who will prevail."

Two cries were heard at the same time; the blades met, and sparks jutted forth; the fight lasted only a minute, yet to me it seemed an age. Kostaki fell; I saw the terrible sword raised, I saw it thrust into the body, and pin it to the freshly dug earth. A last agonizing cry, with nothing human in it, rang through the air. I ran forward. Gregoriska was still on his feet, but he staggered. I supported him in my arms.

"Are you wounded?" I inquired with anxious alarm.

"No," said he; "but in such a duel, dear Hedwige, it is not the wound that kills, it is the contest. I have striven against Death, and to Death I therefore belong."

"Dear one," cried I, "come away from this; and life may

return, perhaps."

"No," said he; "here lies my tomb, Hedwige; but let us not waste time; take up some of the dirt moistened with his blood, and rub it over the spot where he has bitten you; it is the only means of preserving you for the future from his horrible love."

I obeyed with a shudder; I stooped to pick up that blood-stained soil; and as I stooped I saw the corpse riveted to the ground; the consecrated sword was passed through his heart, and a plentiful stream of black blood was running from the wound, as if he had died the very moment before. I applied the horrible talisman to my neck.

"Now, my adored Hedwige," said Gregoriska, in a weak voice, "hearken attentively to my last advice: Leave this country as soon as possible. Your best safeguard is the distance between you. Father Bazile has received this day my last wishes, and will attend to them. Hedwige, one kiss—the last, the only one, Hedwige! I die! Farewell!"

As he spoke, Gregoriska fell down by the side of his brother. Under any other circumstances, in the middle of the cemetery, that gaping tomb, and those two dead bodies lying by the side of each other, I should have gone mad; but God had lent me a strength equal to the events. As I looked round for some assistance, the door of the cloister was opened, and the monks, preceded by Father Bazile, advanced two by two, bearing lighted torches, and singing the prayers for the dead. Father Bazile had just arrived at the convent; he had foreseen what had passed, and, at the head of the whole brotherhood, was going to the burial-ground.

He found me alive near the two dead brothers. Kostaki's face was twisted into a final grimace, whilst that of Gregoriska was, by contrast, calm and almost beatific. As Gregoriska had desired, they buried him along with his brother—the Christian standing guard over the Damned.

When Smerande was informed of this new calamity, and

the part I had taken in it, she wanted to see me; she came to the monastery of Hango, and heard from me all that had occurred that terrible night. I related to her, without, suppressing any particular, the whole of this fantastic story; and she listened to me, as Gregoriska had done, without astonishment or terror.

"Hedwige," she replied, "you have said nothing but the truth. The race of Brankovan is accursed, until the third and fourth generation, because a Brankovan once killed a priest. But the term of the malediction is now come; for although a wife, you are a virgin, and the race is extinguished in me. Follow, without delay, your husband's advice. Return to those countries where God does not permit these terrible wonders. I want no other to assist me in weeping and mourning for my sons. My grief calls for solitude. Farewell! inquire for me no more. My future lot belongs to God alone."

She embraced me for the last time, and left me to shut herself up in the castle of Brankovan.

The following week I departed for France; and, as Gregoriska had predicted, my nights were never again disturbed by the terrific phantom. My health itself recovered, and all I have retained of the event is this death-like pallor, which will ever accompany to the grave a human creature who has sustained the posthumous embrace of a vampire.

THE VAMPYRE BRIDE

by *Edwin. F. Roberts*

THE events of which the following story derives its origin
had their genesis in certain terrible facts which occurred
in Hungary in the beginning of the last century, and furnishes
another illustration of those marvellous and almost incredible
aberrations of human nature which may well make men stagger in their belief, or go to the opposite extreme of implicitly
believing too much.

In a wild and remote district, though in the neighbourhood of one of the chief cities in this country, was builded a
huge old castle, whose high walls, towering turrets, and extent, indicated antiquity as well as great power and wealth. It
was well known to the surrounding country as the Castle of
Auerstadt; and the lords of Auerstadt had lived there for long
and dusty generations past.

The last descendant of this lofty house was a lady, very
proud and haughty—so much so, that all suitors who came
to seek her hand were dismissed with such scant courtesy as
never induced one of them to return: and she was withal very
beautiful, which made men mourn for her perverse and un-
tractable nature, but which had the effect of spreading her
name through that and other countries, and like those fabled
princesses in the old fairy tales, still brought others to her feet,
to be treated in the same contemptuous manner, until it was
asserted that none under the rank of a sovereign king could

ever dare to claim that ambitious hand with any hope of success. Her name was Gouvina, Countess of Auerstadt, and at the period our story opens, she was considerably over thirty years of age, an event that was fatal to her pride.

For years and years, and even to traditionary times far beyond the memory of man, the hospitality of the Castle of Auerstadt had been well and favourably known. No matter for the grade or rank of the party demanding food and shelter; no matter whether business, pleasure, or an errand of love-making to the countess brought them, the great gates opened, food, wine, and shelter were accorded; and so far all was well.

As the countess grew older day by day, and year by year, a change came over her, and an unconscious change also fell on all within and without. Little by little the hospitality of the castle had contracted itself, though neither from necessity or by any order of the Countess Gouvina but because fewer people demanded it. Travellers who used to go some distance from their route to claim the generous shelter of the castle, had actually made beaten roads, leading from every direction to the gates, now not only never frequented them, but would even make a circuit to avoid its neighbourhood; and the grass grew on the once well-worn paths, giving to them an unspeakably desolate aspect.

Gradually also the princely number of retainers who once filled the walls and out-houses of the castle dwindled away to a few; some died off; some left; but of those who left none ever returned, and when questioned why, would only turn pale, shrug up their shoulders, and become suddenly mute. Not half-a-dozen grey heads were to be seen, and these were strange: but on the walls there sometimes were to be found half-armed bravo-looking men, like those brigands in the paintings of Rosa or Tintoretto, and one would have thought the countess herself had turned leader of a horde of robbers, and that she had surrounded herself with the most ferocious ruffians those wild times created, rather than that she was a noble lady; living on her own estate, and the last representative of a lofty line of ancestry, remarkable for courage, loyalty; generosity, and, in fact, every virtue that ennobles men.

This striking change must have had its origins in some potent reason, doubtless, for if this desertion and avoidance had been confined to a few, it might have been said that the pride of the countess had offended them; but when it became universal, so to speak, then men began to ask themselves the cause. Rumours were abroad, of such hideous bloody, and horrible kind, that the hair rose on the scalp, and the skin seemed to crawl away from the flesh, when these rumours were shaped into words and ideas. Those distant districts of Europe have, in common indeed with other nations, been pre-eminently superstitious, and the peasant portion are indeed so to this day. Sorcery, impious rites, conclaves held with the dead, and orgies with evil spirits, were all and each assigned to the countess as being her present condition of existence.

When such rumours as these are vague, one is merely shocked at the jumble of horrors they exhibit; but when they are detailed one by one, and from that detail take a comprehensive form and shape, it is no wonder that the very name of the countess became synonymous with the most ghastly terror itself.

For a length of time past the country around, and soon to distant localities, became alarmed and appalled by the mysterious disappearance of the young village maidens, and even of the higher born. Week after week were parents distracted with horror and awe at missing their best beloved from the household circle, and at last it seemed that no care or precaution was availing, for, either by fraud or by force, the maidens continued to disappear, and none *knew* to any certainty—though men at last pointed with their hands to the gloomy, frowning turrets of Auerstadt Castle, and indicated that there lay the solution of the shuddering mystery.

But previous to this period an event had occurred which

saved the countess from any immediate suspicion, and gave her all the mere immunity (supposing that she was guilty) and made facts and these lately-awakened auspicious quite irreconcilable. We have already stated that her pride pointed to an alliance with royal blood, and the visit and lengthened stay of a certain Prince Wladimir, the future heir of the throne, gave people room to imagine that there was something more than a probability they would be united. The prince himself was several years younger than herself. He was gay, handsome, and accomplished, and in every way a man most likely to win a woman's heart. That he had won the love of the countess was beyond all doubt, for she idolized him. But the disparity of their ages, his almost boyish gaiety, and her almost matron dignity struck her with a painful conviction that she could not tame him down. To a woman like herself, sensitive on the score of her age (there were some seven years difference between them), great undoubtedly as her beauty was, it became to her a source of endless misery, for soon after the prince had taken tender leave (without making any confession of love) it came to her ears that he had spoken of her as an "old woman," and, but for that, he could have adored her for her beauty. She could not, therefore, conceal from herself the fact that she was growing old, that truth so fatal to her vanity. Her pride, her intense ruling passion, revolted at this, and well-nigh drove her to distraction. The insolent remarks of the young prince pierced her to her soul, because she was convinced there was foundation for them. Nothing could destroy the damning truth; and, goaded by the strong passions of a nature unused to disguise its impulses, or to set bounds upon the expression of her will, they thought in the castle that she had gone mad when first she was made aware of the thoughtless and cavalier remarks uttered by the Prince.

Her anguish was the greater because she loved him with a fiercer fervour and intensity than ever. It was not the thought that he had chosen to speak of her with disrespect that wounded so much, as the thought that, in any case, he could never be hers—for how was she to roll back the wheel of time—make herself younger—give to herself the bloom and grace of girlhood, and stand before her lover like Aurora before Tithon—the type of beauty, the adored one enjoying a love that should satiate the hunger of her vast heart. "It is true," she fiercely said one morning, while looking into her mirror,—

"It is true. The canker tooth of time is beginning to indent itself into these cheeks which were so fair and fresh, and I am made a jest of by the man I love. Old, withered, and haggard, what horror is mine to wander forth daily side by side with decay, and to rest at night while its hideous embraces are sapping the foundations of youth and beauty. What is to be done, for something must be done, and that speedily? I will not endure this; something there must be in the range of art, holy or unholy, and to that mysterious something I will have recourse."

Then she spent days and nights in the castle library, prying over old manuscripts and vellums, where the wild dreams of old philosophy in their most distorted forms were to be seen. Alchemy, cabalistic arts, and sorcery, by turns, took possession of her thoughts; and she began to indulge in those visions of rejuvenescence which Medea and the Thessalian witches suggested. In the pages of an old book, now known as the "Golden Ass of Apuleius," she found that women were enabled to change their forms and transform themselves into shapes of youth and beauty as well as of age and ugliness. They could change themselves into birds and animals, and the means by which she could attain this dark and detestable skill occupied her wholly.

She sought with secrecy through every part of the country for those semi-existences—the wizard and the witch, who by an unhallowed art had obtained a mastery over spirits of evil and powers of darkness,—and at last found two old hags who were the dread and terror of the world around, and to them she confided her passionate desire.

The frightful secret which they disclosed sent her from the spot shuddering, panic stricken, appalled beyond the possibility of words to tell. When she arrived at the castle it was remarked that her haggard and pallid face, her horror-stricken and averted eyes, and the nervous terror that seemed to have affected her from some unknown cause, betrayed a mind that was ill at rest; her appearance was, in fact, more like that of one who has committed a mortal sin—a terrible crime, and is haunted by the evil spirits the criminal has invoked.

But for all this, though she carried terror about her, she could not forget the infernal suggestion that had been made; and day and night the grim act that was to re-clothe her in the freshness and the almost matchless beauty of the past was so often done in imagination, that the terror of the deed began gradually to give way, and she now familiarized herself with the idea more and more. The image of Wladimir, too, with his gallant bearing and his handsome face, despite his scorn, added to these diabolic promptings, and made her impatient of delay.

But what confirmed her more than ever in her purpose was the following event:—One day, having looked for some time fixedly upon her image in the mirror, she discovered a grey hair or two in her luxuriant tresses, and traced fresh wrinkles on the still beautiful cheeks. Rage, dread and wounded vanity all combined together, and she dashed the mirror from her with all her force. It struck her waiting-maid, and broke against the poor girl, who fell cut, and gashed, and bleeding dreadfully, to the ground.

Struck with momentary pity and remorse, she hastened to the girl's assistance and in restoring her to consciousness, the arms and hands of Gouvina became stained with blood. Leaving the girl therefore to the charge of other domestics, she retired to wash her hands of the sanguine spots, and to her surprise and even gratification, she saw that the places whereon the blood had rested became whiter, fairer, fresher than the other parts. An exultation of a dire and devilish kind seized upon her; and she resolved that not another day's delay should take place before commencing her almost unutterable project.

Instantly, and for several weeks after, workmen were employed in an unfrequented part of the castle below the level of the ground, demolishing several old dungeons and rebuilding them after a style and fashion which the countess herself had drawn and planned, and which, when completed, was kept a perfect secret from all within the castle, a stranger of forbidding aspect (and an armed guard,) whom she had engaged, having charge over the passages leading to the place of mystery and guilt. The workmen could betray no secret, for two sufficing reasons; they were strangers from a distant country, and sent away thence when their task was over, and in addition, there was nothing apparently in the place itself to give any suggestion of secrecy.

Time went on, and Gouvina's waiting-maid in a most unaccountable manner disappeared; soon other maidens of the vicinity followed, none knew how or where, and the alarm spread abroad. The alarm, the fear, and horror of the people against this unheard-of and unseen agent of desolation cannot be expressed. Unconsciously, as it were, the countess became the object of suspicion. All fled from the castle, and a grim and savage desolation marked the surrounding country that formerly had been gladdened by the feet of travellers going or returning from Auerstadt, full of trust and gratitude; and thus we find her at the commencement of this story.

Up to this time it was known that no less than *three hundred* maidens had disappeared from one place or another without leaving a trace of their fate behind them, without the slightest indications of their whereabouts. No conjecture could by any possibility throw a light upon these tremendous catastrophes, though, as we have said, suspicion and rumour pointed out the Countess and Auerstadt Castle as the agent and place.

But men hesitated here. What end—what purpose could all these terrifying circumstances serve? It was not for wealth or possessions, not from jealousy or rage; for the Countess was rich, and was not usually cruel to any one, until, as we have said, rumour took a definite shape, and the Countess Gouvina was suspected of Vampyrism!

Still this involved a contradiction, and that too almost in direct terms, for it was held as an ascertained fact that the vampyre must be dead—that is to say, must die a natural or an unnatural death; and must also be buried, from which grave he or she, by some preterhurnan means, was to rise up at night, seek for their victims wherever they could find them, and add thus more to the number of these revolting and horrifying creatures, for each one bitten by a vampyre became a vampyre in turn. Had these three hundred virgins, then, changed into vampyres also?

Out of this question arose another defensive side in favour of the countess. The first who had fallen victims to this dreadful condition might have made victims of the others, and the countess was thus virtually exonerated. But, again, it was not necessary that the corpse of the assumed victim should disappear, and this was what added to the impenetrable secret.

An event, however, occurred at this time which brought to light the whole of the strange and mysterious occurrences, and revealed a series of crimes so vast and gigantic that, if committed by a denizen of the bottomless pit, could not have been more abominable. In a little village some miles away, and across a wide forest, stretching between it and the Castle of Auerstadt, dwelt a young peasant whom we shall designate as Huon. He was strong of frame, bold of heart, honest and industrious, and loved as dearly as he loved his life, Ina, a fair peasant girl, the daughter of some poor neighbours.

Brought up together from childhood, the youthful pair

were devotedly attached to each other. This ended in a betrothal, and when Huon should have earned a certain sum of money they were to be wedded. The sum was at this time almost gathered together, and Huon was congratulating himself on the prospective happiness in store for him when he should lead his pretty bride to the church.

It happened, however, that all this dream of joy was destroyed by her sudden disappearance, none knew whither, except that she added one more to the number of those poor maidens who had so unaccountably vanished within a comparatively short space of time. The grief and distraction of the poor peasant at the first intimation of this was intense, but he soon calmed his agony and registered a vow that while life held he would not give up the search for Ina, and ascertain her fate whatever that might be.

He accordingly provided himself with what he needed and set forth to explore the neighbourhood, but as yet entirely without success. This did not discourage him, however. It was evident that there was mischief somewhere, and he was too hard of belief to share the general impression that his fond and dearly-loved Ina had joined the vampyre band.

Rumour that was long afloat reached him at last, and pointed out the Castle of Auerstadt as the most suspicious place. Thither he resolved to go, to gain entrance, to seek, and to dare all, in order to unravel the atrocious secrecy of this horrible castle. Convinced, as he was, that there was a will to dare, and a power to act, in the mysterious sequence of affairs which had robbed him of her he held most dear, he came to the conclusion that he too must be secret and bold, and as he had bidden farewell to the fear of all consequences and the dangers that might surround him, so he was not likely to be deterred by any difficulties that might arise, and to be a dangerous as well as a desperate man when brought to bay. Starting forth, therefore, one morning, unseen to any, and without a word said as to his intention, he dived into the depths of the forest which lay between him and the object of his search, and brooding upon his loss had lost himself in the tangled wilderness, where he sat down to compose his thoughts, for there was a stern duty before him which he must do or die in the attempt.

As he lifted up his eyes and glanced around, an opening in the trees revealed to him a trampled path, where the brushwood had been lately trodden down by the hoofs of animals. A party of three or four horsemen had evidently been by that way, and, springing to his feet, upon the impulse which this discovery gave him, he was soon on the track, pursuing it with fresh vigour and determination. Hope had brought to his breast a kind of conviction, and he felt instinctively that he should ultimately be able to discover Ina's fate, whatever that fate was.

He glanced keenly at the branches on both sides of him, as he plodded on. By the manner in which they were bent and broken, he ascertained that he was going in a direct course. Suddenly he stopped, his lips parted, and his limbs trembling with agitation. Surely he was not deceived! No! for there, fluttering in the broken limb of a tree, was a little kerchief, such as he had known Ina to wear but a day before her abduction. No vampyre had hung out this signal—no supernatural hands had indicated this much to him. He seized it—covered it with kisses, and placed it in his breast, and went on with heart now more hopeful.

He continued to look with the greatest attention, on every side, lest he should pass over some other stray portion of her garments, which accident or design had placed there; nor was his cautious search unrewarded. He had not gone far before he discovered a piece of her garment rent off, and flung as if with the design of pointing out to some one that she had passed that way; another and another, still satisfied him of the fact, until he saw through the now scantier foliage the gloomy turrets of the castle rising before him.

No words—no power could now convince him but that Ina was within the walls; and fatigued as he was with a long and arduous journey, he lay down to rest and think. A broad space supervened between the forest and Auerstadt, and any-one attempting to cross it could be easily seen by the sentinels on the walls. He was cautious, therefore, not to approach too near in the broad daylight; but, climbing up into a high tree, he carefully examined every place before him, and saw that by swimming the broad moat to a particular spot, he would arrive at a low part of the wall, covered with ivy, where a small door lay hidden, and apparently long unused. With the implements that he possessed he would soon force an entrance; and, having carefully noted every spot in the neighbourhood, he descended, in order to take a little rest until the evening came.

"Yes!?" he muttered, shaking his clenched hand at the dark walls, "palace of crime and horror, I feel an instinctive thrill crawling through my veins—creeping over my very flesh, and filling me with an indefinite and awful sentiment, as though by drawing aside a curtain it would reveal to me things that would change men's hearts to stone, as the eyes beheld them. I feel that I shall see and know things within those walls which will make the world execrate the countess, and regard that ac-cursed castle with dread and detestation; and God protect me and direct me, for I shall have need of strength and help—of that, I am quite convinced."

He lay down on the grass, beneath the shadow of the trees, having selected a spot which accident alone was likely to re-veal; and thus committing himself to the care of heaven, slept soundly until the evening came. The sun at last set, and the breeze of the evening woke up in the woods, and began to sing sonorously among the branches. Huon woke, and was startled to see that the twilight was waning in the darkness. The moon was not up, and only a star or two was visible, Huon started from his place of concealment, crept cautiously to the outskirts of the forest, and, bending to the ground, began to creep with the greatest caution towards the edges of the moat. There he partiality undressed himself, bound up his clothes in a tight bundle, so that they should be as little wetted as possible, slid gently into the water, and swam across. By the little postern door, where the wall was built, was a little green knoll, thickly covered with bushes, there he dried and dressed himself, and without loss of time began to seek for the fastenings of the door, assured that if it did not lead to what he sought, it would give him entrance into the castle.

In the dim, dusky evening when the mists were rising on the water, and the distant forest, through which the wind roared, looked like a huge wall, while the scream of the bittern, seeking its nest in the sedges, now and again struck the ear; the bold peasant, with a heart panting with expectation, drew his belt tighter round him, looked to his strong knife and keen axe which he carried in his girdle, and then began with a crow-bar to wrench away the fasteningess of the door.

Thanks to time and the action of the air, the screws were soon torn out, and, by degrees, he felt the door opening, while a rush of damp, unwholesome air struck him on his brow. The next moment he was in some hollow archway, and drawing the door to—the ivy hiding it as before—he began to search for his steel and tinder, which he had kept dry, and soon lighted the lamp that he carried with him. Then he began to explore the place.

It was with a strange conflict of feeling that he gazed on the huge and massive stone-work above, and pierced to the far end of the passage. He then went forward, and came to a narrow flight of stone-steps, which led to the turrets of the castle. At a doorway, however, some little way up, which was evidently of recent origin, he paused. He must seek below, but not above. He sat down to think.

He heard the rats below, and beheld the bats striking against the walls.

The hours rolled on till the castle bell sounded with a hollow boom, and the peasant, with a start, roused up from his reflection, and by dint of strength and perseverance the second door also gave way to his efforts. Through passages that seemed interminable, door after door gave way, and at last he was in the very interior, in the neighbourhood of the countess' chambers.

Dim lights from lamps hung up here and there made his own useless. So he extinguished it, and crept behind the huge hangings, and thus stealthily passed on, until he lost sight of the tortuous path by which he had come. He passed, at last, the doorway of a vast chamber, brilliantly lighted, from whence voices came, and he caught a momentary glimpse of the lovely Countess Gouvina, attended by her maidens. An involuntary shudder ran through his frame as he darted past, and took the first dark corridor that presented itself. Down some steps, by windings and turnings, he came all at once in sight of a man, who, armed to the teeth, appeared to hold guard over a door at the extremity. This was the place he sought, he felt convinced of it.

He crawled on the ground, in the dark shadow, till he came within a yard of the grim sentinel. Drawing his strong knife, Huon held his breath tightly, and, seizing the opportunity, drove it with such sudden force under the left shoulder of the guardian that he fell dead to the ground, without a groan. He dragged the body on one side, took off the doublet, the half-armour, the helmet, and donned them himself; then, seizing the keys, opened the door, locked them on the inside, and felt secure. The place beyond must be luminously lighted up, for he saw that the heavy silken curtain between him and the dread secret was glowing with a sullen and subdued flame.

He passed under the curtain, and the whole iniquitous mystery was revealed to the man who was frozen, for the moment, with involuntary horror, and hid his seared eyeballs with his hand.

Let the reader imagine to himself an immense chamber, of great height, the roof supported by massive pillars that went round, and thus left, between the centre and the frescoed walls, a sort of terrace, which was covered with roughly woven wool. From the top, lamps were suspended, and on each pillar a bracket from the inside also held one. Everything was clear as at noonday; and when Huon had set his teeth, and inwardly defied all the horrors that hell could vomit forth, he prepared himself to scrutinize the place.

The ceiling was painted azure, and was dotted with golden stars. The mythology had been ransacked to find devices for the clouds, whose images of gods and goddesses sat or reclined. The walls were covered with pictures—images of youth and beauty, destitute, let it be understood, of every grossness; on the contrary, the whole reminded one of the golden age of the poets of the Vale of Tempe, of the charming pictures seen in Theocritus and the Eclogues of Virgil, and the whole had been done by a master hand.

But what a contrast was there before him. Stretching from end to end, from side to side, was a dark sullen pool, sustained by a vast marble basin, or rather tank, of Parian whiteness. The inky-fluid, however, which that otherwise magnificent bath held almost revolted sense.

He descended some steps, and his foot was almost dabbling in it. He stooped down, and with a shudder, a terror, a horror unnameable, indescribable, and almost incomprehensibly took up some in his hand, and held it between him and the light. As he let it fall, plashing with a sullen, turbid manner below, he saw that it was red—blood-red!

It was a bath of blood—of human-blood!

✳

When Huon returned to consciousness he found himself lying on the steps which led to the Dead Sea, stretched out in its leaden mass before him, repulsive to the pure white marble which lipped its brim. The soft and radiant light streamed down, and the wondrous and even mythical beauty of the vast room contrasted with a hideous yet grotesque horror, that the man leaped to his feet and stumbled as he fled back from the spot.

What sights flashed across his mind as he stood still there—what ghastly deeds of murder were done on the white edges of the bath as the fore-doomed victims were held struggling on the brink, and with a single gash were left to bleed till the frightful tank was replenished. What!—but no: it is not healthy to dwell upon horrors that are super-human.

Almost unconsciously he had unlocked the door and placed the keys without, in order to lock it up after him, and secure the means of future ingress. He stood without and heard approaching voices.

The next instant he saw the Countess, attended by a couple of withered human-looking things, approaching. She was beautiful, too, pale—but, to Huon's eye that pallor was as abhorrent as if he beheld in her some dead fiend of the pit, disguised in the form of a woman.

What should he do? How escape? for now, even when the secret was but half developed, and he would be detected before discovering Ina! The thought was dreadful. To be murdered—to be butchered in some obscure corner was all that struck him. Suddenly he remembered that he had dressed himself in the garb of the green sentinel. There were only three women to deal with, and he could have brained them without remorse. He recovered his composure, shrank back into as deep a shadow as he could, having seized the weapon the dead man had loosed from his relaxed hand, and waited.

He heard them speaking.

"It is true," the Countess Gouvina was saying, "my skin grows fairer and whiter, and my cheeks fresher—youth—

youth comes back to me again, and so must Wladimir; but, oh! what price! what cost! what terms!"

"Price! cost!" murmured one of the old hags. "How you talk, great lady. What price is too high for renewed youth? what cost too great for the beauty and the radiance of years long gone? Our art is not great enough to turn back time, but it is, as you are a living example of, powerful enough to destroy its effects, and once or twice more———"

"Has the bath been renewed? Is that young peasant girl———"

Huon, whose heart thundered against his ribs like a bell, had started—started into such a picture of intense listening, that he might have been taken by a sculptor as the ideal of the echo which waits ere it repeats.

The countess did not speak the last word, but the shuddering peasant comprehended its purport and heard the answer.

"No, not yet—the bath is well replenished; your grace will need it but a little longer. She will die tonight."

"To say the truth," interrupted the other hideous piece of incarnate horror: "we must completely refill———"

"Hush!" suddenly cried Gouvina; "there stands the sentinel. Open, slave!' she added imperiously and Huon obeyed. The door was opened and they passed in. He drew it to again, but not closed, for he intended to enter again; but he heard a plash.

The plash of that horrible bath unequalled, incredible, and absolutely demoniac, made the strong muscles of the man flaccid as those of a child. His knees shook as he tottered out of the ghastly chamber.

He stood back in the place and position where he had slain the sentinel, whose body lay within a few feet of him in a niche of the wall. One of the old women entered from the bath and passed him.

Soon she re-appeared carrying with a strength almost superhuman, a form that was evidently bound hand and foot, but which was also covered over with a veil. By the power of the same instinct that had already told him so much, he felt that she was carrying the living Ina, to be left there dead!

His muscles became steel, his limbs like a rock, and his heart like adamant not to be affected by anything horrible or hideous. He had passed through *that* ordeal, and was man—was more than man again, for he had seen that which man perhaps had never seen before.

When the hag had entered the chamber and was about to lock the door within, he stepped stealthily forward and placed his hand between the door and its frame that the lock shot falsely—it was still open. Then he heard her with the same unnatural strength bear her burden away.

Away! To the brink of that murder pool, where the vampyre-woman—as the frenzied youth though her—drank of living blood, and bathed her limbs in its sanguine title.

There was no time to lose, and he pushed the door open, axe in hand, and stole in.

It was quite time. Half naked, the pallid form with her limbs bound and her mouth gagged, was held by one half leaning over the basin. The other fury, with fiery eyes, held a gleaming knife in her hand. The countess, clothed in long, dark, loose robes, was reclining on a stone couch.

Another minute and all was over. Ere the minute passed he had cloven one through the skull and the other was flung into the dark, dead sea. The next moment the countess found herself bound hand and foot and securely gagged, and then Huon turned to Ina.

He loosed her bandages, flung them away, and bore her out into the corridor. He restored her for a moment to life, and she sank into a swoon, during which time he discovered that some keys, which the countess carried, opened a private door which led to the gardens of the castle.

✳

When he had borne Ina across the forest, after immense difficulty and dread, and had placed her in perfect security, he went to Presburg, and before the Palatine, accused the Countess Gouvina of having been guilty of murder, together with many other hideous deeds, for which she deserved to die. He described the bath, the incident he had witnessed; and so powerful was his denunciations, that the rank and power of the countess could not save her.

She was condemned to the stake, but this was to be commuted to imprisonment for life. We avoid dwelling on the terrible details of the case, and repeat, once more, that the history of this women who sacrificed three-hundred maidens to a frightful hallucination, is one of those truths against which human nature shudders, but which it cannot disprove.

In conclusion, Huon led his young betrothed, who, thanks to her fright, imprisonment, and swooning, never knew the fact, to a distant land, where the story should never reach her, wedded her, and was as happy as the memory of this unparalleled occurrence would permit him to be.

THE DEAD ARE INSATIABLE

by Leopold von Sacher-Masoch

Thou hast invoked me from my grave,
And through thy magic spell
Hast quickened me with fierce desire,
This flame thou canst not quell.

Oh press thy lips against my lips,
Divine is mortal breath;
I drink thy very soul from thee.
Insatiable is death.
Heinrich Heine

WITH us, familiarity comes easily, for the doors of the peasants are without locks and often their dwellings lack even doors, and the gates of the landowners are open to all. When a guest comes to dine in the evening there are neither sad nor apprehensive faces as there would be in merry Germany, and it does not fall to family members to slip one by one into the kitchen to take their nightly meal in secret, and on feast days when friends and kin come together from afar, cattle, calves, geese, chicken and fowls are slaughtered and the wine flows in torrents as in Homeric times.

So I came freely to the house of the Bardossoski family, just as one nobleman calls upon another without ceremony, and soon I was visiting each evening. Their manor house was situated on a small hill just behind which rose the verdant foothills of the Carpathian Mountains. The family were most congenial, the best aspect being that suitors had already been found by the two daughters of the house, the younger of whom was even formally engaged, so one could talk freely and even, as is necessary with Polish women, pay court to them a little without immediately being regarded as a future marriage candidate.

Herr Bardossoski was a true country gentleman: simple, pious and hospitable, yet not without that quiet dignity, the presence of which requires no outward display. His wife, a petite, voluptuous, still pretty brunette, reigned over him just as absolutely as Queen Maria Kasimira ruled the great Sobieski, though there were a few subjects about which the landowner did not care to joke, at the mention of which a twist of his thick moustache or a puff of blue pipesmoke, that swiftly grew into a venerable cloud, enveloping him like the Olympian Zeus, was enough to quell dissent. I had never seen him without this long Turkish pipe with its head of red clay and delicate amber mouthpiece, which seemed to tell the outsiders amongst us *you are no longer in Europe my friend, here begins that Orient from which all your wisdom originates, from whose inexhaustible wells all your poets and thinkers have drawn.* In the year of 1863 he had sent his only son to fight beside the insurgents and lost him to the murderous thrust of a Cossack lance; mention was never made of this son, but his image, encircled by a withered wreath and a dusty black funerary band, hung over the old man's bed between two arched sabres crossed.

Of the two young ladies, Kordula, the elder, was what they called "intriguing", tall and well developed, with magnificent dark hair, fine teeth, grey eyes that bespoke a penetrating intelligence, and a face that showed unyielding resolve, both in its delicate snub nose and its upturned lips; the younger, Anna, on the other hand, was one of those ever pale, rose-cheeked beauties who seem always so languid, whose blue eyes dream even whilst open, and whose slow, deep breathing sounds like a sigh. It was she who already wore an engagement ring on her finger.

I also became acquainted with the young men who captured the hearts of these two so different sisters. The admirer of the elder was a Herr Husezki, who held the office of adjunct in the courts of a nearby town. He displayed that earnestness and enthusiasm for learning that characterises our younger generation, dressing after the French manner, with spectacles and crisp, white cuffs, the edges of which he was always straightening.

The fiancé of the lovely Aniela was a neighbouring landlord who called himself Manwed Weroaki, a handsome youth with teeth that sparkled beneath a neat black moustache, short, dark curly hair, and soulful eyes, who dressed always in black laced shirts and pantaloons with high leather boots. He smoked cigars, loved to discuss literature and could recite a hundred verses from Mickiewicz's *Pan Thaddeus* or *Konrad Wallenrod* by heart. His favourite routine was the tale of Demeyko and Doweyko, and he knew how to portray their duel over the bearskin so dramatically that a smile of youthful tenderness even stole over the snowy whiskers of the old patriarch.

Now there was a third young gentlemen, who was always in the habit of arriving late, a bad habit which seemed to be his fate, for he had also come too late for Aniela, so now had to be content with gazing at her forlornly and rushing off to bring her all manner of things should she make the least movement to rise; hence it was that although he imagined he was pre-empting her wishes, he would fetch her a footstall when she wanted the scissors and snatch up her little lap-dog by its fur, hauling it through the air before its mistress's gaze, when all the good woman's moist eyes really desired was a handkerchief. His name was Maurizi Konopka, and he rented a neighbourhood property on which he worked with machinery, and generally did everything according to rule, much to the astonishment of the farmspeople, and who never appeared in anything besides his standard costume of a suit, white waistcoat, kid gloves, fretted stockings and evening shoes. As he always arrived only when the rest of us had already gathered and, moreover, made every effort to slip in as silently as a ghost, he was usually only noticed when he stood up in the middle of the room, and, since he considered it impolite to draw attention to his presence with a loud greeting or audible clearing of the throat, this occurrence was so unexpected that it often caused everyone to jump, with the exception, of course, of the old hero, who at the most merely took his pipe from his mouth for a moment, in keeping with his character.

Maurizi was a very pretty, milk-faced youth, of the type preferred by mature, experienced beauties, but little resembling the ideal of a maiden's dream, which is why he bore the bitter lot, evening after evening—and our Galician winter evenings are long—of acting as a helper and playing Tarok with Herr Bardossoski whilst the rest of us chatted with the ladies.

Aniela's fiancée won my sympathy from the start. He was a magnificent story-teller, which earned him the reputation of a boor with many, but he also usually paid the cost of the entertainment without ever being unfaithful to the humble nature that makes Poles so amiable in ladies' company. We quickly grew close, visiting one another often and frequently hunting together. When we returned to his abode, footsore and hungry as the Seven Swabians after their pursuit of the hare, the samovar would be brought in immediately and the good Valenty would be on hand to help remove our muddy boots. Then I had no choice but to don a pair of Manwed's morocco slippers and one of his luxuriant dressing gowns, allow him to refill my pipe and accept that there was nothing for it but to spend the night beneath his hospitable roof.

After this he would play all manner of pranks, painting moustaches on the sleeping maidservants with a stump of charred cork or pulling the sheets off the beds, wrapping himself in them and wandering about the house, wailing and moaning, only to drag the old Valenty, who was by now praying fervently, from under his great woollen blanket by his feet.

✳

Near to Manwed's property, atop a lonely broad expanse of rock, was situated the ancient half-ruined Tartakow Castle, the site of many a sinister legend.

Once, on a gloomy winter's evening, as the snow rapped against the window panes with white ghostly fingers, the wind drew eerie melodies from the ruddy fireplace, and far away there sounded the howling of the wolf, Anna spoke of this subject:

"Have you heard," said she, "that the ruins are said to be occupied?"

"Who could reside in those desolate crumbling walls, aside from maybe owls and ravens," remarked Herr Husetski, with the common sense befitting a young man educated in the sciences.

"Well, there are all kinds of inhabitants," replied Mrs Bardossoski.

"It is true that a grey-haired old man can be seen in the upper rooms, some sort of steward," said Aniela. "He dresses as men did centuries ago, and the farms people say he is a thousand years old. And in the well-preserved great hall there stands a marble statue of an enchantingly beautiful woman with dead white eyes, who is said to come to life on certain nights and walk the corridors with a retinue of a myriad spectres, the eerie voices of which sound now as a bestial howl, now as a tormented moan, and now as a seductive whisper."

"Bah!" cried the adjunct. "An Aeolian harp. I've heard it myself before."

"Who knows? These lands are crowded with demons," said Manwed, "in the cottages of the peasants the *Did* murmurs, secretly helping to milk the cows, sweep the floors, wash the dishes, and groom the horses, only showing itself, a little grey-bearded man no more than a foot in height, when the master of the house is on his deathbed; on the banks of the rivers and pools, in the dark glades, the *Russalka* reclines on the swaying boughs, singing and weaving golden fetters from her hair with which to snare the poor sinner, a golden noose to choke his life away; in the mountain caverns, veiled by green latticework, dwell the amorous and daring *Majki*, who on the high meadows build enchanted gardens girt by fences of gold, raise bridges of pearl to span the rushing waters, and dance naked beneath the sun; they carry off youths to whom they take a fancy, beguiling them with their fragrant gossamer tresses and graceful figures, yet behind their shining eyes, their beautiful countenances, there is no soul. With the wolf packs there roam the wild women whom the peasants call the *Bochinki*, goddesses of forest and mountain, a terrible race that kidnaps the children of men and leaves behind in the cradle their hideous changelings, that tickle old men to death, and cruelly strangle the young bridegroom on his wedding night. Among the people there also dwell the wise, the *Widma*, who command the occult powers of nature, who know the herbs to cure plague and venomous snakebite, who can rob the stars of their light and the men of their strength, who send their souls abroad as birds even as their bodies sleep, and who on certain nights fly atop black tom-cats to Kiev, there to celebrate their sabbats wheeling in the sky high above the holy city. Yes, in this country stars that fall to earth assume human form and become vampires, men bear the evil eye, and the souls of lost children wander the night seeking baptism."

"So, yes, why shouldn't that ruin too be home to all manner of spooks, as well as a beautiful marble woman whose white limbs run with hot lifeblood at the midnight hour?"

"What a dreamer you are!" exclaimed Herr Husezki, "though now even I would like to know the real story of that old castle."

"I can give you the truth of it, you young folk," began the old gentleman after a brief pause, during which Panna Kordula filled the samovar with red glowing coals and Aniela's little rosy-tinged hands picked up the first few chords of a melancholy folk tune on the piano. He began his account by enveloping himself in clouds of blue tobacco smoke.

"The truth of it," he continued, "is that in the great hall of the castle, there is indeed a splendid marble sculpture of a beautiful woman. Some say that an ancestor of the Tartakowski family journeyed to Palestine with the red cross upon his breastplate seeking to liberate the Holy Sepulchre, and that he returned with an image of Venus made by a Greek artist in Byzantium."

"Others claim that a lady of the Tartakowski family, famed for her beauty and for her vices, was carved in this manner by an Italian sculptor, having posed in that costume that need pay no heed to fashion and which was already worn by Eve in Paradise before the Fall of Man. This is said to have happened in the time of Benvenuto Cellini, the beautiful lady being the Starostin Marina Tartakowska."

"So it is," interrupted a deep, soft voice that seemed to come from beneath the ground.

This had us leaping from our seats; Aniela gave a sharp cry and clapped her hands to her face; Panna Kordula dropped a cup which exploded like a grenade on the floor, a stray shard hitting the little lapdog and setting it barking furiously.

"I must fall at your feet and beg forgiveness, ladies and gentlemen," whispered Maurizi Konopka, who had slipped in unnoticed on his dancer's feet and now stood at the middle of our group. "A life sized portrait of the lady in question," he went on quietly, "hangs in a gloomy panelled room in the castle, the ceiling of which features a large mural of

Diana surprised in her bath by Actaeon, the ill-fated hunter transformed into a stag for his transgression. The Starostin is dressed in black velvet, with a Polish cap tipped with a spray of egret plumes. I once saw this portrait, from which the eyes of the Starostin seemed to stare back at me, and it made me feel as if my skin were being stretched over a drum as the Tartars used to do."

"That might have been close to the truth," said the adjunct. "In Krakow there are all manner of curious old records, including many court transcripts from the time of the Starostin Marina, which testify about the despotism of that beautiful widow who once resident in and ruled over Tartakow like an absolute monarch. Once she was charged with the murder of one of her servants, and since they were of noble descent, a royal commission was called to investigate, but the sight of this bewitching woman was enough to disarm the judges, and the court, chased away by Cupid with a switch of roses, returned without achieving their aim. Incidentally, the castle is said to be as good as abandoned now."

"Ah!" said old Bardossoski, removing the pipe from his mouth in surprise, "and what became of the last owner's widow, the lovely Zoë Tartakowska?"

"She has spent the last few years in Paris," answered the adjunct, "but I have heard that she died recently."

"A pity," the old gentleman murmured "she was a woman like the Starostin Marina, only tailored to current fashions, but still a beautiful woman."

"Now, now, don't get too enthusiastic about her," said Mrs. Bardossoski.

For a while no one spoke, then Manwed suddenly leapt up and cried out, "I must go."

"Where to?"

"Why, to that haunted castle!"

"You wouldn't dare to," said Mrs Bardossoska, "what they talk of is frightening."

"Well, I think if Herr Konopka dared to do so, then my courage shan't be found wanting," replied Manwed, twirling his moustache.

"Oh! he's only joking," breathed Aniela.

"I am not joking, my lady."

"Manwed, you will not go seeking that marble woman," cried Aniela with all the force she could muster.

"I will go, and at night, for I wish to see if that cold beauty shall come to life."

"Manwed," said Aniela faintly but with a definite note of conviction in her voice, "I forbid you to go."

"Forgive me," murmured the stubborn youth, "but I must be so ungallant as to disobey you on this occasion."

Aniela looked back at him for a long time, more astonished than angry, then she turned away, her bosom heaving, her breath unsteady, and tears began to flow down her cheek.

Manwed took up his hat, bid the company a brief farewell, and departed. It was not long before we heard the crack of his coachman's whip, and the ringing of horse bells. Aniela fled the room sobbing.

The next morning, I visited Manwed with the intention of making peace, but if possible he was even more set in his views than on the previous evening.

"Our women are tyrants each and every one," he cried, "the only difference is that some trample us beneath their feet and others abuse us with tears. If I yield this once I will be lost. I am all the more determined to visit this mysterious castle, and at this very instant."

He dressed quickly, had them saddle his horse, and bid me goodbye at the steps from his gate.

"So, you are really riding there now?"

"Yes, as you can see."

"Well, I am curious as to what you find there."

"So am I."

We nodded to one another and he spurred his horse, the snowy ground crunched beneath its hooves and sent up glittering particles of ice. I watched him go until he vanished into the white haze.

✳

Manwed remained away for two evenings, returned to us on the third, and was received rather coldly. Aniela did not even appear to notice him, instead she joked and made an uncharacteristic show of playing with the little lap dog, who was utterly delighted by this course of events, by turns growling, whimpering and barking, sitting now on its front paws, standing then on its back legs, its tail wagging constantly.

Manwed sat there in silence, contrary to his normal habits, his face grave, contemplative and very pale, only his dark eyes still blazed with life, the brow above them creased with a grim line like a shadow or the scar from a sabre cut.

Finally, the old gentleman broached the topic, "Well, come now! Did you go up there, Herr Werofski?"

The "Herr" was heavily emphasised.

Manwed contented himself with a faint nod.

"Well, so tell us then," cried the adjunct, hastily tugging his white cuffs from the sleeves of his black shirt.

"It doesn't interest me," broke in Aniela.

"It is interesting all the same," said the lady of the house with dignity, "take a cup of hot tea and then tell us all."

And Manwed accepted a cup of warm tea, loosened the thick knot of his silk kerchief, and began to tell his story.

✳

"If I was not sitting here amongst you, able to hear the singing of the samovar, the crackling of the fire, and the sigh of the good Mr. Bardossoki's pipe, I would believe that I had slept

166

for two days and two nights, and again for a day, and that during that time the weirdest and most sinister dreams had tormented me, yes and I would believe that I was dreaming still, for a fine transparent mist, like an enchanter's veil, separates me from all of you, and in the far distance stands a figure pointing and beckoning——

"It was a bright winter morning, radiant, the golden sunlight playing on the white snow, which gently covered the earth, on the tall furs and spruces with their branches outstretched like black arms from beneath white coats, on the fringes of icicles that brocaded the overhanging thatch of the peasants' houses on their northern side, on the frozen pond then transformed into a silvery meadow, and on the black metallic plumage of the crows which strutted stiffly along the path nodding to themselves before taking wing laboriously, as if with reluctance, to sit again by the roadside or atop a tree covered with glittering needles. Ash-grey vapours slowly rose like the smoke of extinguished candles from all the clefts and crevices of the mountains, obscuring the sun and coming down quickly towards me.

"Through this tide of damp surging mist, my horse seemed not to walk but rather to swim forwards, and from time to time a fantastic apparition wrapped in an impenetrable shroud, or with a flowing white beard, crouched down by the bushes and field edges.

"Yet it was not long before the heavens turned to translucent alabaster, colouring more and more, finally revealing a glowing circle from which the sun proceeded triumphantly. The grey billows gathered into clouds and rolled over the forests. A rosy-coloured tint hanging about them, the trees and bushes were suddenly decked with pearls of light and the snow had the pale sheen of silk to it. Through the dark boughs the mountains could now be seen, as stark and white as chalk, each towering head of rock surrounded by a blazing halo; the sky was a pale green in colour, which gradually abandoned itself into the blue until the purest azure covered me, and only little white clouds, like wandering swans, passed across it.

"And there ahead, too, lay the dark crumbling rock, with the gloomy castle before me.

"I skirted around it, and found a gentle slope down which stretched overgrown parkland, but even here there was no road to be seen, not even a foot trail. My animal had to make its own way through, snorting and struggling. Finally, I came to a great gate with rusted fittings, and sought about in vain for a knocker or bell cord. On both sides loomed the high grey wall, atop the broad merlons of which a small garden had grown over the course of centuries. Individual roots ran down the entire length of the wall and entwined themselves in strange formations at its base. Above the gate was a dark coat of arms, worn and faded by the rain.

"I stood up in my stirrups and gave a loud cry, but before the echoes of the surrounding rocks could return it, there opened, with a horrible creak, a narrow wicket in one side of the great gates, from which came an old man who greeted me with great deference, his head bowed and his hat in his hands. I had not seen his like before, save in age-old portraits and on stage, when dramas depicting Polish history were performed.

"He gave the impression of one of those weathered stone figures which lie with folded hands on the marble tombs of our long-dead nobles come to life. The entirety of the old man was decrepit and decayed, as though it were soon to be coated with mould, the shrivelled face with its yellowing cheeks resembled a venerable parchment, covered with countless tiny wrinkles as if by a script lost to time. His dress was of the old Polish style, from around the period of Johann Kasimir, when the Tartar cut had already totally supplanted the Slavic. He wore high, pleated morocco boots, that might once have been green, over wide pantaloons and a long kontusz, the slitted sleeves of which were tied at the back, a broad metal girdle, and an arched sabre that hung about his shoulders on a strong cord, all of this faded and sombre in colour. On his bald head there stood a tuft of hair; which the breeze gently shook; it was as though in accordance with the time to which he seemed to belong, he had shaved his scalp and was wearing the curl once sported by the Tartar hordes.

"His grey moustache hung down to his kontusz. He bowed once more with great politeness and ceremony.

"'You must be astonished to have a guest, old fellow.' I said, as lightly as I could manage. He shook his head. 'I have been expecting you,' said he, a friendly smile crossing his gnarled face.

"'Put your hat back on,' I called.

"He nodded, set the grey Czapeka back crooked over his left ear, and opened the gate, closing and locking it again behind him after I had ridden in. The great key sang mournfully in the rusted lock.

"'Well, do you want to show me all your treasures then, old fellow?' I said, after I had dismounted and let him take the reins of my horse.

"'It shall be a rare honour for me,' he replied in a voice akin to the creek of a rusted gate. 'And my name is Jakub, if it does not displease you, my gracious sir.'

"Whilst he led my horse into the stable, I had time to glance around the castle courtyard. Before me was a kind of palace with a leaded roof, with a magnificent open stairway and a balcony borne upon the stone shoulders of naked Turks, under which protruded a dragon's head ready to spout rainwater in a broad arc. In a deep recess formed by the wall, the hideous head and manacle-laden hands of a Mongol chieftain could be seen carved in stone. The stone-paved courtyard, then lightly carpeted with snow, had at its centre a brick cistern, over which a great linden spread its boughs; the two crows sitting upon these periodically let out shrill cries of joy, as if calling to hail the worthy stranger. All about was strewn with rubble, shattered bricks and mounds of stones.

"The old man returned, beckoned to me, and prepared to unlock the latticed gate that barred the external stairway. There was something shadow-like about his gait and movements, I fancied that if the sun had shone I would have been able to see straight through him. Only now did I notice that a large raven was quietly and earnestly observing his step.

"He conducted me slowly up the stairway, unlocked an ornately decorated door at the top, and then I was across the threshold of that sinister infamous edifice. We went by sweeping marble stairways and narrow, concealed spiral staircases, up and down, through corridors now as wide and grand as an avenue, and then as stifling and claustrophobic as the shaft of a mine. Large dark-wood doors with metal fittings were opened and closed again, sometimes the pressure of a finger sufficed and a wall swung aside to let us pass, and through the suites of rooms, the shades of bygone centuries passed with us; here hung suits of black armour with white angels wings, captured Turkish banners, Spanish breeches, Tartar quivers with envenomed arrows, in rooms tapestries depicting scenes from the Old Testament hung, faded and eaten by the moths which rose up in swarms, filling the air, at the slightest touch; there, a corridor further on, was enthroned a Rococo beauty in all her capricious charm. We passed dainty boudoirs papered with faded blue silk or yellowing white muslin, in which pot-bellied Chinese porcelain sat atop large fireplaces and mirrors with silver frames atop high dressing-tables; all the ephemera of times past were to be seen.

"From majestic halls decorated with delicate stucco-work and gigantic frescoes one came to bedchambers with opulent four-poster beds. There on a marble pedestal stood a vase only the aesthetic genius of a Hellene or an Italian could realise, and one door on a tall, carved cabinet occupied the width of the wall, filled with all manner of queer glasswork and pottery, brightly painted, lettered with earthy mottos as only the bizarre German tastes of the fifteen and sixteenth centuries could produce. Woodworm ravaged the precious panelling, almost black with age, most of the windows were shuttered, and on the old portraits which adorned the walls, the colours had darkened so much over the course of centuries that the bold knights, the magnificent starosts and the richly dressed ladies all seemed to stand in deep shadow, from which, here and there, a beautiful face shone out as though through the gloom of the night. Everything was neglected, decaying, blanketed with ash-grey dust and hung with cobwebs, the air smelt of mildew, and suddenly it appeared to me as if the old grey man too were covered with mould.

"We came at last to a chamber of moderate size, square in layout and panelled with dark wood, in which there were neither furnishings nor ornaments. On the central wall hung a portrait in a smoky gold frame, which was presently concealed by a green curtain.

"The old man motioned for me to be still—he had said not a word throughout the whole journey and he communicated now only by means of look and gesture—and approaching the green curtain on tiptoe, pulled on a concealed cord.

"Dust rose up and from the grey cloud seemed to step a female figure of uncanny loveliness. It was a tall woman of serpentine slenderness, clad in black velvet, one who could hardly be called beautiful but who bewitched with an expression of smirking melancholy and gentle savagery, her demonically coquettish face framed with dark curls atop which a Polish cap perched delicately. Her great dark eyes burnt with a kind of phosphorescence, and seemed to follow me as I retreated.

"I know not what lay in that look, something incomprehensible that took my breath away, set my heart pounding in my breast and made my knees tremble.

"'It's a good likeness,' whispered the old man.

"I stared at him in horror, just as one looks at a man one suddenly realises has lost his mind. He seemed to recognise this, shrugged his shoulders and covered the picture. At that

171

instant I felt a searing pain in my index finger. It was my engagement ring, which had cut into my flesh for the first since I first wore it. 'Well, Herr Jakub,' I said, 'will you now show me the marble woman too?'

"He reached out a withered hand, resembling a dried-up leaf, from the sleeve of his kontush and gestured to me. 'I know,' he told me in his creaking voice, 'that this is the reason my gracious sir has journeyed here, but it is not the hour. If he should return tomorrow night we shall have a full moon and the dead shall come to life.'

"'Have you lost your wits?' I started, half unconsciously.

"'Very well, my gracious sir,' he returned with a smile which stole into his grey moustache like a ray of sunlight, 'the portrait is a fine likeness and the dead stone resembles her too; yes, I know her well, but who else should know her if not I? It was I who dandled her on my knees, as true I love God.'

"I shuddered at the deep conviction with which the old man uttered this impossibility. I swiftly handed him a gold piece—which he accepted respectfully—rushed back down to the courtyard, saddled my horse and rode back down the slope resolved never to go near this mysterious castle and its crazed inhabitants again.

"This was a resolution though and went the way of most promises we make to ourselves. By the very next morning I denounced myself as a coward, by noon I had given myself an eloquent lecture on the follies of superstition, and nightfall found me seated in the saddle, ready to seek out the woman of marble.

"The night was cold, but the air was calm and without movement. The great pure disk of the full moon already rode high in the heavens, so that nothing could be seen of the golden light and flashing of the stars save for a dim, pallid glimmer. It was as if it were day, a dull day with lead-grey light, but day still, so strong was the silvery brightness of the moon, which flooded over everything, and which the snow, enveloping the landscape in its dazzling whiteness, threw back with piercing intensity. One could see every little thing from afar, only in the distance they seemed to drift like faint smoke, and behind them the mountains stood wrapped in a diamond veil.

"On such clear, calm nights the snow and the moon are wondrous artists, architects and craftsman without peer; they vie with one another to erect fabulous edifices and line our path with their creations. Where otherwise there is a charred, abandoned peasants' cottage with its skewed thatch roof, they raise up a magnificent ice-palace with sparkling windows like that which was built on the frozen surface of the Neva during the reign of Czarina Anna. On a broad hill, dark columns with flashing chapiters loomed in the air like the ruins of a Grecian temple. On the banks of a pond seemed to stand a Tartar woman, wrapped from head to foot in white veils, and inspecting herself in the green lustrous sheet of ice as if in a mirror, whilst in the distance there towered images of the gods, cut from dazzling marble, and on the shimmering plain of the meadow fair elves entwined with one another in a spectral dance.

"In the cemetery, every one of the paupers' graves was adorned with a grand sarcophagus, above which a white cross gleamed, and the restless dead in trailing burial gowns hovered menacingly.

"The mill wheel stood petrified, large pillars of ice supported the chase, the silver fall of the brook had frozen and within it roots and foliage glowed with all manner of colours, like the flowers formed of gemstones in the *Thousand and One Nights*.

"And at last, when there was not a rooftop, not a tree and not a shrub to be seen, no matter how small, only the noiseless radiant flood of moonlight over the white surges of snow, then it felt to me as if I were flying upon the enchanted horse high in the air, above me the stars and below me the white shimmering clouds.

"It was not long before the earth announced its proximity once more, the lights of a village winked in the silver twilight, a forge sent up showers of sparks and from its chimney a column of red flame rose towards the sky, heavy hammer blows pounded with a melancholy beat echoing into the stillness of the night; and by the marges stood a pump-spring covered in a shroud of snow, the frozen stream of which formed bizarre arabesques. Behind the huts rose the slopes of the mountains, and from them a forest of snow-topped firs descended like a Cossack host upon black horses, with tall lambskin hats and burnished lances. To the side, snow-covered fields in which there remained the yellow stalks of corn shimmered like moonlit reed-beds in the bright mirror of a lake.

"Further on by the roadside stood a cross to which the Saviour was fixed with diamond nails, bearing a crown of radiant light instead of drear thorns.

"And then, though hitherto no living beings had made their presence known, there suddenly appeared amidst the snow-covered winter-crops a lively company of grey hares, frisking and making love in the amorous light of the moon. There some were busy digging in the snow for food, there some frolicked, screaming like children and boxing one another with their forelegs; others arrived with light hops, suddenly sat up to look at me, then flicked their ears back and stretched themselves out again playfully as soon as I had ridden by. In the distance an old fox barked hoarse and sullen.

"Thus I came to Tartakow Castle.

"As the old man led me up the broad stone stairway, an icy draught rose, the old linden rustled longingly, deep down below, unmastered even by winter's freezing chains, a mountain stream rushed eerily, and over my head there came fabulous, heartrending tones of sorrowful sweetness.

"'What is that?' I asked.

"'It's the Aeolian harp,' answered the old man, 'it's stood in the tower for a hundred years, as far as I can recall.'

"We stepped into a cosy room with green curtains which was kept comfortably warm; fresh spruce burned in the fireplace, giving off a pleasant narcotic aroma. A covered table was set before a flowered sofa. I noticed precious china and antique silverware decorated with the Tartakow family coat of arms.

"The strange old man invited me to take a seat, set the samovar on and served me with the solid dignity of a grizzled steward. The hand on the archaic wall-clock seemed to stand still. Finally, it drew near the midnight hour.

"'It is time,' said I.

"'Yes, it is time,' agreed the old man. He took the ring of keys from his belt and began to unlock the way, door by door; we walked again through long passageways and endless suites of rooms, only this time everything took on a ghostly life, from the black visors hostile eyes glinted at me, from the golden frames uncanny figures made ready to step down onto the threadbare carpets and even the old banners and hangings seem to stir and whisper.

"After the elder had opened the silver-embossed black door of a large hall unentered on my first visit, he said:

"'Here I must leave you, my gracious sir. Go ahead boldly. At the end of the room you will come to two flights of stairs; that on the left shall lead you to the marble woman.'

"I crossed the threshold and stood in a splendid hall with high windows through which fell the rich light of the moon, illuminating the entire room with its enchantments.

"My footsteps echoed on the marble slabs, and as I slowly approached the twin staircases which climbed upward at the end of the room, two shapes seemed to rise from the floor of the landing above in the silvery moonlight.

"To my right stood the Saviour in a flowing white robe, his beautiful brow wreathed with a crown of thorns, the weight of the cross on his shoulder, his gaze full of gentle grief as he beckoned to me with his outstretched hand.

"On my left, though, there was a woman whose marble limbs seemed to reach out and glow in the moonlight, a woman of that beauty which has something diabolic to it, which grips us with sweet agony, which teaches us to rejoice in suffering and weep in pleasure.

"'You must take up the cross of mankind!' the Saviour seemed to whisper softly to me, but she offered her full, perfumed, unliving lips in a kiss.

"A mysterious compulsion drew me on; I staggered up the stairs into the gentle twilight of her presence, and when at last I was on my knees before her, I pulled my engagement ring free and slid it on to one of her white fingers. She received me silent and cold as a marble image, as a goddess, as a dead woman; and I bowed my head, brought my lips to her beautiful feet and kissed them.

"Then I stood up and reached out my hand to take back the ring.

"It was then the unbelievable occurred, that which froze my heart and befuddled my mind. She closed her hand, preventing me from retrieving my ring.

"Dread seized me, I recoiled and almost toppled back down the staircase, but I managed to regain my balance, telling myself aloud that this was all a play of the imagination, a trick of the moonlight, nothing more.

"The vaulted roof returned my words, but with mockery and in a tone which seemed not my own. I approached the beautiful woman once more and saw that she held out her white hand to me in a gesture of divine gracefulness as before, and I saw the golden circlet on her finger.

"Yet when I tried to snatch it from her again her hand closed, and when I tried to pry it apart I felt those marble fingers clench into a fist at my touch. It sent a chill coursing through me.

"I don't know how I escaped the hall or how I left the castle. The icy bite of the morning wind on my cheeks brought me to my senses, but from then the ghostly woman seemed to follow me. I saw her, delicately caressed by the rosy dawn, standing in a cloud that passed over the pond, and saw her again not far from my estate, her beautiful white body glimmering through the black fir trees. Since then I have seen her in dreams and in waking, with open eyes, I see her as she steps gently into my chamber like a moonbeam, and smiles at me with white, dead eyes."

※

Whilst Manwed recounted his adventure, Herr Konopka entered the room, maybe not quite as a moonbeam, but silently enough, and stood gazing at the lovely Aniela, as was his normal manner. All of a sudden she gave a piercing cry, at which we all noticed that good young man's presence for the first time and there was not one of us who did not start a little.

"What right do you have," asked the elder Bardossoska sister angrily, "to frighten us so every time?"

"I don't know," replied Herr Konopka, who was shaking like a leaf, "all I know is that I am terribly afraid myself."

"You afraid?" scoffed Kordula, "of what?"

"Herr Werofski's story has every hair on my head standing on end," stammered Maurizi.

The old gentleman blew aside a cloud of blue smoke, plugged the tobacco firmer with his fingers, and said:

"A fine ghost story."

Aniela rose and took Manwed's hand.

"Where is the ring that I gave you?" she asked, deep shadows flitting across her normally unsullied brow.

"I don't have it."

"A poor joke!" Kordula exclaimed.

"Indeed," put in her admirer.

"It is no joke," said Manwed, "the dead woman of marble has the ring."

Not a word more was said about the matter, but all were noticeably upset and so Manwed made a hurried exit. I accompanied him to his sleigh.

"Don't you think it's time to change your conduct?" said I.

"Now, you, as well, think I'm joking," he replied irritably. "Fine, but I tell you that I have lost my will, that my soul is thrall to a demon in the form of Venus, and that I love this cold, dead beauty, without voice, without sight, and without a heart, with a love like that of a madman." And so he left.

Upon returning to the house, I found all present in a state of tremendous excitement. Maurizi swore he would not make the ride home unaccompanied; the adjunct spoke learnedly of the powers of autosuggestion; Herr Bardossoski's emotions were conveyed only through the medium of his long pipe, which snuffled and whined like a small child. Suddenly, the lady of the house frowned and looked at the window.

"Who is out there?" she asked meekly. At once we all noticed a white figure, mysteriously lit up by the pale glow of the moon.

"It is her," murmured Maurizi, "she comes seeking him."

"Who?" asked Aniela, suddenly seized with jealousy, her voice trembling.

"The marble woman, who else!" replied Maurizi. He motioned with his hand as if to say that he you are searching for has gone from here, far away, but the white figure moved not from its place.

"My pistols," wheezed Herr Bardossoski, "I will load a consecrated shot, then we shall see——" He did not finish but took his Kuchenreuter from the wall and let the hammer fall.

"Why don't you speak with her?" pleaded Aniela

"Madame," Maurizi began in a truly pitiful voice, "he is not here, he has driven home, if you make haste you might be able to catch up with him." His teeth chattered as he spoke. "But look here," he went on, grabbing my arm, "the fiery breath the terrifying woman gives off; is not that queer?"

"It is even queerer," said the old gentleman, with a merry laugh, "that our ghost has a pipe in its mouth and is smoking from it."

He went slowly to the window, drew it open, and then we had a full view of the ghost standing there with cheerful clarity in the moonlight.

Roguish laughter rang out across the courtyard.

A snowman with a large head and a big foolish face stood on broad legs in a sailor's posture. The coachman and the servants had raised him with all the skills at their disposal, and the Cossack had set his short, smouldering pipe in his wide mouth. Then there was loud, boisterous laughter in the room as well as in the courtyard, where the pranksters had concealed themselves behind a wagon, the samovar was put on, the tarok cards were summoned and we talked to our hearts' content long past midnight.

Manwed arrived at the Bardossoski household the following evening with the firm resolution of reconciling with Aniela. The dreamy aspect of his character, which sometimes bordered on the delirious, seemed to have retreated utterly; everything about him betrayed determination, earnestness and contrition. He wasted no time in explaining himself. When Aniela came down, pallid, her eyes still half shut, he approached her and bowed deeply.

"My dear," he began in a conciliatory tone which spoke to the heart, "I have wronged you with behaviour which is as bizarre as it is unwarranted. I am fully aware of my fault and ask your forgiveness for it."

"Bravo!" cried the old gentleman, clapping his hands vigorously, as if he were a devotee of the theatre applauding a well-executed scene.

"Give him your hand," said the mother.

The poor girl immediately extended both hands, and Manwed clasped them with all the ardour of a lover; he made a motion as if intending to kiss his bride, but in that same instant he grew as pale and rigid as a dead man, his horrified gaze fixed on the empty air, until at last he stumbled backwards, crying out:

"What do you want? Why do you menace me?"

"What has come over you?" asked Aniela fearfully.

"There she stands," he went on, "between you and I, the dead stone woman, she has my ring upon her finger and is admonishing me. And now she drifts to the door—there—there—and now she beckons to me."

At that most apt moment, Maurizi reappeared, wearing a white coat and looking like the Commander in Don Juan.

A cry of terror went through the room, Aniela clasped her hands to her face, and Manwed collapsed into a chair.

"I am very much afraid . . ." Maurizi began, his whole body shaking.

"Are you unable to make your entrance like any other man?" growled the old gentlemen.

"You are ill," said the adjunct to Manwed, "perhaps it is the onset of a nervous fever. Try to sweat it out. Remain in bed and take elderberry tea."

"I am beginning to fear him," Aniela murmured.

Manwed looked about with glazed eyes, rose, ran a hand over his forehead and went from the room. A week passed before he showed his face again. Herr Bardossoski drove out to see him, but each time found him not at home. I fared no better, but he returned my visit later that same evening. His appearance was like that of a man who had just quit his grave, pale, stumbling, his face grimacing; he entered, offered me his hand and sat with me for an hour without speaking, without even hearing what I was saying.

"Come," he cried unexpectedly, "I must get some air, come out with me."

I had two horses saddled and we rode at a light gallop along the country lane, through the snow-covered fields and between the white-clad trees, till we reached the edge of his estate. At this moment he drew up his bay and pointed ahead. "Do you see?" he whispered in a dry voice like that of a fever patient. "Do you see her?"

"I see no one."

"There, the pale lady who rides upon a black horse."

It was that period of twilight which is darker than true night. I strained my eyes in vain unable to detect anything. At last he was satisfied. We came to his courtyard, dismounted, and went and sat in his cosy little smoking room with its large fireplace, the strong red flames of which also provided light. The old manservant filled the samovar with hot coals. Neither of us had any desire to speak. The yellow hunting hound whimpered beneath the divan, seemingly dreaming, the massive clock in the hallway, the wooden case of which rose like a tower almost to the ceiling, held its monotonously serious sermon. A moth rose from the frayed upholstery of the armchair on which I sat and quietly orbited the samovar.

"What was that?" asked Manwed all of a sudden.

"I do not hear anything."

"But now——"

Indeed, there did come a soft tap on the windowpanes, which were covered in great blossoms of frost resembling Brussels lace.

"So, do you still see nothing?" said Manwed with a smile. He rose and went to the window. I looked out and at last saw standing before us, illuminated by the moon's rays, a pale woman who exchanged knowing signs with my friend. Finally, she nodded her head and withdrew.

"What is the meaning of this?" I asked. "Am I mad as well, or are we both prey to a trick of the light?"

Manwed shrugged his shoulders.

"As you must see, I am already wholly in the claws of Satan," he whispered. "It is a story of something that seldom happens, which is why I would willingly tell it to you, but you need not believe I am mad, and still less that I am telling you a fairy tale. I am simply not on good terms with courage. Poor Aniela!"

We took tea, he lit my pipe for me, and caught the moth that flittered around the samovar and tossed it in the red fires of the hearth where it was immediately consumed. Then he began.

"It was a beautiful, unearthly night, the moon full, when I made my third ride to Tartakow castle. I wanted my ring back at any price. The weather-beaten old man was waiting for me at the gateway this time; he nodded in a friendly manner, took my horse and invited me to share this meal.

"I drank one glass of old Burgundy, which ran through my veins like fire, that was all. My head was clear, my heartbeat steady. I was determined and without fear. As midnight struck, the old man opened the door of the great hall and bolted it again behind me. I paid no heed but climbed the stairs swiftly and took the hand of the beautiful marble woman with the intention of retrieving my ring from her, but she took my fingers in hers and I tried in vain to wrest myself free.

"It was an eerie struggle with the cold, dead stone woman in the wan moonlight and the deep silence which held sway over all. At last I let my arms fall and gasped for breath, and then her wondrous bosom rose in a sigh, and her white eyes gazed into mine with a look that humbled me, that robbed me of my reason. Without thinking what I was doing I wrapped my arms around her cold, beautiful body and pressed my hot lips to her icy countenance.

"It was a kiss without end, not as of two souls melting into one another but as of a demonic force slowly sucking the lifeblood from its victim.

182

"I was seized by a nameless dread, yet still unable to break free of those dead lips, which were already stealing the warmth from mine, a gentle breath lifted her elven-white bust, and then suddenly her marble arms wrapped around my neck like a heavy chain, the sweet burden pushing me to my knees as a beguiling smile shone like a moonbeam from her white eyes. Her entire body began to stir softly, like a tree stretching in the spring winds and breathing gladly after its rigid sleep had passed. Her feet made to move, and slowly, as if tired unto death, she stepped down from the pedestal. Overcome by her beauty, I embraced the newly awakened woman and kissed her anew with all the ardour of life and youth that pulsed through my veins. With drowsy lips she returned the kiss, as if still languid, stretched her blooming limbs in Olympian indolence, pulled away and waveringly, with the movements of a sleepwalker, went towards a door I had not noticed on my first visit, beckoning me to follow with a wave of her hand.

"The door seemed to swing open of its own accord and we came into a chamber with a panelled ceiling, ancient wallpaper, oddly shaped old furniture with gilded arms and feet, the floor of which was covered with a Persian carpet.

"By the hearth there stood a daybed hung with blood-red silk, as are found in Turkish harems, a lion's pelt spread out on the floor before it. In the heavy air there was an odour of mould and exotic spices reminiscent of a tomb. Nothing burnt in the ornate candelabras that stood before the large mirror, but outside in the darkened heavens, the moon hung like a silver lantern, illuminating the little room completely. The beautiful woman lay back on the bed and beckoned for me to join her. I went down on my knees before her, caressing her feet with my breath and kissing them, kissing her hands, kissing her neck, kissing her shoulders, until she drew me to her with coy grace and sought my lips once more. It is impossible to describe what I felt as I warmed her against my breast, the current of life seared through her, coursing from the top of her spine to the soles of her feet, and what I felt when she opened her eyelids slightly and blinked sideways at me, as her lips quivered and began to speak with a voice which was so unearthly, so tender, as her mighty gaze suddenly fell upon my soul like a snowflake! And bizarrely, she spoke in French.

"'I am freezing,' she began, 'make a fire in the hearth.' I obeyed and soon the dry wood was blazing brightly, the light of the flames playing about the room delightfully, dancing on the faded portraits, on the old wallpaper, on the yellowing furniture, and on the intoxicatingly lovely body of the white lady, who lay draped in the red silk, enveloped by her own luscious curls. The moon wove white roses in amongst the bloody red roses of the flames, garlanding that divine image. And again we kissed.

"'Bring me something to drink,' she said all of a sudden.

"'What do you command?' I asked.

"'Wine,' she answered indicating a bell-rope near the door.

"I tugged on the cord. The bell's note echoed horribly through the vast desolate building, and soon a voice that seemed to issue from the underworld asked what it was we might wish.

"'Wine, old man,' I said.

"After a short pause, there came a knock at the door, and when I stepped out there stood the steward bearing a bottle still coated with the grime of the cellar, along with a silver tray, atop which two glass goblets rattled softly.

"I filled one of these to the brim with gleaming red Burgundy wine and passed it to her. She took it and sipped the blood of the vines just as greedily as she had my kisses, and when I retrieved the glass at a gesture, she draped her arms around my neck and sucked hard on my lips. A wondrous languor fell upon me, she seemed to steal away my breath, life and soul, I felt as if I were dying, the awareness of being in the bloodthirsty hands of a feminine vampire swept over me like a shadow, but it was too late, for I had become entangled in

184

her curls, my hands digging through her demonic hair until consciousness fled away.

"When I returned to my senses I saw with indescribable astonishment that it was not in the arms of a vampire nor a statue, nor a demon of death that I lay. A lively, beautiful woman of radiant voluptuousness, her supple alabaster skin aflush with warm blood, looked down at me curiously with moist, devilish eyes. The finely shaped oval of her pale face glowed with pure ecstasy, her magnificent hair, at once molten gold and soft silk, flamed about her like a halo, like the blazing tail of a comet. The air about her was heavy with fragrance. Her body was without ornament, without even a simple band, such as that which adorns the arms of sculptured goddesses, but her teeth gleamed like two rows of pearls in that ruby mouth and her eyes cast a green light like that of precious emeralds.

"'Am I beautiful?' she asked at last in her languid, husky voice.

"I was unable to speak. The faint, strange glow of her watchful eyes took my breath away. Her imperious gaze seized my heart with panther claws. I felt my blood ebb away like that of a mortally wounded man. For a moment a predatory fire kindled in her eyes, before fading away like that arcane veil cast over the landscape by the moon.

"'Am I beautiful?' she repeated.

"'I have never before seen any woman like you,' I replied.

"'Fetch me a mirror,' she said at this. I lifted the heavy mirror down from the wall and set it before her, so that she might admire all of her lovely figure. She did so with beguiling delight, and began to comb and arrange her mane of red-gold hair with elven fingers. Eventually she seemed satiated with her own beauty and bid me set the mirror back in its place. As I again lay reverently at her feet and gazed up her face, she murmured: 'I see myself in your eyes,' and her lips brushed a kiss over my eyelids.

"'Come then,' she commanded, 'let us begin anew the tor-
turously sweet game of love.'

"'I fear you and your red mouth,' I replied hesitantly. She
laughed. It was a lavascious laugh filled with sweet temptation.

"'Oh! You cannot flee from me,' cried the woman, as she
pulled my face to her curls violently, and then quickly twisted
the ends of them into a noose, which she draped around my
neck and slowly pulled tight.

"'What if I were to strangle you now,' she whispered,
'and at the same moment drown you with my kisses, as the
Russalka does with her victims?'

"'It would be a sweet death.'

"'You think so? But I shall let you live, to my pleasure and
your torment.'

"She bent towards me, closer and closer, her breath prick-
ling over my skin like a foretaste of hell-fire. My lips traced
her delicate blue veins, everywhere shimmering through the
alabaster of her skin, before I threw my burning face against
her bosom, which was as soft as billowing velvet and as delicate as fresh snow. I let her soft breath wash over me as she
played with me like a doll. She laid her hand over my eyes, she
whispered in my ears, and then placed a finger on my lips and
at last in my mouth, as if she wished me to taste it, her flesh
intoxicating and sherbet sweet. In the following moment, she
twined my curls around her fingertips and then ran both her
hands through my hair, at once so tenderly and so savage-
ly, before resuming her Bacchanalian frenzy and pulling me
again to her lips, which seemed parched with a feverish thirst.

"The swells of love lapping about me softly grew into a
wave which threatened my very being, with which I struggled like one shipwrecked; and when suddenly the bewitching
woman kissed me upon the ear it crashed down, booming,
and whirling me about as if I were a drowning man; enveloped as I was in her fiery tresses, it was as if I swam in an
ocean of boiling lava, which finally consumed me in the ar-

dent, superhuman rapture of love. Through these diabolical kisses all the mysteries of Passion were suddenly revealed to me, lust and fear, pleasure and torment, laughter and tears, until in delirium I sank to the earth once more.

"'Are you dead?' she asked after a pause, and as I did not move she kicked me in the face with her dainty bare foot, and in the next moment laid herself across my back, stretching out and laughing arrogantly, like a lion-tamer atop the beast she had broken.

"I did not stir, not even as she rose and crossed the room.

"When I eventually opened my eyes, I beheld the moon, who had slipped in silence into the chamber, kissing her, then slowly sweeping up to embrace her in his white arms as she offered her lips to him coquettishly.

"Anger and jealously gripped me.

"'What does that pale brute want?' I cried; 'you are mine!'

"'*You* are mine!' she laughed and flung herself down amongst the pillows, her hair flying up like a plume of flame, and I was again seized by the madness of love, pressing my lips to her knees, to her heaving bust, and finally resting my head against her shoulder.

"'What is this?" I asked after a moment. 'I can feel no heartbeat in your chest!'

"'I have no heart,' she said coldly and sullenly. Her noble limbs trembled for a moment as if chilled by a draught. 'As for you,' she went on mockingly, 'yours pounds like mad behind your ribs—and—you love me like a fool too!'

"'Like a fool,' I repeated mechanically.

"We lay there for a long while, shoulder to shoulder, listening to the wind, the gnawing of the mice beneath the floorboards and to the boring of the woodworm in the old wood panelling. The full moon had long since disappeared from view. Only the stars still gleamed through the white curtain of snow, the first wan half-light of morning spreading out as I again collapsed to the ground like a dead man. The beautiful woman set me up again slowly, and used me as her footstool, her languid, husky voice sounding like the soft note of a harp through the room.

"'You have given me life from your life, soul from your soul, and blood from your blood, you awakened sweet lust in my breast, now satiate my love.'

"'You have killed me,' I moaned.

"She shook her head.

"'Death is cold,' she said in answer, 'yet Life is so warm. Love kills, but it also wakes new life.'

"She gathered together her loose hair and struck me with it tauntingly; her foot, which she had originally placed on my hand, now rested on my neck, and as I lay with my face to the ground still, she began to run it gently over my back, sending thrills through my spine comparable to an electric current. Once more she was seized by a divine ferocity. She turned me over swiftly, knelt on my chest and bound my hands with her golden plaits.

"'Now you belong to me and no one can rescue you from my love,' she gasped with a ragged breath. A feral light blazed in her eyes, her lips clasped to mine like red-hot tongs, kiss for kiss and pleasure for pleasure, until the first bright golden ray of morning fell before our feet.

"'Now I wish to take my rest,' she said. 'Go and do not return before the evening.'

"I went from the chamber. I found my horse in the courtyard, the gate stood open, the old man nowhere to be seen. I leapt into the saddle and bolted away from there. Yet I came again as the night fell and returned night after night.

"Ah! This woman is like a labyrinth, all who lose themselves in her are ensorcelled, doomed, damned!"

✳

A few days after giving this strange account, Manwed vanished. No one could say for sure what had become of him.

Herr Bardossoki was convinced that the Devil had carried him away. Aniela told me in confidence that the marble woman had come to her in a dream, this time dressed in a petticoat and with her hair done up in a chignon, and with a satisfied smile having told her in the most perfect French: 'He is dead. I have drunk the soul from his body, and can once more amuse myself for a time on this bright earth.'

A Cossack of his assured us that his master had coughed up blood and had went to "Netalien" at the recommendations of the country doctor.

Aniela wept till her eyes were red—and then took another. One day, as she sat in full Niobian mourning in her little bedroom with its blossom-white curtains, Herr Maurizi Konopka suddenly appeared before her and this time, inexplicably, she was not in the least bit startled. He stammered something that was supposed to be a marriage proposal and was in fact indistinguishable from a lyric poem, and four weeks later the pair stood before the altar. It was a most amusing wedding—I danced at it myself.

It was years later, whilst in Paris at the Grand Opera, that I saw my friend Manwed again. *Robert the Devil* was showing. I had left the house whilst Bertram and Alice were fighting for his soul. Summoned by a servant in blue Cossack dress, there pulled up a coupe drawn by a pair of fierce black stallions, sparks flashing beneath their hooves. I stood by and watched a distinguished couple pass on their way.

It was Manwed, conducting a lady by the arm.

He was dressed in black, as pale as a dead man. Deep shadows lay beneath his sombre, hungry eyes, his hair hung lank on his forehead. The lady was of regal stature, I only glimpsed her noble, beautiful profile and saw that she was very pale with red-gold curls tumbled about her marble neck. She was wrapped in rich furs but still seemed to radiate cold.

Manwed's gaze swept past me as if I were a pillar or dead stone wall. He recognised me not.

At that moment there arrived a Parisian friend of mine, a painter well acquainted with all the beautiful women.

"Who is she?" I asked softly.

"A Polish Princess Tartakowska," was his reply.

In foreign lands all our ladies are princesses, especially if they are wealthy and beautiful. But now I am no longer sure whether my friend Manwed had lost his mind back in those days, whether he had been playing us all for fools, or whether there was some truth in his story.

MANOR

by Karl Heinrich Ulrichs

I.

IN the middle of the North Sea lies a group of thirty-five islands, forlorn and desolate, equally distant from Scotland, Iceland and Norway, named the Faroe Isles; barren, rocky, veiled by cloud, echoing with the bleak cries of soaring gulls and kiers, battered on all sides by the thundering waves, and almost eternally shrouded in fog. During the summer, amidst mountain peaks, eighteen hundred and two thousand feet above the sea, craggy fells, gloomy ravines, and ancient pine forests, thousands of springs, often foaming and roaring from great heights, plunge down from boulder to boulder. The shoreline is riven with bays and fjords; yet nearly everywhere inaccessible due to the high cliff walls. The sea all about is crowded with reefs; here and there completely barricaded; disturbed by whirlpools; swept by fierce currents. Only seventeen are inhabited. Strömö und Wagö are separated only by a narrow strait; swimmable; though certainly only for the bold swimmer. Many a place name recalls the time when no churches stood on the Faroe Isles and the old faith had yet to be banished e.g. Thorshavn on the coast of Strömö, that is Strominsel.

In those days there rowed forth to sea from Strömö a fisherman and his fifteen-year-old son. A storm blew up; their boat was knocked over; the son was cast against the cliffs of Wagö. A young sailor of Wagö sighted this; sprang into the waves, swam between the rocks, grabbed the floating body and dragged it ashore. He sat with him upon a rock; the half-drowned boy laid on his knees and cradled in his arms. Then his eyes opened.

"Who are you?" the sailor asked

"Har; I am from Strömö," answered the lad.

The sailor rowed him back across the sound to Strömö; brought him home to Lära, his mother. As they parted the boy threw his arms around his saviour in gratitude. The father's corpse was washed to shore by the waves. The sailor's name was Manor. An orphan, four years older than Har, he grew to love the boy and yearned to see him again. Now and then, in the evening when his day's work was done, he would row over to Strömö, or swim through the waters now luke-warm with the coming of summer. Har went to the shore, scaled a cliff and waved his scarf when he saw Manor's boat coming from afar. They would spend an hour or two together; row out onto the calm waters and sing old mariner's songs. Sometimes they would strip naked, plunge into the waves and swim to the nearby sandbank across the bay, setting the seals sunning themselves there to flight. Or else they would wander in the dark green forests of lofty fir trees, the rustling limbs of which heralded the speech of Thor, or sit themselves on a stone beneath the single ancient beech tree. Here they chatted and made plans. When once a ship sailed past bound for the whaling routes they both dreamed they went with it. And when they sat together upon the stone Manor would lay his arm around Har's shoulders and call him "My lad," and never was the boy happier than when Manor embraced him like this. If the hour was late when he arrived, he would walk quietly to the lilac bush that shaded Har's window and tap on the panes; Har would then wake and steal out to him. He felt so happy to be with Manor.

II.

Then there came a Danish triple-mast, taking anchor in the safety of Wagö's bay and seeking sailors for a two month whaling voyage. Manor went aboard. The captain accepted the lean, hale youth straight away. Har wished to go as a cabin boy, but Lära wailed and cried, "You are my only son! Your father was devoured by the sea. Why do you abandon me?"

Two months went by. It was already winter once more. Har would mount the cliff and peer into the far distance; one morning he saw the ship coming in and flourished his scarf joyfully. Yet a storm blew up and the breakers rose high. The vessel was steering hard for Wagö Bay. It failed to make Wagö and was driven into the perilous reefs of Strömö, where it foundered before Har's eyes. He saw the shipwrecked sailors battle with the waves. He beheld one of them seize hold of a plank with his strong arms, only in the next moment to be dragged down along with it into the vortex formed by the roaring surf. Har recognised him. It was Manor.

The high-tide brought many bodies to the shore. The village people spread straw on the beach and lay them on it, corpse by corpse. Har aided them, searching those so laid out. At last they brought forth Manor's body and set it before him on the straw. The young sailor lay there cold, his hair sodden and tangled with sea water, eyes shut, with white lips and pallid bloodless cheeks, slender in form, even in death comely to look upon. "Oh, Manor, we must meet again!" Har cried out, throwing himself sobbing over the beloved body and clasping it to him once more in the comfort of a final embrace.

They bore the corpses across the sound and buried them that same day in the sand dunes on Wagö.

III.

As evening came Har sat mute and brooding in the cottage. Lära wished to comfort him, but he desired no consolation; against the gods he cursed. He left for his bed but could find no rest. Towards midnight he lapsed into a half slumber.

He was awoken by a noise. He peered about; it came from outside beyond the window. The branches of the lilac bent and its dry leaves rustled. The window opened and a shape climbed inside. Har knew that figure! In spite of the darkness he recognised it straight away! It came up with slow steps and slipped into the bed with him; he trembled but made no attempt to resist. It stroked his cheek but with a hand cold, oh, so cold, so cold! Feverish chills wracked his body. Freezing lips kissed the boy's warm quivering mouth. He felt the lover's water-logged shroud, and the dank hair which hung down its head. Dread overtook him but with it there came bliss. The figure sighed. To him it sounded as if it wanted to say:

"Longing drove me to you! I can find no peace in the grave!"

He dared not speak. He barely dared to breathe. Yet already the figure rose and murmured as if to say: "Now I must go back!" It climbed over the windowsill; leaving as it had come.

"Manor has been here," Har croaked softly to himself.

On that very same night a fisherman of Strömö had taken his boat out into the sound. The sea shone lustrous. Droplets of flashing sparks fell from his oar. He watched as something shot through the phosphorescent waves, something the shape of which he could not pick out, but which moved with the speed of a great fish in the direction of Strömö. It was not a fish; that much he could tell, even in the dark.

Manor came again the following night, ice-cold like yesterday, yet more demanding. He held the boy in his cold arms;

kissed his cheeks and mouth, and lay his head upon his soft breast. Har trembled; his heart began to pound at this intimate intertwining of their limbs. And Manor placed his head right above that beating heart. His lips sought for the gently swelling mound above the heart, which rose and fell rhythmically with its palpitations. There he began to suckle, desperately and thirstingly, like an infant at its mother's breast. Yet after a few moments he ceased, rose up, and slipped away. Har's breast felt empty, as if a suckling animal had nursed itself from him.

That night too the fisherman was abroad in the sound. At exactly the same hour as on the previous day the rushing thing sped past him again, coming closer this time. The pale moonlight was enough for him to make it out; the swimming form was that of a man, one who swum on his right side, as sailors often swim, but who wore the remnants of a grave-cloth. This swimmer seemed to pay the watcher no heed, though his face was turned to him.

Here was one who swum with unopening eyes! The sight so unnerved the fisherman that he hauled in his unspread nets and rowed back to shore.

Manor returned the next few nights. Occasionally sleep would overtake Har before Manor's arrival, in which case he would hold the sleeping boy until he would awake in his embrace. Each time those lips sought the gentle rise above the heart. When day came Har would notice from time to time that a delicate droplet of blood still leaked from his left nipple, and have to wipe it away quickly lest it stain his shirt. Only on the night of the full moon did Manor come not.

The dead are often suffused with a mighty longing for one of the loved ones they leave behind, so mighty that they forsake their grave in the hours of night and seek them out. For it is said in the old faith that Urda restores to some a brief half-life come midnight, thus granting to them unearthly might from beyond the grave. This happens the most among youths who are mown down by bitter death in the bloom of their years. Those who return are filled with a great hunger for both blood and warmth; they yearn for the fresh blood of the living and for such embraces as lovers do. Yet whilst this can inspire great passion it often brings ferocious torment too.

So too was it here. Har agonised and struggled all day to warm himself, yet awaited the coming of night with impatience, longing for the cold spasms of that midnight embrace.

IV.

Thus passed twelve days.

"What was is wrong with you Har? You are so pallid and so wan," asked Lära.

"Nothing, mother," Har replied.

"You are so quiet."

Har sighed.

In the rearmost cottage of the village there lived a wise woman, knowledgeable in all manner of hidden lore. The concerned mother sought her out and watched as she cast runic lots.

"He is visited by the dead," the wise woman said.

"The dead?" replied Lära.

"Yes, during the night; and moreover someone shall perish if these visits are not stopped before it is too late."

Lära returned home in dismay.

"Is it true Har, do the dead come to you?"

Har gazed at the floor. "Manor has been here," uttered he and lay his head upon her breast in tears.

"May the gods take mercy on you."

"The gods?" Har cried, "Bah! How can the gods help me now! When he clung to that plank, woe! Woe of my life! That was the time to show mercy for me if they had willed. Yet being without pity they left him to sink and drown. Oh, how I loved him so!"

196

But now she too had noticed the traces of blood upon his shirt. She sought out the village elders. Across to Wagö they rowed with both mother and son, and they brought the wise woman also. To the men of Wagö they said:

"Your graves are unsealed. There is one who leaves his grave each night, comes across to us and drinks up the blood of this boy."

"If that is so then we shall fasten him down swiftly," shouted one of the Wagö men.

They brought a stake of fir-wood, as tall as a man and thicker than his arm, which they cut square with an axe, sharpening the end to a point nearly a foot in length. As a group they set out to the dunes; one man carrying the stake and another a hefty axe. They laboured to open Manor's grave, and there the sailor lay before them, motionless and silent, wrapped up in his shroud.

"See! He is still just as we laid him," said a Wagö man.

"That is because each time he must return to his original position," said the wise woman.

"He looks almost more hale of face than when we buried him," said another

"No wonder," said the wise woman, "and in exchange Har's face is now all the paler."

Har clambered down and threw his arms around the beloved corpse once more.

"Manor! Manor!" he called fearfully, "they want to stake you down. Manor, wake up! Open your eyes! Your Har is calling you!"

But his eyes did not open. He remained motionless in Har's arms, just as he had twelve days ago when he lay on the straw on the beach.

Har refused to let go of the body; the men were forced to pull him away. One of them positioned the tip of the stake on Manor's breast. With a moan Har turned and fell around Lära's neck, pressing his face into her shoulder as if to hide.

"Mother," he cried, "why have you done this to me?"

A heavy blow; followed by another blow, followed by half a dozen more blows and——

"Now he is fastened down!" cried the man of Wagö.

"The returning one shall now surely stay put," said another.

Har was carried back half-senseless. "Now, he shall leave you in peace my dear child!" said Lära, when they had returned to the cottage.

He went to bed saddened. "Now he will come to me no more," he said to himself sorrowfully. He felt worn and tired, yet he tossed in his bed without rest or peace. The minutes crept by slowly and hours crawled on. Midnight came and still sleep had yet to fall upon his wakeful eyes.

Hark! What was that? In the lilac bushes . . . Yes; no; that was impossible. And yet! Again, as before, there came a rustling amidst the branches. The window opened. Manor had returned. The drowned man sighed deeply. Upon his chest there was a large wound, square in shape, and going all the way out through his back. He lay down beside Har again, embraced him and began to suckle thirstier and more demanding than ever before.

Lära however had lain awake in the next room and she heard all and trembled. Early in the morning she came in and went to Har's bed.

"My poor child! He has visited you again."

"Yes Mother. He has been with me again."

But the bed-sheets were stained with corpse blood that had trickled forth from the great wound.

V.

Several hours later the boat made another journey across the sound; this time without Har. The group made their way back to the dunes and opened the grave once more. The an-gled stake was still stuck fast in the grave, though no longer through Manor's chest. His body lay bent over next to it, for the stake prevented him from lying out straight.

"That is how he was able to free himself," said the wise woman, "the stake is of the same thickness at both the bottom and the top."

"Twisted himself up along the length of the stake," said one of the Wagö men

"It must have taken inhuman strength to do so," said another.

At the biding of the wise woman that day they cut a stronger stake, which they left twice as thick at the top as it was at the bottom, so that it resembled a nail with a flat head. They withdrew the old stake and drove the new one in place.

"Right, now he is nailed down!" said the man with the axe, as he gave the stake a last blow to its head.

"Let him writhe and twist, he won't pull himself free."

Lära returned to Har and told him what had happened. "Now it is all over," he said to himself as he retired to bed. He lay there without sleep. Midnight came, yet all remained silent. Nothing rustled outside the window amongst the lilacs. No swimmer crossing the sound by night with closed eyes troubled the fisherman.

"Now you will have peace from him. He has tormented you so," Lära said to him.

"Oh Mother! Mother! He did not torment me!"

Har pined, longing in vain. "Mother," he said, "it is all ending for me now." Eaten away by grief, the boy was able to leave his bed no more.

"You look so tired and so worn, my dear son!" said Lära

"He drags me down to him," Har replied.

One morning she was sitting at his bedside whilst he still slept. A month had passed since the shipwreck. It was early. She began to cry, then he awoke.

"Mother," he said in a faint voice, "I must die."

"Oh no, my child! You are not meant to die so young!"

"Yes, yes! He was with me again. We spoke together. We sat on the stone under the old beach tree in the woods as we used to; he lay his arm around my neck and called me 'my lad' again. He will come again tonight to fetch me. He promised me so. I cannot bear it without him!"

She bent over him and her tears fell freely onto his bed. "My poor child!" she said, laying her hand on his forehead.

As night fell she lit a lamp and sat watching at his bedside. He lay there quietly, unsleeping, staring into the distance silently.

"Mother!" said Har.

"What do you wish, my good son?"

"Lay me in his grave! Yes? And pull the dreadful stake from his breast!"

She promised to do so, sealing the vow with a handshake and a kiss.

"Oh, it must be so sweet to lie with him in his grave!"

Midnight approached. All of a sudden his features became transfixed. He lifted his head a little as if harkening to something. With gleaming eyes, he looked to the window and out at the branches of the lilac bushes.

"Look, mother, he comes now!"

These were his last words. Then his eyelids fell shut.

Har sank back on the pillow and passed away.

They did as he asked.

MORE THINGS IN HEAVEN AND EARTH

by Elaine A. Swire

A wild December night at Shotover camp, rain falling in torrents, beating pitilessly on the half-frozen sentries, as they vainly sought to shelter themselves in their boxes. Inside the mess of Her Majesty's 200th regiment all was light and warmth; thick curtains closely drawn deadened the sound of the storm as it lashed the window-panes, a blazing fire diffused a grateful heat into the room. Everything indoors was in marked contrast to the cold and general discomfort that reigned outside. Some idea of this kind crossed the mind of the solitary occupant of this room as, pulling back the curtains, he saw the sloppy pavements and rivers of water that rushed along the gutters.

"What a miserable night," he exclaimed. "I'm precious glad I did not go to the kick-up; those fellows will be half-drowned before they get back."

And drawing the curtains closer he returned to the fireplace, where he ensconced himself in a deep armchair and began to smoke. The function he had alluded to in the above elegant terms, was a large dance given at one of the neighbouring country houses. Regimental business had detained Captain Ellis, and by the time he reached the mess, most of the officers had already dined and started. Not being a very keen dancer, he was not at all put out, so having enjoyed a solitary dinner he retired to the ante-room, where the opening of our story has found him. For sometime he was alone, but at length the sound of an opening door aroused him from his reverie.

"Hullo, doctor, is that you? Come and have a smoke and tell me the news."

The doctor drew another chair up to the fire and stretched his hands out towards the blaze.

"No news that I know of," he answered. "I have been writing business letters all the afternoon and haven't left my quarters."

He looked so thoughtful and pre-occupied that Ellis said: "I hope your business was not of a painful description."

"Well, it was rather," answered Dr. Cameron slowly. "Did you ever happen to meet Fendall, of the ——th?"

"No," replied Captain Ellis, "I have never met him, but I know a good many friends of his and have heard a good deal about him. Isn't he in a lunatic asylum?"

"*Was*," corrected the doctor. "One of the letters I received today was to inform me of his death in the asylum under most extraordinary circumstances. But then, if one begins to talk of extraordinary circumstances, nothing could be more strange than his life itself; poor fellow, he had a hard time of it."

"If it's anything in the shape of a yarn," said Ellis, "you might just as well spin it now; there's nothing else to be done unless we play cards."

"I don't mind telling you about it, more especially as it was never a secret; but I warn you that you will probably disbelieve the whole thing, although it is perfectly true."

"You are raising my curiosity to fever pitch," said Captain Ellis, laughingly. "Kindly begin at once, or I cannot answer for the consequences."

The doctor smiled and settling himself back into his chair began the following narrative:

"I must preface my story by saying that Fendall's family and mine were next-door neighbours in Blankshire and also distant connections by marriage; so that I know more about Roy Fendall's unhappy life than most people, more especially as he and I always hit it off pretty well together. When he joined his regiment and I went to walk the hospitals, we rather lost sight of one another, but always heard of each other's doings from our respective families. One fine day, some nine months after Roy had joined, I received a letter from one of my sisters, informing me of Roy's marriage, and adding that he was bringing his wife down to Fernleigh Hall to make the acquaintance of his family who had heard nothing about her until the wedding was actually over. This sounded rather odd, as Roy and his parents had, up till then, always been on the best of terms. I wrote and asked my sister to send me all the details of the affair, as I could not help thinking that it was a little mysterious. Connie, like the good soul she is, immediately sent me a budget of news; and indeed, if she was to be believed, there was plenty of material for gossip in everything concerning Mrs. Roy Fendall. It appeared that her maiden name was Varesco; she was the daughter of an English-woman and an Armenian merchant of Odessa. Both her father and mother had died when she was a baby, leaving her to be brought up by her father's aunt, a certain Mrs. Arataria, who had an only son. Dina Varesco had run wild till she was fourteen years old; at that age she was the acknowledged belle of Odessa, counted her admirers by the score, flirted with them, encouraged them, and threw them over with the *aplomb* of a woman of thirty. Mrs. Arataria, discovering that her son was beginning a violent flirtation with his beautiful cousin, sent the girl off to England to school and told the youthful lovers they must wait a few years until they really knew their own minds. The separation did not seem to tell much on Dina's spirits; she had been at school for a couple of years when she met Roy Fendall at the house of a mutual friend. To see her was to admire her, and from that to loving her was but one step with poor Roy. He had only known her three weeks when he proposed to her, and she accepted him with an *insouciance*, which to any one less madly in love, would have argued badly for their matrimonial happiness. But he was simply in the last stage of infatuation, and could see no flaw in her anywhere. She insisted on their engagement being kept a secret, and also the wedding, on the plea that she hated a fuss, and succeeded in silencing all Roy's scruples. After the marriage, she graciously permitted him to inform his parents of the event, and after a certain amount of warfare on paper, Fendall *père* asked the newly-married couple to come and stay at Fernleigh.

"Dina's beauty took them all by storm, and she certainly was a most beautiful woman. She had inherited her mother's golden hair and wild-rose complexion, and her father's black almond-shaped eyes with their long covered lashes and finely-pencilled eyebrows. She was small and exquisitely formed, with the daintiest hands and feet, and the most bewitching little ears. But in spite of her beauty, her new relations could not get on with her; they were full of the best intentions, but Dina's manner somehow chilled and estranged them. She had such a curious way of gliding noiselessly into the room just when she was least wanted, and they could never tell how much or how little she had heard. Sometimes her beautiful dark eyes had a positively wolfish gleam in them, and her sisters-in-law and even her husband seemed to feel as if she had something uncanny about her. When she at last left to accompany Roy to Malta with his regiment, they were all unfeignedly relieved to see the last of her, but they were full of anxiety on Roy's account. It was curious how they all seemed to have made up their minds that Roy would suffer in some way from his connection with her. A year passed, however, without anything taking place to justify their alarm. At last, one day a letter came from Roy, saying that Dina's cousin and former lover Mr. Arataria, had come to Malta on business matters, and as he was likely to stay some time, they had asked him to share their house, which was a good deal larger than they required. Roy did not say much about him, but the general impression of the Fendall family, was that he was not particularly fond of his cousin by marriage. From time to time Roy mentioned that Malta did not seem to agree with him, as he was frequently subject to fainting fits; he also said that Dina's cousin was still with them. Dina herself never wrote, as she considered it was far too much bother. When the regiment had been at Malta some eighteen months, it was ordered on to India. Mr. Arataria announced his intention of going too ostensibly to see if he could not extend his business. He could not, of course, obtain a passage in the troopship, so went by a P. and O. steamer. While at sea Roy's fainting fits ceased entirely, but soon after he had settled down in India with Arataria once more as their guest, they began again. Things went on like this for about a year; the Fendalls received very few letters from their son, and those that reached them filled them with anxiety. Eventually they heard nothing for two or three months, and Mrs. Fendall was beside herself with apprehension.

"One evening, the front door bell rang and on going to open it, the old butler was confronted by the apparition of a man so worn and haggard, and emaciated, that it was with the greatest difficulty he recognized Roy Fendall.

"'Master Roy!' he exclaimed. 'Beg pardon, Captain Fendall, sir, is that you? My mistress will be shocked to see you like this. Have you been ill, sir?'

"Roy smiled faintly, and taking the old man's arm, dragged himself wearily through the hall on to a sofa in the library, where he sank down exhausted. His mother was hastily summoned, and after applying restoratives for some time, he revived and was able to speak.

"'Where is Dina, my dear boy?' asked Mrs. Fendall. 'What on earth possessed her to allow you to travel alone in this state?'

"At his wife's name, Roy turned deadly pale, glanced hastily round the room and put his hand to his neck with a queer kind of clutching movement.

"'Hush, mother,' he said hurriedly. 'Don't talk about her.' And pulling his mother's head down to his face, he said in a whisper, 'Send the girls away and let me tell you while I can—before I go mad or she kills me.'

"Mrs. Fendall's astonishment was unbounded, as you may well imagine, but controlling herself as well as she was able, she dismissed her daughters, and begged Roy to explain his mysterious speech. Far into the night they sat, and the mother's heart turned sick with dread and anxiety as she listened to her son's monstrous tale.

"It seemed that from the day that the Armenian cousin had appeared on the scene, everything in the Fendall household had gone wrong. Dina, never demonstrative at the best of times, became colder and colder in her manner to her husband, and finally so indifferent that Roy felt bound to say something to her about it; suggesting at the same time that Mr. Arataria's absence would be very desirable. Mrs. Roy listened to his remarks without moving a muscle. When he had finished, she slowly raised her long lashes and looking at him with an ominous glitter in her black eyes, replied in a clear, metallic voice: 'If you ever dare to speak to me on the subject again, I shall leave you and you will never see me again.' The words in themselves were not much, but the look and manner which accompanied them were so hateful and venomous that Roy felt a cold chill passing through him.

"'I wish you could have seen that look, mother,' he said wearily. 'There was nothing human about it. Ashamed of my momentary terror, I was about to expostulate with her, but she left the room and managed to avoid being left *tête-à-tête* with me for several days. From that day forward, our household became most uncomfortable. Dina ignored my presence systematically, even when her cousin was in the room; to do him justice, Arataria was always scrupulously polite to me, and his ready tact filled up many an awkward gap in our conversation. Still, I was fully aware that he knew of my disagreement with my wife; and at times I caught him gazing at me with an indefinable glance, which I also saw in Dina's eyes whenever I managed to intercept her looks. It was a perfectly indescribable expression, but it always made me feel quite helpless as if I were a victim under the knife and they were the executioners. I bore with this state of things for some time, and at length once more suggested to my wife the propriety of Mr. Arataria seeking a domicile of his own. Never in my life shall I forget the scene that followed. I had always felt that my wife's real character was a sealed book to me, but I then discovered what lay beneath her placid and impassive exterior. White as death, her eyes gleaming and her scarlet lips drawn tightly across her teeth till she looked more like a she-wolf than a woman, she stood and stormed at me for an hour. I felt so sick at heart to think that this furious vixen was really my delicate, dainty, ethereal wife, that I did not even hear what she said. Having at length exhausted her rage, she turned to go; but on reaching the door, she stopped and hissed out between her teeth: "The day he leaves this house, I leave it too; and then beware!"

"'I sank into a chair and sat staring at the door, wondering if by any chance I had taken leave of my senses! Gradually, my stunned amazement gave way and I found myself recalling with disgust Dina's invectives and abuse. What could have caused her sudden dislike to me? For, like all men, I felt certain she had loved me once. What was the secret of Arataria's influence over her? What measures had I better take to rid myself of him without provoking a repetition of such a scene? These and other thoughts whirled confusedly through my mind until, worn out with bootless speculations, I fell asleep. It was dusk when I awoke, and as I sat still for a moment wondering why I should have been sleeping in the drawing-room, the door opened and I heard Arataria's voice in the passage saying, "You can begin tonight!"

"'The door closed and somebody came to the window where I was sitting.

"'It was Dina. "Are you awake, Roy?" she asked in her clear, cold voice, from which all traces of her previous anger had vanished. Her tone sent a shiver through me, I don't know why.

"'I answered, "Yes," adding, "I suppose it is time to dress for dinner," at the same time rising and leaving the room without giving her an opportunity of saying anything more. All the time I was dressing, I kept wondering what the meaning of Arataria's remark could have been. *What* will she begin tonight? I said to myself over and over again without finding any possible answer.

"When I came down to dinner, I thought I had never seen my wife look so lovely. She was a little pale, the result no doubt of her rage in the afternoon, and the filmy black dress she wore only enhanced the whiteness of her skin. Her velvety eyes gleamed like diamonds and her full red lips were even more strikingly red compared to her pale face and black dress. In manner, she was perfect and quite like the Dina of our honey-moon days. I began to think that the quarrel of the afternoon existed only in my imagination; now and again, however, I caught her exchanging glances with Arataria, curiously eager, expectant, longing looks, which puzzled and alarmed me. What could she be longing for? What had she to expect? The bewilderment in which I was kept me very silent at dinner. Dina and her cousin on the contrary were extremely gay and talkative, and their air of good-fellowship and secret understanding annoyed me more than ever. I was angry with myself for occupying such a false position; and yet I could see no immediate way out of it. The dreadful paralyzed and helpless sort of feeling which always overcame me whenever I caught Arataria's steady gaze fixed on me was terrible. I *could* not own to myself that I was frightened of him, and yet it was something uncommonly like it. And, even granting that it was so, what cause had I to fear him? I thought and thought, but I saw no solution to the problem. After dinner, we went as usual to the drawing-room, coffee having been served; Dina, to my great astonishment, opened the piano and asked if I would like her to sing. She possessed a really lovely voice which had been trained to a high pitch of perfection, but, on ordinary occasions, no persuasion would induce her to open her lips; even when we were first married it was only as a great favour that she would occasionally sing to me. Later on, the fact that I was devoted to music seemed to be sufficient to prevent her ever singing a note. So you may guess my utter surprise at this unusual occurrence. I took it as a good omen and replied that I should be enchanted if she would favour us with a song or two. I threw myself down on the sofa and listened with half-closed eyes to the ravishing sounds. Arataria was sitting on the other side of the room and, although I could not see him, I *felt* that he was watching me with that steady, pitiless gaze of his. Worn out by the excitement of the day and soothed by the exquisite "timbre," of Dina's voice, which had a liquid ring in it, suggestive of a physical caress, I soon fell fast asleep, but not to rest; a dream as torturing as the events of the day racked my brain and exhausted my body. At first, I dreamt I was in a fairy-like garden; the scent of flowers, the song of birds, the trickling of a thousand little streams and a radiant roseate glow over every-thing combined to delight my senses. Suddenly I beheld Dina, her arms stretched out toward me, a divine smile on her lips and the love-light in her eyes, just as I had seen it in earlier, happier days, or had *fancied* I saw it. I ran to clasp her to my heart, but as I advanced she retreated, her azure draperies floating round her slender body. All at once she turned and flung herself into my arms, covering me with her gauzy garments. As I pressed my lips to hers, I fancied that her filmy coverings seemed thicker; slowly their azure colour faded, and Dina's yielding figure slipped from my embrace, leaving me enveloped in a thick grey mist which could be *felt*. Thicker and thicker it grew, until my arms seemed bound to my sides, and my legs were stiff and heavy. In vain I tried to extricate myself; choked and suffocated, I gasped for air; my head swam, my very life seemed to be draining from me, when again I felt the velvety touch of Dina's lips on mine; then a horrible, sharp, stinging pain in my neck, as if two red-hot needles had been plunged into it, and with a cry I awoke to find Arataria standing by my side, holding my wrist in his fingers and a smelling bottle in his hand. Dina was sitting in a low chair a little way off, playing nervously with a scarlet hand screen. Her face was colourless, save for two bright red spots on her cheek bones, which burned feverishly, vying with the dewy scarlet of her lips. They both asked if I felt better, and Dina told me that at first they thought I had fallen asleep, and had not wished to disturb me, but on seeing my complete immobility they became alarmed, and looking more closely, discovered that I had fainted. I assured them that I was all right, and rose from the sofa intending to go to bed. I was so weak that Arataria had to help me.

"'Some three weeks after this we were ordered to India, and once there I became a perfect martyr to these fainting fits. Regularly once or twice a week they occurred, invariably preceded by the same dream and the same painful awakening with the stinging sensation in my neck. Tonics of all kinds were prescribed by the doctors, but were of no use, and they soon began to shake their heads, saying that nothing but leaving India would do me any good. The curious thing was that Dina was always at the piano whenever these attacks occurred, until it became quite a joke. Whenever I saw her preparing to play or sing, I used to laugh and say, "I suppose you want me to faint, Dina."

"'Strangely enough she was never angry, but took it all in good part; she had become much more gentle and loving

210

since my first attack in Malta. She had been growing so much prettier of late, too, and it seemed that while I grew more and more of a wreck, she became far more beautiful. Never had she been so lovely nor so affectionate. Tenderly solicitous of me, she surrounded me with the most watchful care; *too* watchful it seemed to me, for my invalid fancy thought it detected in her soft eyes a glance like that of a bird of prey intent on its victim. But I dared not breathe my vague suspicions to a living soul, for had I done so I should have been called a madman, so completely had she fascinated everybody in the place, from the doctors downwards. And, indeed, to all outward appearance, she was a model wife; so devoted had she become that she would even sing without being asked. I grew to loathe the sound of her thrilling, soul-subduing voice, all the more so that whenever I fainted it was, as I have already said, when she was singing, though what connection there could be between these two things was difficult to divine! One morning, whilst dressing, I suddenly noticed on my neck two small red marks, close together. I had never seen them before, and put them down to the bite of an insect of some sort, more especially as they looked as if they were of several days standing, and thus dismissed the matter from my mind. That evening I fainted again, but forbear describing the scene, as everything was an exact *replica* of the first occasion. Had they not been so painful, the attacks would have been monotonous. The queer thing about them was Dina's invariable state of suppressed excitement on my recovery. Her tender anxiety, combined with the steely glitter of her dark eyes and Arataria's cold, curious stare, made me feel certain that some-thing extraordinary was taking place. But *what* could it be? In vain I racked my brain to find some solution. If I had been naturally superstitious, it would have been easy to say that I was a victim of witchcraft practised by my wife and her cousin, and one day that idea *had* flashed across my mind. But, being an Englishman, I laughed at my own folly. The next morning, moved by an unaccountable impulse, I looked at my neck to see if the red marks had disappeared; to my surprise, they were still there and looked quite fresh and vividly scarlet, as if they had just been made. I sat and looked at them in the glass, thinking in a dull sort of way that they were just in the place where I always felt the stinging sensation on recovering from my faints. One idea after another came crowding to my mind. Why were those marks so red? Yesterday they had been quite healed—now they were scarlet and seemed wet!—nearly as scarlet as Dina's cheeks, red as Dina's lips! Why should they be so close together? It was like the mark of a serpent's fang. Arataria was rather like a serpent; his cruel eyes were enough to paralyze anybody! How lovely Dina was growing! Why were her lips so red? Red as blood!—"Blood," I repeated half aloud with a shudder, glancing hastily round the room, half expecting to see Arataria or Dina looking at me, but finding myself still alone. Slowly I finished dressing, trying to shake off the dreadful thoughts that assailed me, but in vain. All day they haunted me, assuming more definite shape until the horror of my own ideas seemed to be driving me mad. Half-forgotten stories of my childish days revived in my memory. Stories of witches, of lingering deaths, of the evil eye, of vampires. I made up my mind I would watch the little marks very carefully, and perhaps that would help me to solve the horrible mystery that seemed to envelope me. Night and morning I looked at them, and in a day or two they were healed, and had the dull red look they had worn when I had first noticed them. The next evening I fainted once more, and on going to my room I went straight to the glass. A cry escaped my lips! The marks were quite fresh, and from one was oozing a tiny drop of blood! I recalled the stinging sensation which invariably preceded my recovery, and even as I thought about it I seemed to feel it again, and saw a second tiny drop issue from the other little wound. How long I sat staring at my livid, horror-stricken face I do not know, but at last I flung myself on my bed to try and snatch a few minutes' relief from the ghastly thoughts which were haunting me. At dawn I rose and began putting together the things I should require for my journey to England, for I had determined to leave at once, without seeing Dina and her partner in crime. As early as possible I called on the general commanding the station, and had a private conversation with him, the upshot of which was that I got leave to go that very day, the pretext being urgent private affairs. Fortunately for my plans, the mail steamer was to leave Bombay the next day. I returned to my house, and, ordering the carriage, started for the station, without inquiring whether Dina had returned from her morning ride or not. The next night found me on board the homeward-bound steamer, and it was with a sigh of relief that heard the waves lapping against her sides, for I had a kind of feeling that, do what I would, I should not be able to escape from the clutches of the guilty pair.'

"With a sigh of exhaustion Roy sank back on the sofa, as he ended his dreadful history. Mrs. Fendall's feelings are easier to imagine than to describe. She could hardly credit her own ears, and terrible doubts as to her son's sanity crossed her mind.

"Roy seemed to guess her thoughts, for he suddenly said:

"'I am not mad, mother, though I confess it seems rather like it; but just look here.'

"Unfastening his collar, he pointed to his neck. Just above the collar bone were two little red marks, quite faint and somewhat larger than the mark left by a pin prick.

"'I have not had any fainting fits since I left India, and the scars have gradually grown less distinct. I used to look at them every day on board ship to make sure.'

"He closed his eyes again with a weary sigh, and for about ten minutes neither of them spoke.

"Mrs. Fendall was terribly agitated by all she had just heard, and scarcely knew what to think or what to say.

213

"Suddenly Roy started up, and flinging up his arms across his face, cried out: 'Here she is! Oh, mother, save me!'

"Whether it was fancy or not, one cannot say, but Mrs. Fendall declares she saw a cloudy, shapeless form hanging over the sofa, close to Roy's head. As she looked she seemed to see the outline of a gigantic bat with outstretched wings, evolving itself from the nebulous mass; but instead of a bat's head she saw Dina's face, her red lips drawn up in a wolfish snarl, her eyes distorted with a bloodthirsty glitter. Nearer and nearer the loathsome monster came, when just as it seemed to be sinking down and enveloping Roy in its misty folds, Mrs. Fendall struck at it with a heavy ivory paper-cutter, which lay on a small table near her. The face vanished, the mist suddenly cleared away, and nothing remained of the dreadful vision.

"On looking at Roy, his mother found that he had fainted. Summoning assistance, she had him removed to a bedroom that had been prepared for him, and restoratives were applied.

"When he recovered, he said: 'Did you see her, mother?'

"Mrs. Fendall, who could not trust herself to speak, nodded fearfully.

"'Well, you have saved me this time, but she is sure to come back.'

"Even as he spoke, Mrs. Fendall's eye was caught by the unusual appearance of one of the corners of the room. She thought she detected the same filmy cloud hanging there that she had already seen downstairs, but on approaching it nothing was visible. On resuming her seat at the bedside, it reappeared, and from that moment the Fendalls' house was never free from the mysterious thing. Whatever room Roy was in, one corner of it was darkened by this cloudlike mass. Once or twice a week the same scene would occur which had taken place on the night of his arrival. Sometimes the apparition had Dina's face, sometimes Arataria's, and on some occasions both together would glare from out the misty apparition with looks of diabolical hatred.

"This went on for some months, and then Roy had to be removed and placed in an asylum. He had a horror of being left alone, and the strictest injunctions were given by his family that an attendant should be with him night and day.

"He died about six months after entering the asylum, and his death was attended by a very strange incident.

"Seeing that the end was coming, his attendant went to ring the bell that summoned the doctor. It happened to be outside the door, a few yards down the passage. When the man returned Roy was dead, and on his neck were two little tiny scars, from which the blood was slowly oozing; only a drop at a time, but as fast as it was wiped away, another took its place, and this went on until the coffin was nailed down.

"Nothing more was ever heard of Dina or her cousin. The bungalow in which they had lived got the reputation of being haunted, and no native would go near it after dusk, for they declared that shrieks and groans were heard there all night, and terrible creatures were seen.

"Of course I can't pretend to explain the story, and most people say that Roy was the victim of a delusion. If so, it was a delusion that was shared by everybody who entered the Fendalls' house: for the curious shapeless cloud was visible to anybody who went into a room where Roy happened to be. But I shall have to let you find a solution for yourself, as I see it's two o'clock, and I must turn in; so good-night, old chap, I shall leave you to dream of the fair Dina."

"Heaven forbid," replied Captain Ellis so seriously that the doctor went away laughing.

OUR LADY OF RED LIPS

by Aimée Crocker

THE place was Paris.

A man stood in front of an art-dealer's window, and looked at the painted picture of a woman.

The man was about twenty-five years of age, and extremely handsome.

He was big and brawny.

His hair was brown and curly, and his eyes were blue and frank.

The woman was about thirty years of age, and exceedingly beautiful.

She was small and slender.

Her complexion was creamy white, her hair was inky black, her eyes were dark green, and her lips were bright red.

If you were French, you could tell that the man was American.

And if you were an American, you could tell that the woman was French.

The man stood and stared at the picture.

He stared at the white complexion—but he had seen a complexion like that before.

He stared at the black hair—but he had also seen hair like that before.

He stared at the green eyes—but he had even seen eyes like that before.

He stared at the red lips—and he had never seen lips like that before.

He had never thought of such lips.

He had never even dreamed of such lips.

Of course their vivid crimson colour was unnatural, fantastic, grotesque.

The picture must have been designed for a poster.

But nevertheless it fascinated the man strangely.

The white face seemed to turn to him.

The green eyes seemed to look at him.

The red lips seemed to smile at him.

The man hesitated.

And then he went into the shop.

"What is that picture?" said the man.

"That is the portrait of a lady," said the proprietor.

"Who painted it?" said the man.

"Paul Gaspard," said the proprietor.

"Is he well known?" said the man,

"He would have been—had he lived," said the proprietor.

"Is he dead?" said the man.

"Yes," said the proprietor, "he died six months ago, under peculiar circumstances."

"Tell me about it," said the man.

"He was young, and he was clever, and he was handsome," said the proprietor, "men admired him, and women loved him. The lady who posed for this portrait was one of those who loved him. She had loved other men. She had loved an Italian prince. But he died. She had loved an English lord. But he died also. And then—she loved Paul Gaspard,"

"And then he too died!" said the man.

"Yes—and he too died!" said the proprietor.

"How did he die?" said the man.

"Nobody knows how—or why," said the proprietor. "He was found dead in his bed one morning. That was all. There was some sort of a wound, or a scar, on his breast, over his heart. For a time the coroner was puzzled. At first there was some thought of suicide—or even of murder. But, in the end, the authorities decided that Paul Gaspard had died from natural causes, and there the matter ended."

"And the picture," said the man.

"The picture had just been finished on the very day he died," said the proprietor, "by a strange coincidence."

"Very strange indeed!" said the man.

"Paid Gaspard had from time to time borrowed sums of money from me, until he owed me in all some fifteen hundred francs," said the proprietor, "so when he died, and left no money, I claimed the picture—and I got it."

"And the lady who posed for it?" said the man.

"She left Paris as soon as Paul Gaspard was in his grave," said the proprietor.

"Where did she go?" said the man.

"To St. Petersburg—with a Russian duke," said the proprietor.

"Is she there now?" said the man.

"No, she is at Monte Carlo," said the proprietor.

"With the Russian duke?" said the man.

"No, she is there alone," said the proprietor.

"Where is the Russian duke?" said the man.

"He is dead," said the proprietor.

"Dead?" said the man.

"Yes, dead," said the proprietor, "as dead as all the rest of her lovers!"

"The devil!" said the man.

"Quite so!" said the proprietor.

"And the name of this woman," said the man, "what is it?"

"She calls herself Elise Du Barry," said the proprietor, "but other people call her something else."

"What do they call her?" said the man.

"'Our Lady of Red Lips'!" said the proprietor.

The man thanked the proprietor, and left the shop.

In the street he stopped before the window once more, and stood and stared at the picture.

"'Our Lady of Red Lips'," muttered the man.

And, as he left the window, and walked away, he murmured, "Monte Carlo!"

That night the man dreamed a strange and startling dream.

First he dreamed of black hair.

Hair as black as night.

It covered the heavens and the earth.

There was nothing else in the world but black hair.

Then he dreamed of white skin.

Skin as white as snow.

It covered the heavens and the earth.

There was nothing else in the world but white skin.

Then he dreamed of green eyes.

Eyes as green as the sea.

They covered the heavens and the earth.

There was nothing else in the world but green eyes.

Then he dreamed of red lips.

Lips as red as blood.

They covered the heavens and the earth.

There was nothing else in the world but red lips.

The lips kissed him on the brow.

He felt as though he were swooning.

The lips kissed him on the mouth.

He felt as though he were dying.

The lips kissed him on the heart

He felt as though the world were coming to an end.

His soul was full of terror.

He uttered a shriek.

And then—he awoke.

The next day the man left Paris.

He went to Monte Carlo.

The man's name was Howard Leslie.

He was a New Yorker.

He was an only son, and his father was a millionaire.

This was his first visit to Monte Carlo.

He walked into the Casino.

He looked at the people.

They were strange to see.

And the people looked at him.

He was good to behold.

The celebrated habitués of the place passed before him.

He saw Madame de Lara, the Italian singer.

And La Belle Bolero, the Spanish dancer.

Yvonne Yvette, the French model.

And Olga Maronoff, the Russian poetess.

And then—with a bound of the heart, and a gasp of the breath—he saw her!

Elise Du Barry—Our Lady of Red Lips!

She wore a white satin evening gown.

There were big pearls in her hair, around her throat, and on her fingers.

Her complexion was as white as her gown.

Not a touch of colour, in her dress, or in her face—except her mouth.

But, just as the setting sun will dominate an evening sky, so did this crimson mouth dominate this ashen face, and this pallid figure. One was conscious of the woman's mouth, first, last, and all the time.

One could not help but be conscious of it.

Howard Leslie stood and stared at her.

And she paused and glanced at him.

How like she was to her portrait!

Or rather, how like her portrait was to her!

At last the white face did in reality turn to him!

At last the green eyes did in reality look at him!

220

At last the red lips did in reality smile at him!

And then Elise Du Barry passed by.

Howard Leslie followed her.

She sat at one of the tables.

He stood beside her.

She put down some gold—on the red.

She lost.

He put down some gold—on the black.

He won.

She looked up at him.

He looked down at her.

Their eyes met—his so frank and blue, and hers so strange and green.

He spoke to her.

She answered him.

He didn't know what he was saying to her.

He didn't know what she was saying to him.

He only knew that he and she were talking together.

He only knew that he and she were walking together—out of the Casino.

One month passed.

And then, one day, all Monte Carlo, all Europe, and in fact all the world, was surprised and shocked to learn that Elise Du Barry, a celebrated French beauty, had been strangled at Monte Carlo, and that the man in whose company she had been much seen of late, Howard Leslie, a young American millionaire, had become a raving maniac. The madman, in his paroxysms, constantly clutched his breast, where there was some sort of a wound, or a scar, and he continually cried,

"Heart's blood! Heart's blood! Heart's blood!"

The throat of Elise Du Barry had been dreadfully disfigured by the strong hands that had crushed the life out of her, but her mouth was still a bright crimson colour, thus entitling the woman, even in death, to the name by which she had been popularly known in life—that of "Our Lady of Red Lips".

THE VAMPIRE

by Leonhard Stein

I.

HERMANN SAMASSA was thirty years of age, tall, broad shouldered, and employed in the law offices of Doctor Herzfield. A deep, sonorous voice, calm and firm manner, clothes that were ever more fashionably selected in accordance with his increasing salary, and a head of wavy light brown hair all won him the reputation of a ladies' man, which he accepted with nonchalant satisfaction. But his flirtations were conducted and regulated according to species, the servant class was avoided in general, students and nicer girls were given several weeks, bored wives with pleasant apartments were given months, and adventuresses or worse firmly rejected.

These however were but passing rungs and steps on the stairway to the luxury top-floor apartment property that was his future marriage to Klara Gärtner. Samassa had settled on this union as if at his desk under the yellow gaslights of the office—his worth, Klara's maidenhood, his earning capacity, her less than substantial but still sufficient dowry, his masculine virility, her inclinations; all these factors were clearly considered and weighed against one another before the final calculation was made. Only despite all his prior experience Samassa had failed to take into account the effect his courtship was to have on Klara: he had entered the engagement with a cool head and believed she had too, yet Klara's skin flushed yieldingly on contact with his newly-cut suit and glowed spellbound at his deep bass tones. Samassa magnanimously gave in response to those unspoken pleas, that which should have only been permitted after his next promotion and the wedding. But he consoled himself with the soon to be expected announcement of said advancement, welcomed the pleasure as if it were a bounty to which he had all lawful right, albeit one others need not know of, and continued tranquilly in the thought of their future alliance.

Just now Samassa stood beneath the yellow gas jet of the offices, throwing delicate figures on to the voluminous sail sheet of the ledger page and daydreaming of meeting Klara in an hour, of her buying them fruits and cakes, and maybe their going for a coffee in the Gartenkaffee, before instinctively laying down his pen and straightening his tie at the entrance of Doctor Herzfeld, who emerged from the boardroom ushering a small, unfamiliar woman ahead of him through the murky semi-darkness.

"Here, Herr Samassa, our new typist."

Samassa dipped his pen in the inkwell again and muttered a few words over the book as he leaned over it to add a few more entries. He heard Doctor Herzfeld leave and the new employee slowly and awkwardly grope her way to the typewriter. He finished the present entries, went up to the stranger, handed her some letters to be typed and lit the gas jet for her. Once the bluish flame slid from the match down into the mantle he was able to see her more closely: a ragged blouse hung off a body which appeared even scrawnier due to the way she sat hunched in her chair, and a rheumy sunken face peered up at him from amidst tangled patchy red hair. It was her eyes which unnerved Samassa, dark green eyes, murky and stagnant, the gaze of which seemed to cling to him like masses of algae. But at least the progressive decline visible in her hollow face and the feeble rattling audible from her weak chest reassured him. "She won't be here long," he thought to himself, giving her more letters along with instructions to which she listened almost devotedly. When he returned to his desk, he was surprised to notice, via a side-ways glance, how her long-nailed fingers scrabbled over the keys at a furious speed, and still more so when, after being called away for a moment by Doctor Herzfeld, he came back to find his briefs already typed up, and on top of them a note, also typed, which read: "Would you like to wait for me by the entrance after hours?"

"Shameless!" thought Samassa, who then turned his back on the new girl, who still shook like a red-haired puddle before her typewriter under the dirty gaslight, and loudly screwed up the note in his hand before tossing it in the waste paper basket.

He then set himself to the evening's work with increased zeal until he heard Doctor Herzfeld depart, at which point he closed his books and locked them away, took a brush from his locker, spruced and smoothed his hat and coat, rolled down his sleeves, pressed a cigar between his lips and left the room, ignoring the inviting gestures from the new employee on the way out. Strong and composed, exhaling smoke, he strode down the stairs and greeted Klara, who already stood waiting in the hallway, with a light kiss on the brow; he slipped his arm into hers and they went out into the street together.

Klara spoke of her day and other inconsequential matters. Samassa did not fail to observe the way in which passers-by looked at her figure, the soundness of his investment reflected in her fine features, and subsequently found himself in a pleasant, satisfied mood and Klara prettier and more pliable than ever. So, with the mute surrender of her pearl grey eyes, he brought a supper of cold cuts and a bottle of red wine; together they went to an apartment belonging to a single girlfriend of Klara's, an older actress who—it must be confessed—only returned home very late at night. Yet Klara locked the door behind her earnest and unspeaking, turned on the light, set the table, placed cuts of meat on plates and filled glasses with wine. Only later did they allow themselves release from this pretence, falling ripe into one another's arms. Afterwards Samassa rose from the warmth, smoothed her hair and saw her back to her home. Then he too set out homewards, humming tunes to himself as he walked through the half-lit alleyways, animated and drowsy at the same time.

He had a single bachelor's room set alongside many others of the kind at the end of a long, woodblock tiled corridor. Upon arriving Samassa noticed that, in the room situated at a right angle to his, a light still burned, dimly flickering through the uncurtained glass door. Without thinking he glanced inside and recognised Dr. Herzfeld's new employee, her wretched body still swaddled in her work blouse, sat before a mirror plaiting her ruddy hair, her green eyes shooting him glances from her cadevourus face. "Shameless!" though Samassa, turning away, "now she is living next to me too!" He went into his room, threw the door closed with a crack and began to undress.

Once in bed he read a newspaper, smoked till all the after-images of the day were blurred and effaced from his mind, and passed out. But his sleep was restless, hot and weighty as lead; Samassa felt the blood roll and pound in his veins like muffled drum-blows upon metallic cymbals, surging as it was drawn in the direction of the next room. He tossed from side to side, soaked in sweat, until all of a sudden he sensed someone cross the threshold into his room, bumping into the furniture as they moved closer, pull back the blankets and then run their hand up over his throat. At last the fumbling and groping ceased, the bed creaked softly as if someone were sitting on it, and Samassa felt a sharp stab of pain in his chest. He grasped for the lamp and froze at what he saw, for the new typist was sitting on the edge of the bed, leaning over him so close that her red hair brushed his face, the emeralds of her eyes shimmering vibrant green from out of the livid tangles.

She had drawn back the fabric of his shirt and lowered her mouth to his chest. As her lips parted Samassa distinctly perceived her only well preserved canine tooth, grotesquely oversized, elongated into a long bony spike which the stranger now drove into his breast. Samassa felt it penetrate the skin but experienced no pain, and then felt his blood rush audibly towards the bite-wound, the redhead's lips sucking it down greedily. Samassa could only watch powerlessly as the blood left him, his fear growing as he grew ever weaker. Finally, the intruder appeared satiated, and lifted her mouth from the wound, a round pale mark which bled not, the lights went out and she departed.

Samassa felt hideously innervated, though without any other after-effects, he lay there, his eyes open and glazed, his pulse unsteady, sleepless till the coming of morning, when the daylight brought something like a faint respite; gasping, he managed to raise himself against the dresser and throw down several glasses of wine, which warmed his insides. Then he threw his cloths on with haste and, trembling as he went, managed to bolt down a double breakfast in a coffee house, and stagger unwashed into the offices with haunted eyes.

II.

The new typist was already sitting at her place when Samassa entered. Doctor Herzfeld emerged stout and jaundiced from the boardroom, grumbled at him for his lateness, and presented Samassa with a pile of documents to deal with. It was futile, Samassa still felt utterly exhausted, his heart, a lifeless pumping motor, laboured to squeeze droplets of thin blood to his brain, barely sufficient to enliven it for the work at hand. Dizzied, hands frozen, Samassa struggled to collate numbers which flickered blue, danced and fluttered again into the haze of bloodless delirium; he was forced to clutch onto the desk with both hands in order to prevent himself from collapsing. Exhausted, his head resting on the desk beside a ledger, he noticed the new typist crouched like a strange reddish beast before her machine, periodically tapping out a letter with her rattling claws.

At length he managed to collect himself again, and hurried from the chambers to the nearest street canteen, gulping down a garland of sausages and multiple glasses of schnapps. At last, as he lay resting on a bench, he felt his blood begin to flow anew, vibrant and wild, in sympathy with the strains of a military band marching past; overjoyed beyond words he hurried back to the office, made his entrance with a swagger, stood tall on his heels and in a curt tone ordered the new typist to complete twice her allotted workload, only to be amazed at how quickly she accomplished just that, her waxen features wrinkled into a grin as she worked. Now under the full light of day he fancied that her face was no longer as haggard as it had been yesterday, that deposits of soft fat already showed beneath her pallid freckled skin.

Then came the lunch hour spent in the brightly lit eating house; clean plates, a meal, repose and space for rational reflection. The waiters, dark and nimble as ever, darting between tables, the familiar guests and table-mates, absorbed in their newspapers or beer glasses, black and yellow, the bill, the tip: all leant the events of the previous night a haze of unreality. A dream? Samassa, who had never before dreamed of such evil apparitions, inwardly rejected this most reasonable method of explanation, and sought for some external factor. Dream and indisposition, all knew the food in the restaurants was growing worse and worse, every now and then one might read something about the effects of food poisoning in the unbribed papers, that was it, the ham from yesterday's cold supper could have been off, this evening he would have to ask Klara whether she had also felt queasy. And with the intention of avoiding any similar experiences he left the eatery and returned to the offices, coming through the door whistling and clicking a tune with his fingers. The typist was still at her place, bent over the machine; evidently she had taken no lunch at all. Samassa looked her up and down, a feeble creature one ought to be ashamed of being frightened of, even temporarily. With that he walked, straight-backed, hand on his watch chain, over to Doctor Herzfeld, and excused himself for the morning's delays, speaking to him with the confidence of an equal about dates and business matters, before collecting some recently delivered documents.

And as he presented these to the typist, he even tried to say a few kind words, as a demonstration of his contemptuous surety. However, he was shocked when the woman responded by twisting her mouth open in a rictus grin, flashing him a sight of that enormous canine tooth with its elongated needle-like tip, and broke off his conversation abruptly before plunging back to his desk, there to spend the rest of the afternoon in a state of melancholy, brooding, sapped of will, and barely able to rouse himself for a few mindless bursts of work. At last the shadows lengthened, the gas jets burnt brighter, the evening draped black flags over the walls; the noise of the street grew, and Doctor Herzfeld departed, Samassa left soon after him, departing into the sweet warmth of Klara's moist breath. But despite his earlier resolution he avoided asking about any digestive troubles from yesterday evening, and likewise remained deaf to Klara's mute supplications, tearing aside the amorous threads which she waited longingly for him to continue spinning, all in unspoken dread of the coming time which reached for him with scintillating claws, as green and dead as the typist herself.

Klara had departed hurt, leaving him alone, in a state of limbo at the back of a coffee shop, filled with the mute resolution not to return home. But when the lights began to dim at midnight and the waiter politely but firmly pointed him on his way down the street, he set out for home in sudden defiance of this self-imposed eviction from his own room. The room that the stranger had taken next door was silent and unlit. Samassa slipped past it, quietly removed his boots, climbed into bed still fully clothed and, with a profound sense of relief, soon fell asleep. But soon, as if in a dream, he sensed the typist rise in the next room and make her way to him, his blood was seething once more, spurting its way to the bite wound; the red-haired one was already crouched on his chest, snuffling at the wound with pursed, funnel-like lips. And then there began again that cycle of deathly weakness, gazing motionless into the grey dawn, desperately forcing down wine and vast quantities of meat, spasmodic bursts of work in the office seated beside the predator, Klara making eager and uncomprehending eyes at him, a new night, a new episode of bleeding to death.

Samassa, who had postponed his next meeting with Klara, offering excuse after excuse, studied his reflection in the mirror of a barber's shop; coldly examining that haggard face, from the dark furrows of which his nose and cheekbones protruded like lumps of fieldstone, and noticing too how his coat, cut to fit his once athletic limbs, fluttered loose over his ruined frame. Later, whilst sat at an eating-house surrounded by the many plates of meat he was now forced to consume daily in order to regain his depleted blood, he calmly undertook some calculations. A race for his vitality was taking place and sooner or later he must fall. Probably soon, for neither could his salary sustain the tripled expenditure on wine and meat for any length of time nor was his body capable of converting that which he consumed into blood at anything near the rate at which that fluid was drawn from him. And still what was occurring remained incomprehensible to Samassa, an enigma, something impossible outside of nightmare. One evening, torturing himself with hope, he brought a bottle of ink home from the office with him and left it open in front of his bed: when he rose the next morning, feeble and bloodless, it lay spilt, so it was true, the apparition and the fate it brought were real, he was forced to acknowledge them. Whilst at work he noticed how the new typist, her body saturated with his blood, was gradually losing her pallor and sickliness; her figure grew visibly fuller, her hunched back straightened, she began to wear nicer clothes and even a blue bow in her hair. Only her eyes remained as green and hungry as they were at the beginning. Samasa's only hope now was that once she regained her vitality she would cease the nightly pillaging of his blood. But this too was betrayed: the vulture hovered insatiable over him, panting for every droplet of new life he acquired, uncorking him with its spiked canine, feeding gluttonously, unconcerned as to whether the body it sucked dry was still capable of rebuilding itself.

III.

Samassa felt Klara begin to drift away; his career and manhood crumbled away beneath his feet. He gathered his remaining strength and on the eighth morning approached Doctor Herzfeld in his office.

"I request that the new typist be dismissed if you continue to value my presence here."

But Doctor Herzfeld pulled himself up from his chair abruptly, as if he had received an insult. "I am of the opinion, Herr Samassa, that our new employee is fulfilling her duties most diligently, which is more than has been said of you of late."

And then, after wedging his pince-nez tighter into his fleshy nose, he added: "Really, I am surprised at this unfavourable change that has taken place with regard to your appearance. Gambling or women is it? You may find this ques-

230

tion unwarranted, but I place great weight on the fact that my staff uphold the reputation of the firm outside of office hours as well."

Samassa shrugged his shoulders and staggered out, brushing past the red hair of the new typist, who looked him up and down as if he were her natural item of prey.

He felt a sudden yearning for human warmth and walked to Klara's apartment. She rushed to meet him at the door, throwing her arms round him.

"What is wrong with you?"

Samassa tried to reply, but a red haze filled with flashing green specks flickered before his eyes, dimming his consciousness. When he awoke from his faint he found himself lain out on the sofa; Klara, her parents, and an unknown gentleman, presumably a doctor, stood over him, as the former silently poured a measure of rum between his lips, eyes red and swollen from crying. Then the doctor leaned over him.

"You must have experienced a severe loss of blood very recently. Do you recall how this happened?"

Samassa opened his mouth, intending to tell them about the new typist, but quickly closed it again after he realised how ridiculous it would sound. For the time being he wished only to rest; as he pretended to sleep he heard the deep, concerned tones of Klara's father, the high-pitching tinkling voice of her mother, Klara's own sobbing, and the departure of the doctor. So he lay in this state till noon, when the doctor called again and he was carried into a wagon, where he writhed and twisted in a half-dream in which he thought he beheld the typist gliding on vast wings behind the vehicle as it drove towards a great white building, the rooms of which were also white and filled with men in white gowns. Then he felt the surface of a bed beneath him and another stabbing sensation, this time different from the canine of the typist, two hours later he found two men in white coats leaning over him once more.

"Extraordinary, this man has only two million red blood cells and yet still lives," said the first.

"We will have to feed him on iron and arsenic. Perhaps——" the other replied.

Samassa was treated with arsenic and concentrated iron solutions which his stomach was barely able to stand. Yet he bore this all with calm. He saw only too clearly that his recovery was only to be temporary, for often the typist leaned over him to check whether his blood was sufficiently replenished, he would fend her off with his hands only to recognise from her sobs that it was in fact Klara, whom he subsequently forbade to visit him if she wore that red hat. But after a week he was already sitting with her in the asylum garden and conscious that her grey eyes were wider, deeper in spiritual depth, and that her hand rested in his with unwavering longing. They discussed marriage and three days later Samassa was discharged as recovered. He passed the evening with Klara and then walked calmly back to his room.

It appeared clear to him that the previous state of affairs must not be permitted to arise again, that the typist appeared as a human being capable of human language and activities promised hope, for one might bargain directly with such an adversary, convey risks, set conditions, or at least find out more of the nature of the foe. Samassa strode determinedly down the dark, wood-tiled corridor leading to his room, knocked on the glass door, now lit up, and waited till a voice called him in. Samassa opened the door, and there again was the vampire sitting before the mirror, arranging her tousled red hair with a comb, as pallid and infirm as the day they had first met. With a wave of her emaciated hand, she invited him to take a seat. Samassa remained standing.

"I would like to know the conditions under which I might obtain peace."

The vampire threw her withered arms in the air and shrieked with the voice of a crow:

"That is difficult! I have gone hungry for two weeks and am almost completely decrepit again. You would have to offer me a substitute. And every night!"

But Samassa had learnt enough; he thanked her and departed.

IV.

The next day he persuaded Klara to move in with him before the wedding. He still felt weak and would require close care and support after his demanding work at the offices. He said all this with an earnest eloquence which sprang from that most powerful of sources, his desire for survival, and with certain confidence of its achieving the desired results. Klara agreed to this proposal almost from the first words, offering none of the token protests customary in such situations; with her mother's aid she overcame the resistance of her father, and a day later, taking with her only a few dresses and other items of clothing, moved in with Samassa, who let her take his room whilst he rented the adjoining one, which stood opposite to that of the vampire.

Their first evening at home together was one of gentle intimacy, Klara's lithe movements washed the environments in tinted forgetfulness, and her concern for his barely restored health leant nobility to her affections. After she had sunk back into her pillows, flushed and sighing with voluptuous pleasure, Samassa made his escape into the next room, where he smoked and waited with cold anticipation. At midnight he heard a creaking sound, and watched as the vampire slipped through a crack in the door into the room and leant over Klara's sleeping form. And, come the morning, when he too bent over the enfeebled sleeper and recognised the pale wound upon her breast, he pulled her chemise up over it and fled to the office. At noon Klara received him wan and tired, neither speaking a word. Samassa bolted down his food and left.

And now he watched the same drama he had once been part of repeated day after day with Klara: her skin lost more and more of its lustre and suppleness, her flickering eyes sunk ever deeper into her ruined countenance, and again the vampire of the office flourished, swelling in stature and shapeliness. The only difference was that the process took much longer than it had with him. Samassa sought to account for this by the fact that by nature women are perhaps better capable of producing blood rapidly in the case of an emergency, even if it is at the expense of the other tissues. Yet soon Klara's vitality also began to wane, he could calculate the impending disaster almost to the day, but, vigorous and able to work like never before, he kept putting aside the thought of rescue, knowing all too well what its execution would cost him. Klara's behaviour encouraged this, for never did a word of the deadly nights pass her lips. Maybe she recognised sub-consciously that her duty was to bleed to death here for him, and clutched the will to live tight between already stiffening fingers, spending it only in a kiss to Samassa, to her parents and finally to her other kin. And then one morning he came to her bed and found her colder than normal; a few hours later he was accepting condolatory handshakes from friends, acquaintances, and even Doctor Herzfeld, who had deigned to visit him in his apartment.

Even the vampire seemed to mourn, but two days afterwards Samassa was visited in his new room by that stabbing pain and enervation. At least his own vessels seemed to an extent used to such depletion, and for the next two weeks he managed to maintain a tolerable balance with the aid of arsenic and iron pills, which enabled him to work well enough, but after that he was left empty and on the edge of ruin. A coincidence saved him: Iglseder, Doctor Herzfeld's second clerk, a delicate, dreaming soul who lived only on vegetables and played the flute during his leisure hours, had recently been evicted because he could not afford his landlady's increased rates. With kind words Samassa bid him take the empty room, an offer Iglseder gladly accepted for fear of the approaching frosts of winter. But the notes Iglseder's flute became thinner and fainter along with his body, until one day they fell silent, for his delicate frame, nourished only from plant-based foods, could not satisfy the vampire's hunger for long.

Samassa no longer gave any thought to his appearance, his dress, his career or his social relations; instead he raced about the city pale-faced in search of new, invigorating food stuffs and medicines. The idea of moving apartments or of hiring men to protect him was soon rejected, for it was clear the vampire would follow its prey anywhere and bypass any bodyguard for its nightly feeding. Instead Samassa discovered another refuge, one which brought him respite for an entire night and sometimes for longer. After bringing colour to his sunken cheeks with rouge, bolstering his ruined posture with girdles, plunging his grey hair in dye, wrapping covetously shaped clothes around crumbling bones, he would go forth and seek out women of the street, daughters of night, luring them to his room with promises and enticements. The tones of Iglseder's flute were replaced with the rustle of skirts and the cooing giggle of light sinners, who knew not what lusts they were brought here to satiate. At first Samassa undertook regimes of half-hearted introduction and caresses, the amorous responses to which left him feeling disgusted, before finding the answer in drink: he would ply the victims with glasses of wine mixed with powerful sedatives, depositing them roughly on the fatal bed, and sending them on their way in the morning, pale and ruined, with a bite wound on their heaving breasts.

But talk of the unprecedented exhaustion Samassa's company entailed spread all too quickly through that underworld of women, enticing a few curious individuals but repelling the majority. Samassa raged; ever larger grew the rewards he promised, the honouring of which drove up torrents of debt, throwing him into the hands of usurers, but eventually neither offer nor rouse availed; the threat of the police approached, slowly for lack of concrete evidence, but moving ceaselessly closer. Shunned by former acquaintances, driven from his old social circles, he was forced to resume the struggle again alone, to contest the mad race by secretive means and arts. Great changes took place within him: his body was transformed into an enterprise concerned only with the constant rapid production of blood, all its other functions neglected and allowed to wither away. His muscles, tissue and bones had atrophied, serving only as a support frame for the swollen tubular ducts of his veins, which wound around Samassa like pulsing serpents prior to their decanting in the evening, only to lay like empty tubing in the morning, deflated and rotten. His heart expanded its pumping operation beyond the right half of his chest, trembling under the weight of the dark tides it had to draw forth, crushing the lungs and constricting his diaphragm to bursting point, only permitting him short gasping breaths. Yet it did its duty, for whilst in the office Samassa noticed with horror how the vampire's hump had disappeared, now she stretched her limbs, laughing heartily, complete with a flood of unruly red hair and deep sea-green eyes that shimmered like the shores of song. But the broken man had no time to contemplate this, for he was called to the director's office by Doctor Herzfeld, who informed him curtly that he had been dismissed on account of failure to perform his duties and because of the depravity of his private life.

V.

Samassa staggered into a tavern, emptied several glasses of schnapps and regarded his tattered suit. This vision of his downfall brought with it an idea of such clarity and simplicity that he could only fault his shrivelled brain for not having thought of it earlier: to kill the vampire! If he succeeded he would be free and could work his way back up again; if he was caught, then imprisonment and execution were in any case preferable to his current fate.

So he set upon a plan and went the rounds of the city's gun-shops, only to be refused with suspicion at each due to his torn clothing, until after hours of wandering he managed to obtain a pistol and cartridges from a Jewish junk dealer, after which he lurched back to his room and spent the rest of the day practising his aim with a piece of cut-out paper.

When the last of the sunset sank behind the snowy roof-tops exhaling flame as it went, he piled his clothes together in a heap beneath the bed-sheet, so that it would appear as if he himself were hiding beneath it in fear, and stood in wait with his pistol behind the fire-screen, his other hand poised on the lamp-switch.

Night fell dark over the room. At last at around one o'clock Samassa heard the door open and the vampire, now a beautiful lithesome woman, flitted her way to the bed. As she reluctantly lifted the blanket Samassa raised his pistol, took aim, and fired—the vampire fell back on the bed, wailing and clutching at its perforated chest.

Samassa lunged forward and began pummelling her face into the pillow with his fists, when the red jet spurting from her left breast struck his lips: her blood, his blood! He leaned dizzy over the woman, thirstily drinking back down his stolen blood, feeling triumph as it coursed wildly through his empty veins. The dying vampire lay her arm around him. Samassa stared down into the gleam of her green eyes, which were now growing blue and pure, like the gaze of a woman redeemed; the red of her hair also faded, dissolving into a soft blonde. Samassa felt an inexplicable impulse, almost that of love, for the vampire, who gradually dwindled away beneath him from loss of blood, and then fell still, white as the linen hanging from the bed, and died.

Samassa sprang up, frenzied in his freedom, and allowed the regained blood to dance his body out of the door. He plunged forward disorientated, falling, rushing down the steps into the alleyway, where the shapes of the wintry houses threatened to plummet into the moon, buckling towards him from above at impossible angles and swaying apart again, as the street-lights circled him like fireflies! Samassa felt himself hoisted up, shot in a drunken arc through the heavens, flung through endless, howling subterranean passageways.

What was the cause of all this? None other than his own blood which, grown toxic in the body of the vampire, now raced again through his own veins, ripping him apart from within. How idiotic! He should have realised that the vampire was venomous and that all it ingested was saturated in its deadly germs. What could he do? He ran around in circles, gripped by convulsions, at last he was able to grab onto a passer-by, deliverance! But then many hands pushed him down into the snow, darkling shapes clustering around him.

"I have been poisoned—you must to fetch the rescue services!"

A shadow hurried forth. But Samassa waved it away as the first spasm crippled his brain. For a long time, he stared up at the window behind which the vampire, robbed of the blood that now swam in both of them, hung limp and lifeless from the edge of the bed, and at last felt a connection to that being, exhaling his soul upwards through the cold air towards it as he died.

THE VAMPIRE

by Toni Schwabe

HE could not accept that Erinna was dead, for there had been moments when the light of life everlasting had shown in her gaze, moments when they had experienced such a fulfilment of one another's innermost being as only that moment of searing, ecstatic love is capable of bringing about between two human beings.

He knew without a doubt that she could not be dead. At the same time, he endeavoured to persuade himself of the absurdity and impossibility of this assumption. He told himself: it is only natural that I cannot accept this death, for our hearts have beat too often and too long in unison with each other. It is a purely bodily failure of my reasoning faculties. I cannot conceive of this death any more than I can conceive of my own dying. Was there any human being who truly believed their own death to be possible? We all recognize that one day we will be delivered up to the final hour without mercy, and yet at the same time, there is within each of us the indestructible lie of self-preservation which continually defies it: that I, I alone, will never die.

You my other self, you—self of mine that has abandoned me, how does all the knowledge of death's inevitability aid me if my blood tells me that you live?

I write because I cannot see you beside me and cannot speak to you. As I write, so I believe that you are in some place where my letters might reach you. I only have to begin as normal: I have to place the letter in an envelope, have to address it to you and then have to drop it in a post-box. In one of those innumerable blue bins which each day accept thousands of seemingly living words, bound in characters upon any scrap of paper, and speed them on to their destination. One needs not concern themselves with what happened to the letter afterwards. Then events take care of themselves.

Our deeds never went further than taking this living, pinned down and artificially-bound cry of longing to that narrow dark maw, which swallowed it up in order that it might rise once more from the unliving paper, when finally opened by the one to whom it is addressed.

I write to you Erinna, I call to you. I am calling upon you to return.

Now the letter must be with you soon. The address was somewhat difficult. Whither to should I dispatch the letter? It struck me that I should send it to the place that we both love most of all and where our fondest memories were made. If only you were there! Yet you went a different way. Where to must this letter go? Why did you forget to tell me whither to your journey takes you?

Yet still within me is that great, all-beguiling falsehood which will not permit me to accept your death. I know where you are bound, and there too shall I send my letter.

That fearful address is now written thereupon it, naked and starkly bare.

I was nervous and ashamed to take the letter to the place I normally send my other letters. I went another way, the way which leads to the place where they lowered you into the earth.

Against this very wall did your living fingers brush, back when we once passed in the blazing sunlight and you said that the chill of the stones was good for your warm, living hands; on this very wall did I find the right box into which I placed my letter. I had never noticed it before, since it lacked the bright blue colour of the other post-boxes and that is as it should be. For it is for the other letters, the letters from the lost and the forsaken, and its colour is that of the chill grey stone. Something in me knows with resolute certainty that this letter will reach its destination.

✳

In the night you came to me as I knew you would.

"I am frozen," you said.

"Lay down beside me."

You hesitated and gently shook your head.

"I am too cold," you said.

But how glad I have always been to keep you warm. I felt your feet, cool and soft as silk. I held you close until you grew warm. And you did grow warm. Only it was different from before: then it was the warmth of life to life, both of us glowing embers. On this night though my warmth flowed into you softly like running blood, seeping away, leaving me in a never-ending stream, until I was left dead and hollow.

I fell asleep beside you. Forgive me for falling asleep, despite such happiness. When I awoke you were no longer with me. What happened to you? Why am I alone and frozen to my last drop of blood?

What is this? Have I been dreaming? I understood, I understand, that you are dead and that for the dead there is no way back to this life. What is happening to me? How can this be?

When my longing grew too great, I took this letter too and sent it where I sent the other. Have I earned an explanation from you now?

I await the coming of night. I lay down to sleep.

You did not come to me. I now see my mistake: I did not call out to you.

I conclude the letter I started with a cry to you: come to me, Erinna, come, I yearn for you.

I was already awaiting you that night. And you did not deceive me. You have never deceived me—how could you wish to make an illusion of my joy this night?

Thank you, thank you for coming.

I think now of you: why did you smile so sadly (regretfully) when I called out for you and you came to me so willingly? You approached with cool, wavering hesitant motions, as if it were merely the night air brushing against me.

I thirst after you so! I think never before in my life have I needed you in my arms as I do now. Would that all of us who seek after Life and Life's highest joy in Love's embrace know of this ice-cold bliss . . .

Come back again, come back again, I need you so dreadfully!

You left my presence warm that night too. You warmed, from my own life warmed, and I left cool because my ardour has flowed into you!

To know that I now fall asleep by your side! To know that sleep is the shrouding veil of your farewell! It is so good of you to let me sleep through your departure.

What have I done, have not I called you? I, oh miserable wretch that I am, was so weary that I could not walk the path that brings my cry to you.

You must have been frozen that night, that night you lay alone whilst I rested and slumbered.

Guilt, remorse and longing eat away at me.

Erinna, I shall await you again this coming night.

All my warmth I have spent on you, and yet you continue saying you are cold. I held you firm in my arms, clasped you tight to my heart, I felt the life run out of me, yet you would not grow warm.

"Tell me, what can warm you?"

"You know what—or maybe you do not."

"Must it be so, because you, you—come from that other land?"

"Because I come from that other land."

"What must I do?"

"You know not—for now you do not comprehend—but you shall know."

"Let me, let me know."

"I cannot."

That is what we spoke of. And now I think of that which you understand and which I cannot. I ponder and brood on how lovers long for a further and deeper form of union.

Come back to me, come back swiftly, for perhaps a new knowledge will be born from my blood.

A further aspect of your wisdom unveils itself, both for you and for me. It is an intimacy, a more profound and total intimacy than the erotic intimacy of the living, which lies distant and empty behind that which I long to reach with you.

On that last night I took your lips to mine and exchanged my breath for yours. It was not merely a kiss but a long flowing exchange of life for life—no, there is no use in lying: of life for death.

Your breath filled me chill and as if blowing from far away. After waking I find that even as the day slips by I can still taste your breath on my tongue like the fragrance of a cool, bitterly scented bough of blossom.

Yet still this was not the union to which I am ever drawn.

This night you came to me without my having to call you.

"You came?" I asked drunk with bliss.

"Your blood has called to me."

"What is this that I long for?"

"Let me still withhold it from you."

I was seized anew by that passion for you, that passion which passes in your train from the passion for life to this obsession with the cold bliss of death.

Oh my days! What is there left for me to do in all this?

Far away is the blaze of human voices: comfort, zeal, the struggles of friendship. All these call not to me. My time is dedicated to nothing besides the devotion I have to you and to our nights together.

By night all is a fast flowing torrent, which by day settles into a dark stagnant expanse of water. There is no purpose other than to flow, to flow into you.

✳

It must be done tonight. How many nights will rush by, will it be on this or on the next that you take me to your land?

✳

This night recognition and knowledge came upon me.

Life and death rush forward to that point of transference, of merging, of union beyond all else.

"You understand—grant it to me now."

That demand was uttered from my heart.

There was some offer in your eyes, some demand. And then you made a small, reverent gesture—as of someone who offers, and as of someone who receives.

Then I felt your cool lips above my heart. A small fountain jet of red sprung to your mouth.

So at last my blood found its way.

DOCTOR HORDER'S ROOM

by Patrick Carleton

THE college of SS Cosmas and Damian, though among
the smallest, is by no means the most recent foundation
of the University of Cambridge. Originally endowed, by a
noble lady, at the commencement of the fifteenth century,
it owes—as so many of the houses of both universities—the
most striking features both of its architecture and its constitution to the zeal of a famous Master. This was Doctor Nicholas
Horder who, like his great contemporary Doctor Caius, seems
almost to have re-founded and entirely to have rebuilt the college over which he ruled. To him is attributed the charming
wine-red brickwork of the college's two older courts: him the
Fellows, at their annual Founders' Feast, thank for the rich
endowments which enable them to dine on turtle and roast
swan, served on silver; and his arms, impaling those of the
original Foundress, are displayed above the college gates.

It is a curious and lamentable fact that next to nothing
is known of the life and antecedents of this worthy scholar.
Born in approximately 1508, he graduated at the college of
which he was the Master in 1527. For some years afterwards
he appears to have pursued his studies abroad—noticeably at
the University of Toledo, where he familiarised himself not
only with Hebrew and Aramaic, but also with Arabic, a language then little understood in Europe. Subsequently, he trav-

elled in Turkey—he is known to have been in Constantinople in 1533—and, on his return to England, was admitted as a Fellow by his old college. In 1548, the then Master, Doctor Foxhill, died very suddenly, and Dr. Horder was appointed in his room. He immediately set about the rebuilding of the College. The old buildings, contemporary with the original foundation were incontinently destroyed, and in their place there arose two splendid courts, surrounded by brick buildings with white stone quoins and casements, a towered gateway, and a chapel of noble proportions. Opposite this last, on the north side of the first court, was the doctor's own residence—a humble enough lodging consisting only of three large panelled chambers on the first floor, approached by a steep and narrow staircase. Here he lived and exercised authority for the astonishing period of sixty-seven years; that is, until, on the lowest reckoning, he was considerably more than a centenarian. How much longer he might have continued to enjoy the work of his hands, it is impossible to say. He was found at the foot of the staircase leading to his room on a morning in 1615, with his neck broken and skull smashed, evidently as the result of a fall. The grave, on the south side of the college chapel, is marked by an inscribed slab.

The college, indeed, appears at times to have been continually under the shadow of wings. During the last forty years of the great Doctor's mastership, no less than five undergraduates died in residence, and one of the few contemporary records that we possess speaks of the moving sermon which the aged master preached at the funeral service of the last of them, on the text *Remember now thy Creator in the days of thy youth*.

It is time now to leave this delving into college history and turn to a typical Cambridge afternoon—grey, damp and dubious—when two members of the Governing Body of the college were discussing matters of policy for the coming term. The younger of them, Mr. Milligan, was the Dean and Senior Tutor, and the elder, Dr. Hollywell, was chiefly famous for his work on the Targums. When—at infrequent intervals—he could be exhumed from this study, he delivered valuable but inaudible lectures on Old Testament Exegesis and coached Divinity students in Hebrew.

"Well, Hollywell, and how do you like your new rooms?"

"Disgusting," replied Dr. Hollywell. "The fact is, Milligan, they don't *want* to learn. They just don't care."

The Dean knew his man.

"Your new *rooms*, Hollywell, not your new pupils."

"Eh? What rooms? What's wrong with them?"

"I hadn't heard anything about it. No one tells me anything."

"*Your* rooms in the second court: how do you like them?"

"Oh—them! Thank you, yes, very nice and convenient, very suitable. I never could stand the Horder rooms; glad to be out of them. Who's having them now? One of these horrible scientist-people we're giving Fellowships to nowadays I suppose. I tell you, Milligan, the temple of the Lord is become a den of scientists. Disgusting."

"As a matter of fact, we've decided not to put another member of High Table into them. They're to go to one of the second-year scholars."

Dr. Hollywell raised his large bald head and stared at the Dean as though he were seeing him for the first time and found the spectacle unwholesome. He asked slowly:

"Did I understand you to say, Milligan, that my old rooms—Dr. Horder's rooms—are being assigned to an undergraduate?"

"Yes—Lake's to have them: that nice young Classical scholar. We really ought to have all the Scholars in college, don't you think?"

Dr. Hollywell's already cracked and tremulous voice quavered like a parrot's.

"Well! Five-and-forty years have I been a Fellow of this college, and never before have I heard anyone—anyone—

suggest that a young man should be allowed to occupy the Horder rooms. Upon my word, Milligan, I don't know what's possessing you. Why, I remember the old Master saying . . . but never mind that now. Just oblige me, Milligan by getting out the Conclusion Book for—now let me see—for the year seventeen hundred and sixty-two.

When, after a certain amount of further argument, conducted, on Dr. Hollywell's part, to the tune of "No one ever tells me anything," the book had been produced, the old man turned to an entry in faded ink and stately Italian script, which read: "Agreed: that Dr. Horder's rooms be no more assign'd as a lodging to persons *in statu pupillari*, but reserve for some Senior member of the College." The Dean groaned in spirit. Dr. Hollywell's familiarity with the unprofitable back-alleys of college history was a proverbial nuisance. He said patiently:

"Well, well, I never noticed that before. Still you can hardly expect us to be tied down by an old enactment like that. *Autre temps, autres mœurs*, you know."

"Don't talk French to me," snapped the Doctor, "and don't go and put an undergraduate in Dr. Horder's rooms. Reverence for the past I've long ceased to look for, but common sense is common sense. I've no doubt at all it's these physicists or scientists or biochemists or whatever they call themselves who're at the bottom of this."

Poor old Hollywell, thought the Dean sadly, it was really tragic, the way he was breaking up.

Frank Shelton drank beer and looked admiringly about him.

"*The* complete Ritz," he said slowly; "*the* complete Ritz, Peter. Fancy them giving you two sitting-rooms just because you're a lousy scholar—and me crouching among the aspidistras in Hills Road and arguing with my landlady about the price of bacon. You're a lucky hog."

Peter Lake smiled and stretched his arms. He was an attractive-looking boy of twenty-one, slim and strong, with grey-blue eyes and a quantity of curling yellow hair.

"They're decent rooms," he agreed. "Did you know, Frank, the old chap who built the college used to live in them? He broke his neck falling down those stairs. So will you, if you gulp your beer like that."

"Cheerful thought! Does he haunt?"

"Not so's you'd notice it. Pious old bird: he's probably safe in heaven. Had a pretty taste in interior decoration, I must say."

Indeed, the sitting-room, which had been furnished by the college authorities in a style appropriate to its period, was an impressive place. The walls were panelled with oak to their full height, and the heavy overmantel was enriched with masks and garland, and supported by two teams of Caryatids with grotesque horned heads—satyrs, no doubt, or fauns. The old flooring creaked a little when trodden on, and the whole place bore gallantly but perceptibly its weight of years. It was, perhaps, a little gloomy, a little inclined to hug the shadows in its corners, and almost—if the expression be permissible—to avoid the eye like a dog with something on his conscience.

But this, no doubt, was due to the thickness and heaviness of the shades on the electric lights.

"I had," said Shelton, "a hell of a queer dream last night."

"What was that?" asked his host.

"Dreamt I was riding a tricycle down Petty Cury in my pyjamas, and playing the saxophone. Then the scene suddenly changed, and I found I was the Bishop of Birmingham. I forget what happened after that."

"There's probably something revoltingly wrong with your subconscious. As a matter of fact I had a dream, too."

"Give me an opportunity of retaliating, then."

"Righto: it was dam' queer really, and rather foul. It began with a most horrible stink—ever dreamed about a smell before? I haven't—then I distinctly felt somebody turning back the clothes from my bed. I woke up, and sure enough I'd kicked all the clothes off and I was shivering. It was awfully real whilst it lasted."

Shelton's proposed explanation was a ribald one and the conversation took a turn we need not follow.

✳

Henry, the head porter of SS Cosmas and Damian pushed his bowler-hat to the back of his head and blinked. Then he shouted across the morning stillness of the court to his assistant

"George, 'as anybody been in the Chapel this morning?"

George, sorting the letters in the porter's lodge, said no.

"Well, that's a queer thing, then, because somebody's gone and unlocked the door, which I'll swear I 'aven't, nor you neither."

"Nor me neither; did you remember to lock that last night, now?" Henry snorted.

"'Ow long 'ave I been in this 'ere college? And 'ow often 'ave I forgot to lock anything? Somebody's been in, and that's a fact."

"It'll be the Reverent."

"'Im, what's never out of 'is bed before nine of the morning, exceptin' when it's early Service? No, that's one of them young devils, that's 'oo that is. I shall report this."

In his comfortable study, the Dean was reading an old book. It was a reprint, prepared specifically at the request of the college authorities, of a number of documents relating to the history of the Foundation. The passage which at the moment occupied on Dean's attention, even to the exclusion of his breakfast, was an entry in the diary of one Master Richard Claye who had been a Fellow of the College during the later years of Dr. Horder's rule. It read as follows:

"It hath agayne pleas'd Almightie God to visit this poore House with a sad Stroke; this daie young *Andrewe Bonner*, yt lodg'd in ye First Court, was found by his sizar on coming to rowse him dead and colde in his bedde: he being at that time not above XIX yeares of age and an honest worthie young Gentleman and moche loved of all who knew him. Wch hath greatlie distressed us all and in especiall ye Master, for when I and M. Northe, having received from ye sizar intelligence of ye sad Fact, did wayte on him and advis'd him of it, he look'd verie gashfullie upo' us, repeating sundrie times (as tho' he did speak with himself) some words in ye *Hebrew Tongue* (wch he is accustomed moche to use) and thereafter saying in ye most solemn fashion: *My Masters, I am heartilie sorry for it.* And indeed it was observ'd of all yt he did cherish a notable tendernesse for ye young Gentleman and had shew'd him sundne kindnesses, wch did put me moche in mind of yt other Tragic Fact of seven yeares since or there-about: I mean ye Death of young James Sturmie yt deceas'd in ye First Court and after ye same fashion, for whom ye worthie Doctor had alsoe a great affecioun, as I recall."

The Dean rubbed his forehead. It was queer, he thought, how one deplorable circumstance had followed another in the first court. There had been the Doctor's own tragic end of course, and then surely there had been a fatality of some sort in the eighteenth century? He turned the pages of his book rapidly, and found what he sought in another and drier diary, that of a certain Randolph Gibbons, Fellow of the College and afterwards a Canon of Ely. The entry, made after a gap of several days, was terse: "Had some talk with Mr. Rose about the sudden decease of Mr. Harrison, he being the first that viewed the poor young man. He told me he supposed him to have died of some sort of seizure of the nature of an apoplexy, basing this upon the circumstance of his finding him, not in his bed, but lying upon the floor beside it, and with his face much contorted. He was the first young man to lodge in

Dr. Horder's rooms, as they are called, within my memory, this being accorded him on account of his being a Fellow-Commoner, and from the willingness of the Master to show some courtesy to his Guardian, Lord Mountgraine. He was an amiable and studious young gentleman, and his loss is indeed distressive. After serious reflexion, I did not think it amiss to petition an All-Merciful Providence for his repose."

The year of this entry was 1762, and the Dean recalled with an uncomfortable suddenness that it was in this year, and evidently after Bonners death, that the enactment had been made to which old Dr. Hollywell had referred him. Probably, he thought, young Lake was the first undergraduate to occupy the Horder rooms since then. Hollywell, no doubt was aware of this. Poor old man, thought the Dean, he must be getting superstitious. I dare say he expects we shall find Lake dead in his bed one morning.

That Lake was, at present, still tolerably alive and active became apparent to the Dean, when, at about ten o'clock that evening, he stepped into the first court for a breath of air. Lights were shining from the windows of Dr. Horder's rooms, and there was a noise of young men's laughter. The Dean looked up quickly. Should he send a porter to request less noise? He thought that he would not. It was a raw and cloudy night, and there was something strangely poignant in this sound of young happiness floating out into the charnel dark. It made him feel old. *Remember now thy Creator in the days of thy youth* . . . what on earth had put that text into his head? His liver must be out of order, for the court seemed suddenly to have put on a very sinister and unfamiliar look. Those shadows, for example, round the Chapel door—one would positively say they were malevolent. The Dean shivered and returned with hasty steps to his own place.

About midnight, Peter Lake's friends began to leave him. Frank Shelton, living some distance from the College, had been the first to go. Lake remembered his asking with a laugh, as he went out: "Been dreaming again, Peter?" He rather wished that he had not asked that. He had given his party chiefly because he felt the need of going to bed in a cheerful frame of mind. The dream *had* recurred, on the previous night, with certain circumstances of an added vileness. Again, there had been the revolting stench and the sensation of the bedclothes being drawn gently back. These had been followed by a conviction—which was retained vividly when he awoke—that something or somebody was bending over him with a sort of eagerness or greediness most unpleasant to recall. He looked round the splendid gloomy sitting-room in which he was now alone. The dark oak of the panels gave back the glitter of the lights, and sudden spurt of the coal fire made the faces of the satyrs under the mantelpiece appear to smile. Peter felt suddenly very helpless and very young.

He undressed slowly before the fire and found a small number of small excuses to potter about the room, first in his shirt and then in his pyjamas, replacing books in their shelves, mustering empty bottles and glasses and generally tidying up with a meticulousness that his bedmaker could not have too highly commended. At last, however, he was left with no alternative but to go to bed, which he accordingly did, not readily, but certainly with no absolute repulsion. The evening's jollity had made him very tired, and it was only a little time before he was asleep.

George the porter, who was on night-duty at the College gates, was accustomed, even bitterly so, to every noisy form of undergraduate activity. He could gauge by ear, and at a considerable distance, the number of young men who were amusing themselves in any given room, and the length of time that would elapse before the Dean sent word to him to go up and take their names. When, however, he was making his final round of the building prior to stretching himself gratefully upon the truckle-bed in the lodge, he heard a cry from Dr. Horder's rooms, no thought of Deans or discipline crossed his mind. On the contrary, as the wild noise died away into a bubbling and moaning very disturbing to hear he began to run. He reached the stairs at the moment when the oaken outer door of the Horder rooms was burst violently open—began to climb them—and was thrust aside, choking, by a heavy shape that moved quickly but with no sound. The smell of this hurrying thing was so unpleasant that he remained for some seconds, gasping and retching at the spot where it had passed him. In this way, he was able to hear the great doors of the Chapel—which he himself had locked a quarter of an hour before—slammed with a noise that echoed round the court.

Peter Lake did not die. True, his condition, when he was found lying senseless, half in his bedroom and half in the adjoining sitting-room, was acutely dangerous; but his magnificent constitution saved him, and in a week he was able to tell as much—it was little—as he ever did tell of what had hurt him. The business began, he said, with the now familiar nightmare—the smell, and the sensation of the clothes being stripped gently by some bending figure, and the cold that now attacked him ended his sleep. He is insistent on this point—that he was fully conscious and awake before he realised that a cold and heavy body, whose stench was beyond all description, lay outstretched upon his own, mouth greedily to his mouth and its hands fastening his wrists.

When asked to describe this horrid bedfellow in detail he vouchsafes nothing except that its flesh was damp and rubbery and that it had a long rough beard. What he suffered at this point cannot be guessed. It was a terror and hatred far beyond the common experience of men that gave him strength to wrench himself out of that flaccid and yet vigorous embrace. For reasons that may already be clear to the reader, it seems certain that, had he not done so, he would have suffered the same fate as young Harrison.

There remains still a little to be told. On the day that Lake was sufficiently recovered to tell his story, the Governing Body of the College, at an extra-ordinary meeting, unanimously adopted two motions proposed by the Dean and seconded by Dr. Hollywell. These were: that the Horder rooms should in future be used as an annexe to the College library, to which undergraduates should have admission only at stated times; and that certain repairs should be undertaken to the floor of the Chapel, on the south side. These latter were at once begun and occasioned no little adverse comment in the University. It was commonly stated that the work of moving the old floor had been so carelessly and irreverently carried out that a grave had been broken into and its contently cruelly disturbed. Some, indeed, even alleged that a certain object—it was generally described as a leaden cylinder of the type used, sometimes, for preserving manuscripts had been removed from the grave and was now in the possession of the Governing body.

The last scene is laid in the Master's Lodge, a pleasant mansion adjoining the second court built in the time of Queen Anne. There were present in the study, on a certain evening, the Master, the Dean and Dr. Hollywell. The latter had in his hands a roll of ancient and yellowed parchment inscribed in staring Hebrew characters and wrapped round a small stick. Presently, he spoke in a clearer and more incisive tone than was his wont.

"The manuscript which you required me to examine, Master, is written in unpointed Hebrew, and has the signature of a certain Kabbalist whose name—Ahimelech-ben-Gittai—may not be familiar to you. It appears to have been written at Constantinople in the early part of the fifteenth century, and its title is *Sepher-Hannephesh*, which, er, with reference to the context, I would venture to translate as *The Book of the Essence of Life*."

"And its contents?" asked the Master.

"With your permission, Master, I shall not offer you a translation. The work is a species of Kabbalistic or magical commentary upon the miracle of Elisha. After describing how the prophet stretches himself upon the body of the dead boy and breathes the breath of life into his mouth, this abominable—er, the writer of the book goes on to discuss a reverse process by which, subject to certain magical conditions which are minutely specified, he claims that an aged man could absorb the, er, vital essences of a vigorous youth and so prolong his own life beyond the normal span. Certain formulae and instructions are given. They are atrocious. With your approval Master . . ."

Dr. Hollywell, whose face wore a very serious expression, leaned forward and thrust the roll into the midmost of the study fire. It crackled brightly and was soon consumed.

ABOUT THE AUTHORS

A. BEE was the pseudonym of an unknown writer who occasionally contributed verse to *The Court Magazine and Monthly Critic, and Lady's Magazine and Museum*, during the first years of the 1840s. "Zuverlein; or, The Prediction", subtitled "A sketch after the German fashion" appeared in the April 1840 issue of that journal.

PATRICK CARLETON was the pen name of Patrick Railton (1907-1942), an English writer and historian. Throughout the 1930s he wrote a number of novels including *Desirable Young Men* (1931), a witty story partly dealing with student life at Cambridge. His antiquarian interests focused on the Assyrian and Hebrew peoples, on which he eventually published a study, *Buried Empires—The Earliest Civilisations of the Middle* East (1939). He died from tuberculosis exacerbated by alcoholism in 1942. "Dr Horder's Room," his only known attempt at supernatural fiction, first appeared in the Charles Birkin edited anthology *Thrills: A Collection of Uneasy Tales* (1935).

AIMÉE ISABELLA CROCKER (1864-1941) was an American socialite, mystic and adventuress. A daughter of one of the railway magnates, she was sent to finish her education in Europe, during which time she became engaged to but did not marry a German prince. Upon her return to America she made a name for herself as a lavish and unconventional salon hostess, winning admirers from all walks of life. King Kalākaua of Hawaii granted her the title of Princess and honorary dominion over one of the islands. In the 1890s she toured India and the Far East getting involved in romantic and political intrigue as well as developing a lifelong interest in Buddhism and Theosophy. In 1936 she published an autobiography recounting her adventures, *And I'd Do It Again*. "Our Lady of the Red Lips" appeared in her only collection of fiction, *Moon-Madness and Other Fantasies* (1910).

ALEXANDER DUMAS (1802-1874) was one of the most popular novelists of French Romanticism. The son of a celebrated general of the Revolutionary wars and the grandson of a freed slave he rose to fame writing for the theatre under the July Monarchy and remained beloved even after his exile under Napoleon II in 1851. The numerous historical romances and plays he wrote, amongst the most famous of which are *The Count of Monte Cristo* (1844) and *The Three Musketeers* (1845), helped popularise historic adventure as a genre and remain read by many to this day. He died in 1870 leaving behind him a vast body of work. "The Pale Lady" first appeared in the portmanteau novel *Les Mille et Un Fantômes* (1849).

WILLIAM HENRY GILES KINGSTON (1814-1880) was a popular travel writer and children's author. The son of a wealthy wine merchant, Kingston took to writing travel essays whilst in the service of his father's company, in the course of which he came to settle in Portugal, where he was decorated in 1842 by Queen Dona Maria the Second for his diplomatic role in helping resolve trade disputes. His book of observations on that land, *Lusitanian Sketches* (1845), won him the freedom to live by his pen alone, which he did by editing magazines and writing adventure stories for children, often about seafaring or exploration. Towards the end of his life Kingston and his wife, Agnes, translated several of Jules

Verne's novels. "The Bruxa" first appeared in the July 1846 issue of *Ainsworth's Magazine*.

JOHN WILLIAM POLIDORI (1795-1821) was an Anglo-Italian physician who served as a companion to Lord Byron during his travels in Europe. In the summer of 1816, he and Byron were present at a meeting with Percy Bysshe Shelley and his fiancée, during the course of which the four read from Jean-Baptiste Benoît Eyriès' anthology *Fantasmagoriana* and entered into an agreement to write their own ghost stories. This friendly wager lead to Mary Shelley writing *Frankenstein* and Byron a fragment of a story about the mysterious wish of a dying nobleman. Upon returning to England Polidori took Byron's fragment and developed it into *The Vampyre* (1819) making explicit the subject of vampirism and basing the appearance of the title character on his former employer. The novella was published in *The New Monthly Magazine*, supposedly without Polidori's consent and bearing the misleading sub-heading "A Tale by Lord Byron". The same year Polidori published a further Gothic novel, *Ernestus Berchtold; or, The Modern Oedipus*, this time dealing with a doomed incestuous love affair. Despite the success of his first novel Polidori found himself increasingly burdened by debts; faced with financial ruin he took his own life in 1821.

THOMAS PECKETT PREST (1811-1859) was one of the earliest and most prolific writers of penny dreadful publications. After a brief career writing musical materials for the stage Prest teamed up with the London publishers such as Edward Lloyd and George Drake to produce "novelizations," of popular stage plays under the collective title of *The Penny Play-Book; or, library of dramatic romance* (1836). Through the 1830s and 1840s he wrote over a hundred novellas covering all popular themes of the time, from nautical adventures to Gothic horror to pastiches of Dickens. In 1847 he served as one of the co-authors for the serialised *The String of Pearls: A Domestic Romance*, which introduced the character of Sweeny Todd, "the demon barber of Fleet Street" into popular culture. "The Wood Devil; or, the vampire pirate of the deep dell" appeared in the sixth issue of *The Penny-Play Book*.

EDWIN ROBERTS (1818-1864) was a journalist and author who contributed articles and fiction, including many Gothic and supernatural stories, to several of the Penny-Dreadful papers. In the late 1840s he collaborated with the radical publisher and Dickens plagiarist George W. M. Reynolds to provide content for the latter's newspaper, *Reynolds's Miscellany of Romance, General Literature, Science, and Art*. A supporter of the Chartist movement along with his publisher Roberts also authored *A New History of England* (1850), which attacked the institution of monarchy, and novelised accompaniments to Hogarth's cautionary print series in *The Complete Works of William Hogarth* (1861). "The Vampire Bride" first appeared in the November 23rd, 1850 issue of *Reynolds's Miscellany*.

LEOPOLD VON SACHER-MASOCH (1836-1895) was a novelist and social reformer whose fiction often explored the theme of feminine power and cruelty, as displayed in the corrupt high society of Imperial Vienna, as well as subjects from Slavic folklore and mythology. His principal work was the long and unfinished cycle of novellas which he published under the heading of *The Legacy of Cain*, the most famous of which was *Venus in Furs* (1869), an archetypical decadent work which became an important text of the Sexual Revolution and was an influence on artists as diverse as Franz Kafka and Lou Reed. "Die Todten sind unersättlich" (tr. "The Dead Are Insatiable") was published in 1875.

TONI SCHWABE (1877-1951) was a poet and novelist who was amongst the first to argue for the rights of lesbian and bisexual women in the German speaking countries. During the first decade of the twentieth century she published several collections of verse on the theme of lesbian love and androgyny. She was an active member of the Wissenschaftlich-humanitäres Komitee, an early LGBT rights group, and argued for the validity of same sex love between women at a time when this was disregarded by many of those sympathetic to masculine homosexuality. From 1918 to 1924 she edited and contributed to a number of ghost story anthologies, including *Das Landhaus* (1918) and Das *Gespensterschiff* (1920). Her greatest literary success came in the thirties with a trilogy of novels about the romantic life of Goethe. "Der Vampir" (tr. "The Vampire") first appeared in *Das Gespensterschiff.*

LEONHARD STEIN was one of the major figures of German supernatural horror fiction in the early 20th century. Despite this accolade, virtually nothing is known of this writer's identity, with scholars considering the name likely to be a pseudonym. The writer was active for a brief period from 1918 to the early 1920s, submitting weird and science fiction pieces to various magazines, as well as publishing the short novella *Die Feuerlilie* (1918) and the collection of short stories, *Das Ballett des Todes* (1918) which include "Der Vampyr" (trans. "The Vampire.")

ELAINE A. SWIRE was a writer who contributed a number of ghost stories to several London magazines during the first years of the 1890s. Not much is known about her other than that she possessed an interest in history and that her husband held the rank of Major in the British Army, possibly being stationed in India for a period. "More Things in Heaven and Earth" appeared in the June 1892 issue of *A London Society: A Monthly Magazine of Light and Amusing Literature for The Hours of Relaxation.*

KARL HEINRICH ULRICHS (1825-1895) was a classisist and legal scholar who was amongst the first to argue for the rights and protection of homosexual men as a special class before the law. In 1856 Ulrichs was forced to resign his position as assistant magistrate at the court of Hildesheim in the then kingdom of Hanover when faced with a blackmail attempt over his sexuality. Over the next decade he undertook a multivolume study and defence of homosexuality, *Forschungen über das Rätsel der mannmännlichen* Liebe (1864, tr. *Research into the Riddle of Male-Male Love*). After being forced to move from state to state for his controversial views, Ulrich finally went into exile over his support for Hanover against Prussian expansionism. Eventually he settled in Italy, during which period he edited a literary journal, *Alaudæ* (1889), and wrote essays promoting this use of Latin as a universal language. "Manor" appeared in the collection *Matrosengeschiten* (1884).

A PARTIAL LIST OF SNUGGLY BOOKS

G. ALBERT AURIER *Elsewhere and Other Stories*
CHARLES BARBARA *My Lunatic Asylum*
CHARLES BARBARA *Stirring Stories*
S. HEZOLNRY BERTHOUD *Misanthropic Tales*
LÉON BLOY *The Tarantulas' Parlor and Other Unkind Tales*
ÉLÉMIR BOURGES *The Twilight of the Gods*
ADA BUISSON *The Baron's Coffin and Other Disquieting Tales*
CYRIEL BUYSSE *The Aunts*
JAMES CHAMPAGNE *Harlem Smoke*
FÉLICIEN CHAMPSAUR *The Latin Orgy*
ARMAND CHARPENTIER
    Claustrophobic Madness and Other Stories of Death and Love
BRENDAN CONNELL *Metrophilias*
BRENDAN CONNELL *Spells*
RENDAN CONNELL (editor) *The Zaffre Book of Occult Fiction*
BRENDAN CONNELL (editor) *The Zinzolin Book of Occult Fiction*
RAFAELA CONTRERAS *The Turquoise Ring and Other Stories*
DANIEL CORRICK (editor)
    Ghosts and Robbers: An Anthology of German Gothic Fiction
ADOLFO COUVE *When I Think of My Missing Head*
RENÉ CREVEL *Are You All Crazy?*
QUENTIN S. CRISP *Aiaigasa*
QUENTIN S. CRISP *Rule Dementia!*
LUCIE DELARUE-MARDRUS *The Last Siren and Other Stories*
LADY DILKE *The Outcast Spirit and Other Stories*
CATHERINE DOUSTEYSSIER-KHOZE *The Beauty of the Death Cap*
ÉDOUARD DUJARDIN *Hauntings*
BERIT ELLINGSEN *Now We Can See the Moon*
ERCKMANN-CHATRIAN *A Malediction*
ALPHONSE ESQUIROS *The Enchanted Castle*
ENRIQUE GÓMEZ CARRILLO *Sentimental Stories*
DELPHI FABRICE *Flowers of Ether*
DELPHI FABRICE *The Red Sorcerer*
DELPHI FABRICE *The Red Spider*
BENJAMIN GASTINEAU *The Reign of Satan*
EDMOND AND JULES DE GONCOURT *Manette Salomon*
REMY DE GOURMONT *From a Faraway Land*
REMY DE GOURMONT *Morose Vignettes*
GUIDO GOZZANO *Alcina and Other Stories*
GUSTAVE GUICHES *The Modesty of Sodom*
EDWARD HERON-ALLEN *The Complete Shorter Fiction*
EDWARD HERON-ALLEN *Three Ghost-Written Novels*

www.ingramcontent.com/pod-product-compliance
Lightning Source LLC
Chambersburg PA
CBHW020127120726
47903CB00007B/2135